# CHUSEN BOY

HANNAH GRAY

# *playlist*

Listen to the music that inspired *Chosen Boy* on Spotify.

"Snooze" by SZA

"Monster" by Shawn Mendes and Justin Bieber

"All of Me" by John Legend

"Shirley Temple" by Lauren Watkins

"Thing for You" by Hinder

"she's all i wanna be" by Tate McRae

"Chemical" by Post Malone

"Perfect" by Ed Sheeran

"Bad Blood" by Taylor Swift

"Close to Me" by Ellie Goulding, featuring Diplo and Swae Lee

"Wine into Water" by Morgan Wallen

"This Feeling" The Chainsmokers, featuring Kelsea Ballerini

"Playing with Fire" by Thomas Rhett, featuring Danielle Bradbery

# prologue

## SUTTON
## AGE SEVENTEEN

The rain pitters on the window as I pull my blanket up a little higher, curling my legs in on the plush chaise lounge. This has been my favorite place to read since my father had it built years ago. It's also the only place where I can feel invisible because aside from our maid, Gert, no one else ever comes up here. I've never been able to understand why though. At the highest point of the house, the view overlooking the creek behind our home is my favorite. I've never been much of an outdoorsy sort of girl. So, I long for rainy summer days like this one.

The rain grows heavier, suddenly turning into those huge raindrops that hit off the window, making it impossible to see through the glass. I sigh, silently hoping that my family will cancel their annual barbeque later on today. Knowing good and well that it's not likely. My parents would move the entire shindig inside our home before canceling. Because *it's the event of the summer*. On the bright side, there will be plenty of liquor. And I have gotten damn good at sneaking it.

"Knock, knock," Gert's voice says before she saunters in. "Child, you're still in sweatpants. It's time for you to shower and get ready for the cookout."

Gert has been with us since I was a baby, and despite that I am now seventeen and going to be heading into my final year of high school in a few months, she still talks to me like I'm a toddler. She is in her late sixties now and slowing down all the time. It's clear her years in this household are limited. She has kids and grandkids of her own, but I know my family pays a pretty penny to keep her around. She does everything for us.

I flop onto my side, putting an arm over my face, and groan. "It's literally a downpour outside. And I know I heard thunder and saw lightning. It'd be a shame to drag everyone out here and get their *expensive* shoes ruined." I pretend to gag before peeking up at her. "What if someone gets struck by lightning?" My eyes widen. "Now, *that* would make things interesting."

"Okay, Miss Attitude." She shakes her head and fights a smile. "I know this isn't your cup of tea, but there would have to be a tornado, and even then, they probably wouldn't cancel." She sits on the end of the bench and pats my ankle. "Besides, it's going to clear off in the next hour and get hot again."

"Perfect," I mutter.

"Look on the bright side. The Thompsons are coming. Which means you get to see Haley. Aren't y'all friends?"

"We are—sort of." I pause. "She's nice."

Her eyes narrow. "But?"

"But with her also comes her parents. *And* her brother." I inhale, shaking my head the smallest bit. "And honestly? I think that guy's a tool."

She's quiet for a moment before she gives my ankle one last pat and stands. "I don't think he's nearly as bad as you've convinced yourself he is. You have to remember, like you, his family puts immense pressure on him to succeed. You know the weight of those kind of expectations." And then she heads toward the door. "Start getting ready soon. The guests will be arriving before we know it, and I set the dress your mother wants you to wear on your bed." She gives me a small look of warning. "Wear the dress she chose, Sutton. If you don't, I'll be the one to hear it."

"Yes, boss lady," I huff.

The Thompson family is made up of some of the wealthiest people this side of the state. All because Hunter's dad, Henry, along with his brothers, are considered to be the most elite doctors in Tennessee. And it didn't just start with them. No, it went back generations upon generations. Which is why Hunter and his sister, Haley, are expected to follow in their footsteps. All the way to medical school.

My family is among the richest families in Tennessee as well. I suppose it was only natural for our families to become friends. Especially since it was obvious that they could help each other out. When the Thompsons need a little extra push to get a new building permit approved, my father, as a senator, has some pull. And when my dad needs a little more backing for his campaigns and fundraisers, the Thompsons are there to lend a few million.

But while the Thompsons are shallow and conceited, Hunter is different. He doesn't fit into the picture-perfect image they strive to achieve. Though he sure looks flawless. His smile, too seamless. His abs? Does he ever eat carbs? And don't even get me started on the swagger. Ugh, rude. No one should have the audacity to walk through a room like they know every female—and probably a number of males—is ogling them. But he does. And it's obnoxious. His brown hair is just long enough to run his fingers through. And he is always flashing around his cocky, boyish grin for some stupid reason. He is crazy hot because he doesn't need to try.

But the most attractive part of him? He's no sheep. His parents made the honest mistake of allowing him to play youth hockey when he was a kid. And then being on the ice was all he saw. Being a doctor? Forget it. The only time he'll be hanging out at a hospital is after he inevitably gets injured while playing in a game. That boy has his sights set on the NHL. And that drives his family crazy. To them, there is no future in anything besides joining their practice. Their insanely large practice. One that is always growing with new locations popping up all over the state. With his mom being a scientist, always trying to cure something, and his dad being one of the top ranked surgeons in the South, they are well known. But that isn't what Hunter wants. And he has made that pretty clear.

And I guess I understand him in that sense. After all, I have spent my days waiting for the moment I can be my authentic, true self. Because for my entire life, I've been a fraud. From being a student at an all-girls private school since before I can remember to being a cringy country-club member, walking in with people who look like they have a literal stick shoved so far up their ass that if the doctor told them to say *ahhh*, the doc would see the top of the stick in their throat. I'm forced to wear the most expensive clothing. And, sure, I attend all these obnoxious fundraisers for my father's campaigns. But someday soonish, I'm going to break out of my little cage and be free. Free from the unattainable expectations. Free from constantly having to pretend to be perfect just because I'm the senator's daughter. And hopefully free from my parents' future plans for me.

I'm a ballet dancer. It's who I am. But at what cost?

What started off as something to make me look more sophisticated ended up being the only thing that gave me a real sense of purpose. But even I have had my share of getting burned out from it over the years. I guess when you push yourself to literal perfection, that's what happens. Especially since everyone knows perfection is just a fantasy. It isn't real. But still, I need to get as close as humanly possible to it. Though, I'll admit, right now, my shitty lungs haven't exactly made it an easy journey. It appears asthma and intense dancing don't really mix all that well.

But like my mom has said, I can use asthma as an excuse to be mediocre, or I can try harder.

And because I can't stand the look of disappointment on my parents' faces when I don't make the cut, I guess I'll just try harder. I'll try harder and hope it doesn't break me for good.

# HUNTER

*I'm so glad I am about to get the hell out of here in a few weeks. God, I hate this shit.*

My shirt makes me look like a douche. Not that I don't fit in—everyone at this thing actually is a douche. But Senator Savage and his wife have been best friends with my parents for years. They aren't bad people, but they care more about things they own and where they sit on the social ladder than anything else. They are shallow. As a fucking puddle on a paved driveway.

I shove my hands in my pockets as we walk out to the huge backyard that's set up similar to my own. A swimming pool with plenty of seating areas and umbrellas surrounding it. Making this the perfect place for a stuck-up party where only the most elite are welcome. I don't belong.

My sister bolts away from my parents and me, and I don't have to look to know where—or rather who—she's running to. But still, I look anyway. Taking in the girl in the pale blue dress, her dark hair pulled up into a loose braid, flowing over her shoulder.

*Sutton Savage.* Stoic angel with a major resting bitch face. Too beautiful for this fucked up world, yet too stubborn to realize it.

Each step she takes is calculated. She floats toward Haley, graceful as always because she has been trained to literally float through a room.

Ever since she was just a kid, I've watched her parents push her to the point of breaking her when it comes to dancing. Yet there is an ease in the way she moves that makes it clear she loves doing it. That it hasn't yet been spoiled for her because of her parents' need for perfection. I understand her. Sort of. But I also hate everything she stands for. She does what her parents tell her. If they yell jump, she asks, *How high?* If they say smile, she flashes her perfect white teeth. But it is clear that, deep down, she is a lost soul.

One I have no sympathy for because she has no fight in her. Not an ounce. A little bird shut in her cage, too scared to push open the door and fly outside. And because of that, no matter how beautiful she is, I'm not interested in her romantically. How can I be attracted to someone who stands for nothing? Even if it is so openly obvious in her eyes that she is dying inside.

Besides, I have a girlfriend. The same one I've had for six months now. Who I love and trust. And the best thing about her? She doesn't come from *this* world. She comes from a normal-sized home. She is allowed to go to college for whatever the hell she wants. She is perfect for me. And I don't care that my parents hate her.

Let's not forget to mention that my brother, Holden, had been in love with Sutton since he was seven years old. And since he's dead now, that makes Sutton even less appealing. After all, what sort of brother would I be if I wanted the girl my dead brother did?

Sutton's eyes find mine, and she stiffens. She tucks a loose strand of her nearly black hair behind her ear before turning her back to me, focusing on what my sister is rattling on about. My presence alone has always made Sutton uneasy, and I suppose that's because since we were kids, I've been a dick to her. Our parents always hoped she'd marry my brother one day. And when he died, I guess I was the next best thing.

*Fuck that.*

I agreed to take medical classes at Brooks University to appease them, but the biggest reason why I go to a school with a decent medical program is strictly because that college just happens to have one of the best hockey programs in the country. And they also happened to offer me a full scholarship to play. It didn't matter to me that my family rolled their eyes and scoffed at the word *hockey* and chuckled at the idea that I could actually go pro because I knew the truth. I'm not going to be a doctor. I'll never come back to Tennessee and carry on my family's legacy. I am going to play in the NHL.

And despite what they think, I'm sure as hell not going to give that girl a chance.

# SUTTON
## TWO YEARS LATER

I stare out the bus window, asking myself what the hell I've gotten myself into and if it's all a mistake. One that's potentially going to haunt me for the rest of my life.

Leaving Juilliard after just one year and transferring to Brooks University in Georgia might have been the most impulsive decision thus far in my life. Okay, scratch that. It was *definitely* my most impulsive decision. And coming from someone who typically doesn't leap without weighing the risks—unless it was while I was dancing—I shocked everyone. And that shock—and sheer disappointment—is what led to my parents' decision in cutting me off. Literally. Financially. Emotionally. Any way they could slice my existence from their lives ... they did.

Apparently, when your daughter has worked her entire life to get into a prestigious school like Juilliard, it isn't exactly ideal for said daughter to transfer out so soon. But while, on one hand, this decision seemed impulsive, on the other, I was tired of the unrealistic expectations my family had put on me since the day I was born. I was exhausted. And that exhaustion was crippling. Couple that with the fact that my asthma was being a miserable bitch, making it hard for me to compete to my full ability, I was breaking. Slowly losing myself. It was walk away or end up completely losing my mind.

*Now, I'm wondering if the latter would have been easier.*

Brooks's dance program, compared to Juilliard's, is like comparing McDonald's to Chick-fil-A. Everyone knows that even though both are fast food, there's still no comparison. And in this case, Brooks is certainly McD's. But I'm okay with that. Because truthfully, I didn't have it in me to dance somewhere like Juilliard anymore. There I was, a small fish in a big pond. At Brooks, I'll be a big fish in a puddle. I like those odds better.

The good news is, because Brooks was so excited to have me on board, they set me up in a house rather than a dorm. The downside of the house is ... it houses three other dancers. And one thing I've learned over the years about dancers is, we're every bit as bitchy as we are intense.

I don't think it helped that the school I chose is also where our family rival's son attends. The Thompson family might have been best friends with my family for most of my life, but nearly two years ago, it all changed. And now, I'll be sharing a campus with a guy who literally hates me because of my last name. And that's okay. Because the feeling is mutual.

The last time I recall seeing Hunter Thompson was at my family's barbeque a few years prior. The one when it had rained all day, giving me hope that it would be canceled, only for the sun to come out just before everyone arrived. Which left me stuck to mingle and chat with people, most of whom I couldn't stand. That night, before the Thompsons left, Hunter's parents and mine got into some sort of disagreement. Words were exchanged. And from that moment forward, we were sworn enemies. Which worked out for Hunter and me because we hated each other anyway. But Haley ... that was a different story. She was kind, sweet, and thoughtful. Everything I wasn't, she was. And now ... she hates me. And I'm supposed to hate her, too, but deep down, I can't. Maybe if she was a little more like her dickhead brother, I could easily do it.

Taking my phone out, I check the time. I still have hours left on this smelly bus. My eyes grow heavy, and I allow myself to doze off to the sound of the humming engine, the rattling seats, and the endless chatter surrounding me.

I stare up at the yellow house. The white window trim is slightly chipped, as is the black door. But it has character. Flowers are planted in front of the porch, and I wonder who exactly put them there. The walkway to the house is slightly overgrown, in dire need of some TLC. But this place is homey. And I don't hate it. The chicks on the inside? Now, that is still up for debate.

Pushing my shoulders back, I inhale and tilt my chin up. "It's fine," I mutter. "They'll probably be super nice. It's going to be great."

"Hah, tell yourself that all you want," a female voice says from right behind me, and I shriek, spinning around.

"You scared the hell out of me!" I gasp. "I thought—"

"No one could hear you out here, talking to yourself?" The girl with strawberry-blonde hair and Levi's overalls raises an eyebrow as she jerks her chin toward the house. "Girl, when you live in a house with three other bitches, someone is *always* around." She takes a bite from her green apple. Literally the only kind of apple I can't stand. "On one hand, that's not a bad thing because there's always an endless supply of tampons. On the other, if we're all PMSing at the same time, it's one big ol' bitchfest." Smiling, she holds her hand out. "I'm Ryann. Ryann Denver. And, yes, I have a boy's name. No, my parents didn't hate me when they picked it out."

Studying her for a moment with my guard up, I eventually smile before shaking her hand. "I'm Sutton."

Releasing my hand, she heads toward the house, nodding for me to follow. "Trust me, homegirl, I know who you are. We all do. You're Sutton Savage. Senator's daughter. Elite dancer. Juilliard dropout. Like Frenchy from *Grease*, but a much, *much* bigger deal, and your hair looks more gothic than an Easter egg."

I frown, rearing my head back as my feet follow her up the paint-chipped stairs. "Um … thanks?"

Her hand reaches for the door, and she looks over her shoulder. "Who said it was a compliment?" Nodding toward my single duffel, she looks confused. "Where's the rest of your crap? I know the freaking senator's daughter isn't rolling in here with one measly bag."

Shrugging, I follow her inside. "Well, this one did. And it's a duffel. Holds a lot of shit."

We walk through the entryway and into the living room, where one girl is lying on the couch in an oversize hoodie and workout shorts.

"Yo, Lana, our new roomie is here," Ryann calls to her, and Lana clicks the remote to pause *One Tree Hill.*

It's the episode when Nathan finally pulls his head out of his ass and forgives Haley after she ran off to be a singer. I sort of wish she had let it continue to play so I could relive it for what would likely be the tenth time now. Still, no matter how many times I've watched it, my heart squeezes inside of my chest each time.

Lana's eyes rake over me, up and down, sizing me up. "Are you Alabama's governor's kid or whatever?"

"Senator," Ryann corrects her before I can. "And Tennessee, dumbass, not Alabama."

"Tomato, tomahto." Lana shrugs. "In the South, it's all the same, isn't it?"

"Not really," I mutter, trying to keep my resting bitch face at bay and attempting to smile, though I'm sure it looks like I'm having a stroke. "Are y'all from around here?"

"Fuck no." Lana breathes out a laugh. "New Hampshire."

"Canada," Ryann says nonchalantly, looking down at her nails.

Gazing around the house, I shrug. "Where's the fourth roommate?"

"Poppy isn't home right now. And while her name sounds sweet and innocent, like the little pink troll from the movie … she's actually a bitch," Ryann says, completely unaffected. "Just stay out of her way, keep on her good side, and you'll be all set."

I start to nod, but Lana's laugh stops me.

"Ryann, I was kidding when I pretended I didn't know where Sutton was from. She's Sutton Savage. We all know she left Juilliard to be here. At Brooks. She's already on Poppy's shit list just for leaving the school she's always dreamed of attending and for being the feared dancer that she is." She gives me a half-sympathetic, half-tough-shit grin. "Poppy is intense. And judging by how far your dancing has taken you, so are you." She shrugs. "I don't need to tell you this is like *The Hunger Games*. Just do you, boo. Don't let Poppy get to you. Because trust me, if she smells weakness—even just a pinch—she's going in for the kill."

"Like literally or …" I say, eyes wide.

She simply shrugs. And at that, she stands, stretching her arms over her head before flipping her long blonde hair over her shoulders and practically skipping away.

Ryann must sense my unease because she pokes my shoulder. "Don't worry about what she just said. Poppy is bitchy, but she's not an awful person. She just wants to be the best." She gives me a sad smile. "And I hate to break it to you, but now that you've arrived … she isn't."

"Y'all haven't even seen me dance yet," I deadpan.

"Oh, trust me, we have. There's been a lot of buzz about you since you were, like … eleven years old. We know how good you are." She scrunches up her nose. "But you also left freaking Juilliard to be here. Which makes me question your sanity."

"Brooks has a good dance program too!" I throw my arms up. "It might not be Juilliard, but it's still one of the better dance programs in the South."

She gives me a sneaky smile. "I'll let it go. For now. But one day, you're going to tell me your real reasons for leaving New York." Heading toward the stairs, she holds her finger up. "Now, let's go. I'll show you around the house and your room. Maybe even help you hide the knives before Poppy comes home."

When my eyes widen, she barks out a laugh. "Kidding. Sort of."

*Great. I got rid of my mother, and now, I have to deal with a she-devil named Poppy. Awesome.*

# HUNTER

I finish dressing and close my locker. Even after a shower, I'm still out of breath. Maybe Coach is right; maybe we do suck this season. I never stopped training from last season, yet here I am, huffing and puffing like I've never played hockey before and I smoke a pack and a half a day. Just like I was after practice yesterday. And the day before that and the day before that.

Link Sterns darts past me, headed for the exit.

I frown, throwing my arms out. "Dude, where's the fire?"

Turning, he grins. "What the fuck are you talking about, Thompson?"

I look around. "Well, you're running out of here like your ass is on fire. Fuck, I'm not even sure you had time to properly scrub your ass. I'm sure you still smell."

"Trust me, I scrubbed my ass. And my balls too, just in case my girl's feeling frisky." He wiggles his eyebrows. "The fuck would I waste time hanging out with you Debbie Downers, sulking around because your asses are out of shape since y'all didn't train hard enough this summer? Besides, I'm taking Tate out to dinner."

And before I can answer, that motherfucker is gone. And I get it—he's madly in love with his girlfriend, Tate.

For years, I had a girlfriend too—Paige. But my family ran her off, constantly making her feel like she was less than us just because her family didn't have the kind of money mine did. The day she broke up with me, I'd never been that angry with my parents before, and that's saying something because they do a lot of shit to make me mad.

Paige was everything I'd ever wanted. She was normal and had a typical upbringing. She was sweet and warm. She didn't have crazy expectations for me. She simply loved me for who I was—until a year and a half ago, when she dumped me. Saying some bullshit about how it was for the best, but the truth came out weeks later. My parents had scared her away, basically threatening her to stay away from me. I told her I'd cut my family off if I could just have her back, but she refused.

What's crazier is that up until a few years ago, my parents were dead set on me getting together with bitchy Sutton Savage. All for their own personal gain. Now, our parents hate each other's guts, which is ironic because I've hated Sutton since I first laid eyes on her.

Now, Paige and I hook up sometimes. And after, when she leaves or I go home, even a year and a half later, it's not fucking easy. But if our random hookups are all I can have of her, I'll take it. Even if it is completely mind-fucking me.

One day, I'll get her back. When I get that phone call from the pros, I'll be off the hook as far as my family's legacy is concerned.

# SUTTON

I head into my Business class with unease growing in the pit of my stomach with each step I take to find a seat. I settle for mid-row. I likely won't be called on, but I'm not in the back of the class, looking like a slacker. Quickly sliding myself into a seat, I toss my bag onto the chair next to me and take my things out. This isn't exactly a class I want to be in, but in case things with dance don't work out, I need a backup plan.

Now that I've had a few days to settle in and explore the campus, I'm finding that it's pretty cute and very clean, and it has a sense of security.

"Is this seat taken?" a familiar voice asks sweetly a few minutes after I sat down.

Looking up from my phone, I find Ryann, and it makes me feel better, having someone here in class that I actually know. With her strawberry-blonde hair, piercing green eyes, and freckles sprinkled across her nose and cheeks, she gives me a wink.

"I suppose not," I joke. Pulling my bag from the seat, I give her a small smile. "I didn't realize you were taking this class too."

"Oh, yeah. I'm going to be a badass business-owning bitch someday. Just don't ask me what I'll be doing with my business because I have no clue." She smiles, sitting down. "Thanks for the seat. My options were sitting next to you; that dude up in the front row, who looks like he might keep panties in his pocket and sniff them from time to time; or that chick who looks like a Karen, ready to ask five thousand questions and demand to speak to the manager."

"Glad I was the safest choice." I chuckle. "I mean, I know you've only known me for a week, but I tend not to sniff panties or talk to managers, so you're safe there."

So far, living with three other women hasn't been awful. I try to stay busy so that I'm not home every hour of every day.

Dance started a few days ago, and as the other girls had warned me, Poppy is frosty. But she's also mega-talented, and I think that if she stopped viewing me as a threat, we could be friends. I've asked the other girls about her enough to know her parents have also been the driving force behind her ballet career. So, I'm sure if anyone else knows what it's like to be pushed to the point of breaking, it's her.

"Glad to see Poppy hasn't stabbed you in your sleep yet," Ryann whispers before giving me one last grin as the professor comes to the front of the room.

And just like that, day one of classes has officially begun.

Closing my laptop, I yawn, stretching my arms behind me.

"So, Business, huh?" Ryann asks, raising an eyebrow. "Not just here to study the art of dance?"

"Figured, what the hell? Doesn't hurt to have a backup plan, right?" I shrug.

"True that." She agrees. "Hey, so I know I could have asked you this at the house, but I didn't want the others to hear. You aren't looking for a job, are you? I mean, I know with a last name like Savage and a dad who's a senator, you don't need to work. But … it's still good money."

"What's the job?" I say, raising an eyebrow.

Standing up, she jerks her chin toward the door. "Why don't I show you? And then you can decide if you're willing to work."

"Are you going to murder me?" I follow her to the front of the classroom and out the door. "Because that's not really how I want to start my school year. I mean, I haven't even gotten to try the bakery on campus yet."

"Nah, you look like you could outrun me anyway. And if you ask me, the bakery is overrated. Their shit is dried out, and their coffee is fucking gross," she tosses back unapologetically. "This job … well, it's easier for me to take you there than to explain it. But I'll warn you, it isn't for the faint of heart.

And growing up like a princess, as you did, it's probably going to be way out of your comfort zone."

"All right, color me intrigued." I hike my messenger bag up a little higher on my shoulder. "Let's go."

"Don't say I didn't warn ya," she coos as we head toward her car. *What am I getting myself into?*

"Somehow, I feel like this could have been explained." I look at her once we're seated in the large, U-shaped booth. "With one word even," I deadpan. "One. Single. Word. The word being ... *stripper.*"

"What fun would that have been?" she calls over the music. "Also, we don't like to be called strippers. That's so ... old school and degrading. We're exotic dancers."

"I feel like that's the *exact* same thing. What's the difference?"

"Difference is, I'm not sucking anyone's dick in a back room!" She raises her eyebrows. "We dance. We get paid. That's it."

"Why does everyone have a mask on?" I nod toward the dancers, all wearing delicate masquerade-ball-like masks over their eyes. "Is that something y'all always wear? Or is tonight a special occasion? Like some *Fifty Shades of Grey* type of shit?"

"Most of the dancers here are students at Brooks, seeing as it's only a half hour away from campus. The owner is a woman who likes to protect her girls. Because of that, it was decided a while back that every dancer would wear a mask. A ... disguise, if you will."

In a strip club called Peaches, I stare as the women flaunt around the different stages, wrapping their bodies around the poles in the most seductive way. I've never danced like this before. Actually, I've never even *considered* dancing like this. But let's face it; since getting cut off ... I'm broke. And not only that, but if I earned money from doing this, it would give my mother a coronary. Something this scandalous and forbidden would make her clutch her pearls and point her nose to the sky. God, I'm grinning, just thinking about it. Especially since it was her decision to cut me off from the family.

"I can't believe I'm saying this ... but I'm in." I nod, keeping my eyes on the dancers. "I'll try it anyway."

"Bitch, you don't need to try. You're a dancer."

"Not a strip—"

"Exotic dancer," she corrects me. "*Exotic* dancer. You gotta get that right, or you'll be meeting a fist from one of these chicks in here. And trust me, you're going to do great."

"I don't know," I mutter, looking around at my new job. "I've danced my entire life. But not like *this*. Why'd you choose me anyway? Looking at me, what made you think, *Yep, that bitch will totally get onstage, strip, and shake her ass?*"

"Well, for starters, we're short-staffed. We lost five girls last spring because they graduated." She sits back in her seat, completely relaxed while being in a strip club. "Apparently, being a doctor, RN, business major, or teacher was more appealing than this."

"What? Noooo." I laugh. "Does Poppy or Lana know you work here?" I widen my eyes. "Do *they* work here?"

"Fuck no, they don't work here." She snorts. "Lana knows I work here. She has a boyfriend; he gets jealous, or she'd probably dance here too. As for Poppy, she knows, but she doesn't ask questions. She probably thinks it's beneath her to speak about it." She snorts.

"So, when do I start?"

"As soon as the boss lady says so," she tosses back instantly. "Ready or not."

"Ready or not," I mimic.

Punching my arm lightly, she squeals. "Annnnd the best part is, we can ride together to work!" She scowls. "But, like, where's your car? I figured you'd have a Mercedes or something."

"Nope. I used to have an Audi." I point to my feet. "Now, these are my means of transportation."

"Shit, really?" She frowns. "Where'd the car go?"

I relax in my seat. "When you drop out of a school your parents made you work so hard to get into … sometimes, life changes." I tilt my head to the side. "Fuck 'em, right?"

Nodding, she pats my knee. "Yep. Fuck 'em. You and I, we're going to have us some fun, and we're going to make some money."

As I turn my attention back to the dancers, my eyes widen, and I swallow—hard. *I guess I'm really doing this.*

# HUNTER

"For the past month, I've told you guys that this season will be hard and that I need one hundred ten percent from everyone. I'm still not seeing it, and it's starting to piss me off. We've got our work cut out for us, and I really hope you all know that." Coach LaConte speaks to the team, looking around at each and every one of us.

"Last season, we lost O'Brien and Hardy, along with others. And Cam Hardy was a damn good captain and center. He also led us to a Frozen Four and helped us win. So, if you think I'm being too hard on you, guess what. Tough shit. We still have a lot of work to do to get ready for our opening game."

Nodding toward Link Sterns, he leans against a locker. "Despite securing a spot in the pros, Sterns decided to stay at Brooks for his senior year. He is experienced. He's a hard worker. He leaves everything on the ice when he plays. And most of all, he's a stupid-talented winger with a good attitude. Which is why he's your team captain this season." His gaze sweeps around the room again. "Respect him. Respect me. Respect the assistant coaches. Respect the staff. And for the love of fuck, respect each other." Nodding, he claps his hands together. "Understood?"

"Yes, Coach!" we all cheer before he sends us out onto the ice for yet another practice.

We've had similar speeches given to us since we started training again, but it's clear he's still frustrated with the shape we're in as a team. With a brand-new center, we need to learn to play together the way we all did last year when Cam Hardy and Brody O'Brien were here.

Coach LaConte is the toughest coach I've ever had. But he's my favorite too. He gets shit done, and I think Brooks University is lucky to have him on board. But I also know he's going to ride us hard this season if he doesn't think we've unlocked our full potential.

And if there's one thing I hate, it's feeling like I'm failing at something. I go hard at anything and everything I do, to the point that it's really stressful. But that's who I am. And hockey is the most important thing in my life—even if my parents don't want it to be.

"It's been months of practicing with the new team, and I still can't get used to not having those guys here," Link says, coming next to me. "Thank fuck we still have Gentry, Huff, and you because, goddamn, a lot of these guys are so green that I might just call them broccoli. I'm worried about this season—I ain't gonna lie about that."

"We'll get it done, Cap." I slap his back. "You know LaConte handpicked everyone here. He knows what he's doing. Have a little faith."

"If you say so," he sighs.

"Hey, your ass is the one who decided to stay here for another season instead of playing in the pros in Cali."

He cracks a smile. "What can I say? I love my girl. She had another year, so that meant I had another year left in me as a Wolf."

He skates away, ready to start practice.

I personally think he's completely nuts to play another season of college hockey. It puts him at risk of being injured and losing his secured place in the NHL. But I guess I get it. Sort of. He has his old lady here at Brooks. And he must love her enough that waiting another year and staying with her outweighed playing for the pros sooner. It's romantic. And sweet.

But I still think he's fucking insane. I've never in my life loved anyone more than I love Paige. And even with her, I don't know if I could do what Link did.

# HUNTER

The smell of weed hits my nostrils before I even leave my room. Which means Cade is planning to party today. And by party, I mean, party by himself. We practiced this morning and don't have to be back at the arena until tomorrow afternoon. In Cade Huff's brain, that can only mean one thing—get fucked up.

He doesn't care that we can get drug-tested at any given time. Or that I'm pretty positive that people who have been to rehab aren't supposed to get high or drunk. And he certainly isn't concerned about a possible hangover. If I thought Brody O'Brien was crazy, Cade is ten times worse. The dude is wild and unpredictable. But, fuck, he's funny—just as long as you don't get on his bad side, that is.

Our house is made up of three of us—Cade Huff, Watson Gentry, and me. Watson is timid, polite, and I'm pretty sure he's never even smoked weed, much less tried drugs. Certainly never done cocaine or prescription pills, like we all know Cade went to rehab for in the past. Maybe that's what makes us all work together so well. We are nothing alike, yet we have each other's backs at the drop of a hat.

When I head down the stairs, there sits Cade. Sprawled out on the couch, playing his Nintendo Switch with his shirt off and a joint hanging out of his mouth.

"Whaddya say, Thompson? Play a game of Call of Duty with me?"

"Fuck no," I scoff. "You know I don't play that shit."

"Fine. Smoke a joint with me and get the munchies?"

"No," I say bluntly.

"Nothing like it, my friend. Get a little high. Hop on here, play a little COD, and then go get some cheeseburgers. It'll be a damn good time."

"I'll take your word for it. But maybe consider taking it easy, yeah?" I mutter, looking at him in sheer horror, worried that he's spiraling. "What's Gentry up to?"

"Hard to say with that boy. Probably eating cookies his mama made him. And if they were pot cookies, I'd make him share." He inhales before exhaling the white smoke into the air. "Where are you headed?"

"Just need to run a few errands before class."

"I've heard that before." He smirks. "Off for a booty call with your ex, are you? You've got the best fucking setup I've ever seen. She doesn't want to date you, both of you can do as you please, but you can fuck her when she's horny."

Sending him a glare, I reach for the door. "Later, Cade. I'd say behave, but I think you've already blown that for the day."

Going outside before he can respond, I close the door behind me and start toward my truck. Climbing in, I head to the library. I need to use the printer because the one at the apartment is a raging pile of shit, and I think Cade took a hammer to it yesterday. Which leaves me no other choice than to use Brooks's library.

I park my truck, looking around at the fairly full parking lot. There're a lot of people nerding out right now.

*Great.*

Walking in, I don't miss the eyes that look up at me. Some chicks wink, and dudes give me the head nod, holding their hand up. Hockey is basically a religion at Brooks. And even though I don't love the attention, it comes with the territory, and I try to always be polite. Even when the last thing I want to do is talk to random people about the upcoming season.

I carry on, continuing to the back room, where the computers and printers are. I'm rounding the corner into the room when I collide with a small body. I instinctively wrap my arms around her as she flails around, preparing herself for landing. I catch her, pulling her against me before she can hit the ground.

When I look down, I can't believe what I see. Sutton Savage's angry blue eyes land on mine, shooting me a death glare. As she rights herself, she makes sure to shove me away, tiny fists and all.

*What the fuck is she doing here?*

At first, I can't hide my stunned expression. It's like seeing a ghost, only … she's alive.

As she kneels down, scurrying to get her papers, I plaster on a smirk to mask my pure shock.

Bending down, eye level with her, I hold out one of the papers for her, still warm from the printer. But when she attempts to grab it from my grip, I let it drop to the floor.

"Whoops, sorry, Little Bird. It must have slipped."

She snatches it quickly as her eyes narrow to slits. "I bet you are, asshole."

I watch her stand, smoothing herself down. Her tight-fitting black cotton dress is short enough that her ass is barely covered. Her dark hair is pulled up into a bun, matching her no-nonsense personality.

She smells delicious, like a fucking dessert.

And when she brushes past me, I catch her wrist, spinning her toward me. "Look, I don't know what you're doing at Brooks, but understand one thing. You're at my school now, brat. Remember that."

Her nostrils flare, and she pokes a finger to my chest. "Oh, really? Last I knew, this was called *Brooks University*. Not Hunter Thompson University, *dick*." She steps back, clutching her papers to her chest. "And guess what. This is just as much my school as it is yours now. I suggest *you* remember that."

Every cell of her being is sharp. Her cutting blue eyes. High cheekbones. Hair as dark as night. Bold, plump red lips. And a bitchy personality to top it all off. She isn't soft and sweet, like my Paige is. No, this chick is something completely different.

There is nothing sweet about Sutton Savage. That's for damn sure.

She struts off with enough attitude to fuel a jet plane. Her dress hugs the curve of her ass. It's not a soft curve either. Her ass is profound, begging to be looked at. And as much of a she-devil as I think she is … I can't stop my eyes from gazing. Or my cock from twitching.

I could make her life hell if I wanted to. After all, her family is the reason why my parents never got to build their new establishment, which was going to help find the cure for my brother's cancer. If the Savages hadn't pulled the plug on the building permit, who knows what could have happened? She might not be her parents, but she's still a Savage. And all Savages match their name.

My parents needed the rights to build on land. And the Savages just so happened to have the ideal spot. It couldn't be just any old property for the place my parents were planning on building. It had to be the perfect location. It needed to be a place so promising that it would draw in the maximum sponsorships and investors. Endless funding to help them get what they wanted. A cure.

That was the only way they were going to beat the devil that had taken my big brother's life when he was fifteen and I was thirteen. Having an establishment where they'd cure rhabdomyosarcoma. And even though I think my parents took it all too far, I know they had the best intentions. Even though he was gone, my parents thought that stopping this cancer from taking other people's lives would make the fact that he'd died hurt less. I guess they needed something, anything, to make sense of his passing, and he deserved to have his name next to a promising treatment.

And when he died, they were stuck with me and my sister.

Out of the three of us kids, Holden was the one who had so seamlessly fit into the Thompson name. He didn't shy away from the pressure of perfection and the constant need to meet unrealistic expectations. He'd stood tall, carrying the weight of my parents' hopes like they were as light as a feather. He was going to be a doctor. We all knew he would have never strayed from our family's legacy.

Holden was the golden child.

And me? I wouldn't call myself the black sheep of the family. Perhaps maybe a grayish hue? I was the kid who just wanted to play hockey.

So, even though the Savages did my parents dirty, making Sutton's life hell isn't going to help me feel any better about the fact that my brother is dead. Especially since Holden would roll over in his grave if I tormented her. After all, he had been in love with her for years.

So, as long as she stays the fuck out of my way, I'll leave her be.

Maybe.

# SUTTON

"Asshole. Jerk. Pompous douchebag," I mutter to myself, walking home from the library. "Ugh. It's not your school, prick. It's an entire campus's school. *Thousands* of people."

Hunter plowed into me like he owned every inch of that building, and whoever stepped in his way, well, they would be roadkill. And then he caught me in his arms, trying to act all nice. That was, until he saw it was me. Then, that *nice guy* act went out the window real fast. His light-blue eyes darkened with rage. He dropped my paper just because he could. *Dick.* The most annoying part is that even though I hate him, my heart betrayed me for a split second—pounding in my chest as he caught me in his arms.

He and I shouldn't even have beef. We should just be indifferent—that's all. But because our parents are insane, we've been dragged into it. And that's something I've never had control over—my parents and their issues. Their shit becomes my shit. And really, who wants that much shit? Not me.

But the more I've thought about everything with my parents lately, the more I've realized one thing. I can decide for myself how I'm going to make money from here on out. And how I'm going to do it is by being a stripper.

*Sorry, Ryann. That's what it's called.*

Exotic dancer might sound nice, but at the end of the day, it's the same damn thing. And *stripper* just rolls off the tongue much easier than taking the time to say *exotic dancer.*

I'll admit, doing something that would make my parents so angry that they'd probably burst into flames, it brings me joy, just thinking about it. And after a lengthy lesson from Ryann last night, I'm ready for my first shift next weekend. I think so anyway.

I arrive in my driveway with only a few minutes to spare before I need to leave again for dance. Only this kind doesn't involve a bunch of pervy men and I get to cover up my boobs and ass.

Heading straight to my room, I change into my leotard. Pulling some sweatpants and a loose T-shirt over it, I toe my sandals on.

"Slutty Sutty, you riding with me?" Ryann chants, but I know she's just being herself and means no harm just by the tone of her voice. Plus, it's Ryann. "That was a good one, you have to admit."

When I swing my door open, she's standing just outside it.

"I'm ready. But unless you want to meet my Taser, come up with a different nickname, dink. We've known each other for, like … five seconds. Don't call me a slut."

"Geesh, fine. But take it from me—there's nothing wrong with being slutty. It keeps life interesting." She shrugs. "Let's go. The other two already left. Poppy was determined to beat you there." Looking at her Apple Watch, her eyes widen. "We have to go! You're going to make us late."

Trudging behind her down the stairs and outside, I pull the car door open. "Sorry. I lost track of time at the library. I ran out of ink."

"Dude, I have ink. Next time, just use my shit and save yourself the walk." She shoots me a look as we pull out of the driveway. "Poppy's in a mood today. Consider yourself warned."

"Awesome," I groan. *As if this day hasn't already been filled with enough assholes.*

The drive to campus only takes five minutes, and before I know it, we're pulling into a parking spot and booking it into class. We aren't late, but as a trained athlete, I think we all like to arrive early to most things. It's a blessing and a curse. Pulling the doors open, we head down the hallway to the dance studio and walk inside. Quickly setting our things down, we grab our shoes and take our positions.

Our instructor, Jolene—who is a tall, slender lady with her salt-and-pepper hair that is almost always in a neat bun—looks around the room to make sure we are all there.

"Ladies, before we begin, I have an announcement. Brooks is doing a fundraiser to raise money that will go to the One Wish program. The goal of this program is to provide resources for less fortunate children in the community. It helps provide financial support for them to participate in sports and take lessons in something they are interested in. This foundation was started by Brooks's very own Brody O'Brien last year, and it has taken off immensely." She looks around, her eyes widening. "This is completely unorthodox, but after speaking to Coach LaConte, I've decided on something. Given that Brody was a huge part of the hockey team, we're going to team up with the hockey team and put on a show."

She can hardly contain her excitement. Me? I can hardly contain my disdain.

"Each of you will be matched up with a hockey player, and the two of you will perform a dance together! You'll have six weeks. This will give you time to come up with a routine and practice together. The main event will involve dinner, followed by a show, featuring you and the hockey player dancing!" She looks around. "How awesome is this?!"

Ryann snorts. "I don't—wait, so we have to basically teach these giant men how to dance? That's what you're saying?"

Jolene gives her a reassuring smile. "Everyone knows hockey players aren't the best ballet dancers. So, your job is going to be to make them look good! But the hockey team is so loved that having them involved will already give this fundraiser an edge. Besides, it makes sense because of who started it to begin with. But I want to add, part of this will run into their season. One thing Coach LaConte stressed is the need to keep his players healthy. So, please, nothing too strenuous in your routines. You all are the dancers; they will be the entertainment. Make them look good. Heck, it can be comical even." She sweeps her gaze around to each of us. "As more information becomes available, I'll fill you in. But until then, let's get to work."

Most of the girls look thrilled. Others look scared. And then there's me and Ryann. Both completely annoyed.

From the little time I've gotten to spend with Ryann since we met, I've gathered one thing.

She really, *really* hates hockey players. Actually, athletes in general, I think.

I have nothing against puck boys. In fact, a lot of them are stupid hot, and I wouldn't mind getting an up-close-and-personal look at their abs. I just have to hope and pray that I don't get matched with Hunter *freaking* Thompson. Because that would suck balls. Big, smelly, wrinkly ones at that.

24

# HUNTER

The professor dismisses us, and I have to fight myself to not fucking cheer because I'm so excited. This might be my only class of the day, but this one class was too much. To be honest, I hate anytime I have to be in a classroom. If I'd had it my way, I would have entered the draft in hopes of being picked up from the pros as soon as I turned eighteen. But I made a deal with my parents. I'd wait until I was old enough to be considered a free agent, and if the time came and I didn't get a call from the pros, I'd carry on with the five million years of school needed to become a doctor.

Now, that time is here. And if I play well enough this season, maybe, just maybe, I'll get picked up. It's now or never. If I don't make it this season, it's probably not going to happen, and I really, *really* don't want to be a doctor. Even if it is my family's legacy, that doesn't mean it's mine.

Obviously, I'm scared of being a failure. I know I have what it takes, but I'm up against the best in the nation. I also know not making it will mean a lifetime of feeling like I lost my shot by not entering the draft to begin with. All I can do is play my heart out this season and push myself harder than ever before. Which is exactly what I plan to do.

Walking by a large picture window, I stop when I see dancers. Until this moment, I didn't realize the dance studio was even in the Finnigan building. I kind of assumed it would be … well, not in a building with regular classes, I guess. My eyes move around, searching for Sutton because I know she has to be in there. I find her after just a few seconds. The black fabric of the leotard hugs her delicate yet curvy body seamlessly. Practically becoming one with her skin. She moves, paying attention to nothing else around her, solely focused on whatever the hell she's doing, and I find myself intrigued.

There's a sadness in the way she holds her shoulders, though I'm sure no one else would see it. And her eyes look lost as she floats around flawlessly. She walks on her tippy-toes before leaping into the air and doing some twirly shit. I've never watched ballet. Never wanted to either. But Sutton Savage makes it look like a work of art. And a real, actual sport.

Unlike a few hours ago at the library, her hair is now tied up in a neat bun, like it usually is.

I might hate her because of her last name. But there's no denying that she's a beautiful, fascinating creature. Even if she is a spoiled brat.

When the music stops and she comes to a standstill, I take one last look at her before heading outside. The last thing I want is for her to catch me watching her. I'm not giving her the satisfaction. But, holy hell, she makes it hard not to stare.

# SUTTON

"This is actually a very good milkshake," I say, taking another long sip and closing my eyes. After my first time really dancing in weeks, I needed this. "Mmm."

"I know, right? They have the best around." Ryann pokes at her fries. "What do you think about the whole *dancing with a hockey player* thing?"

I sigh. "I think it's annoying. But I also get it. I've heard the buzz about how loved the Brooks hockey players are. Even if most of them are likely shitheads, it'll bring in a crowd; people will want to watch them dance. Besides, Brody O'Brien created One Wish. And for good reason too." I scrunch my nose up. "I just wish I didn't have to be involved. Hell, I'd take the football team over the puck boys."

"I don't want any of them," she huffs. "All athletes are assholes as far as I'm concerned." Her eyes widen, and she sits up a little taller. "Oh, speaking of dance, I have a bag of goodies at home from the boss lady. She said if anything doesn't fit, just bring it in on your first shift, and she'll return it for the appropriate size. But when she does measurements on new girls, she's usually spot-on when she goes shopping."

"How skimpy?" I mutter. "On a scale of, like, nun to porn star."

"Oh, porn star, for sure. You just won't have to take any dick. And we get to cover our nips up, so that's kind of nice."

"Oh boy," I grumble. "Thank God for the masks. My parents would literally strangle me if it got out that their daughter was an *exotic dancer* now. Not like it matters, I suppose, since they aren't speaking to me. But still, they'd probably start digging my grave if they knew I was doing this."

"Strict parents?" she asks, finishing her shake and pushing it toward the end of the table.

"You have *no* idea."

"I guess that comes with the territory of being a senator's daughter. But since they aren't talking to you anyway … fuck 'em. Right?"

Nodding, I smile. "Right."

"And side note: the only chicks whose cover gets blown while dancing at Peaches are the ones who want people to know who they are. Trust me. Oh, and the ones who have boyfriends that can't keep their mouths shut. As long as you, one, don't rip your mask off and tell everyone who you are, and, two, don't get a man who has a big mouth … you'll be fine."

"Noted." I clear my throat nervously. "Speaking of the hockey team, do they come in much?"

"Not as much as you'd think. But occasionally, we'll see some boys from the team. I feel like we get more football players than puck boys." She smirks. "Like I said, both are assholes. But both are also pretty good tippers, I'll admit."

"Sweet." I relax a little.

I know Hunter couldn't pick me out in a crowd, but the thought of having to dance for him is annoying. And something I don't really want to do.

"Why do you ask?" She looks me over, narrowing her eyes. "I feel like I should know this already since we're roomies and all, but do you have yourself a boy toy on the team or something? If you got paired up with him, that'd make this whole performance thing easier."

"No." I laugh. "Nothing like that."

Her eyes widen. "I can read people like a book. I've been doing it my entire life. So, go on. Tell me."

Resting my back against the booth, I huff out a breath. "Hunter Thompson."

"You're *boning* Hunter Thompson?" she hush-yells. "Like *über-talented winger for the Wolves* Hunter Thompson?" She shrugs. "Still think he's likely a prick and I hate his guts. But he is fine as hell. Do you, girl. Do you."

"No! Our families used to be close. Really close." I pull my lips to the side slightly. "Now … they are enemies. And even though it's probably my family's fault, he's still a dick. And if I have to be his partner … well, I'm going to be pissed."

"Shit," she mutters. "Well, hopefully, you'll get paired with someone else then. Right?"

"Right." I nod quickly. "All right, roll me out of here. I'm full, and I need a nap."

I groan, and she laughs.

Even though I'm having a good time with Ryann, I still have this bad feeling in the pit of my stomach. A feeling that I'm going to get stuck working with a hockey player I hate.

# HUNTER

Club 83 isn't just a place for dudes to sit at the bar and shoot the shit while chicks shake their asses on the dance floor. It has pretty good food too. It's definitely not the same without Bria Collins's beautiful face behind the bar though. Unfortunately, when her man, Brody, got drafted, she left too.

"I'm sore. I need someone to massage me," Cade whines.

"Well, I'm gonna go ahead and pass, but I'm sure Watson will fix you right up." I grin, elbowing Watson's side. "Right, Gentry?"

"Fuck off," he groans.

"Relax, asshole. I was thinking more along the lines of one of those leggy blondes over there." Cade jerks his chin toward the dance floor. "Hell, even that redhead is looking pretty good."

My eyes move to the dance floor, and my jaw clenches as I take in Paige dancing slow and sexy with her friends. Her back is to us, so I can't blame Cade for not knowing it's her. But I'd know that ass and those thighs anywhere.

"Shut up, Huff," I growl. "Look at the blondes all you want, but don't look at Paige."

He looks harder, rearing his head back just as she turns to the side. "Oh fuck, man. I didn't know that was Paige. I was just looking at that ass and all that red hair." He turns toward me. "But for real, my man ... how long are you going to pine over her? It's been nearly two years."

"Yeah, but she sneaks in and pays him a visit from time to time." Watson grins. "Isn't that right?"

"Does that mean you're, like, her own personal sex puppet?" Cade says, serious as can be. "She uses you for the D, but won't commit? Fuck, how's it feel, being the chick in the relationship?"

"Shut up," I mutter.

I know she isn't using me. Not really anyway. It's a two-way street. Some nights, I get drunk and miss her, and I call her up. Sometimes, she comes over. I fuck her until the sun rises, and then away she goes. Other times, she calls me. She sounds sad and lonely, and I run to her like my ass is on fire. It always ends the same way. She leaves, or she asks me to.

Because of my family, now, we're stuck in this weird fucking place where we aren't together. I have no say in what she does. Yet, every now and then, we fuck. Sending me right back to square one.

When we were a couple, for the first six months, my family was still good with the Savages. And that meant that our families spent a lot of time together. No matter how many times I told Paige I couldn't stand Sutton and that she had nothing to be worried about, Paige was jealous when Sutton was around. I couldn't blame her because my parents were always very vocal that they wanted me with Sutton and not Paige.

When Sutton walked into a room, every set of eyes would be on her, and she knew it. Paige was beautiful, like a girl-next-door sort of look. With tanned legs and long red hair. They were polar opposites on every level. But it didn't matter because I only had eyes for Paige.

"I feel like you're setting yourself up for a restraining order, staring like that, bruh," Cade mutters, hitting his elbow to my side. "Gawking that way, it's just plain weird. You look desperate. Chicks don't want desperate. They want an asshole."

I turn, and he smirks.

He nods his head. "They want ... *me*."

"The man misses his old lady. What would you suggest he do?" Watson says, leaning forward on the bar to look at him. "Hit her over the head and drag her home?"

"It's been, like ... almost two years. She ain't his old lady anymore." He frowns. "And actually, she might be into that. Bitches love the caveman shit." Cade shrugs. "If it were me though, I'd walk right up to those two blondes she's dancing with, and I'd ask them if they wanted to go into the restroom. I'd tell them one could suck on my cock while the other let me play with her tits."

"What in the fuck good would that do?" Watson says, clearly confused.

"I'll tell you what it would do. It'd make her ungrateful ass jealous. Because you know those chicks wouldn't pass up a chance to show Thompson here how good of a blowie they could give. And who knows? Maybe she'd want to join, and he could finger-fuck her while the whole thing went down." He takes a swig from his beer before slamming it down. "I'm a fucking genius, I know."

"Jesus," I mutter, shaking my head.

"Too far?" Cade shrugs. "My bad. Wishful thinking for my night, I suppose." Suddenly, a grin spreads across his face. "I'll make you a deal. I'll take the Barbie twins off your hands for the night, and that'll leave your ex–lady friend all to yourself."

Before I can answer, he's heading out onto the dance floor. His energy is always unmatched, and even though it's clear he's got demons, he's damn good at hiding them from the world when he wants to.

When he wedges himself between the blondes, Paige's eyes find mine, and she smirks, holding her finger up, signaling for me to come over. For a moment, I just sit there. But finally, I give in to temptation, and I finish my beer and move toward her.

"I wondered how long you were going to watch me before you came over." She giggles, throwing her arms around my neck. "You look so handsome tonight, baby."

The slur in her words proves she's drunk. Which seems to be the only time she wants me lately. How long can we keep doing this? I'm not sure. But if giving her what she needs when she needs it keeps her from moving on, I'm okay with it.

"You looked like you were having fun. I didn't want to bother you," I shout over the music, holding her waist with my hands. "I was watching your ass sway, imagining sliding my cock between those legs, and now, my jeans are too fucking tight."

Giving me a little smirk, she spins around, poking her ass up against my crotch and making me hiss with need.

God, she's sexy.

She cranes her neck up to look at me, pursing her lips like she wants a kiss. So, I don't make her wait. I bend down, planting one on her before my tongue teases hers, making my cock stir even more.

When she pulls back, continuing to push her ass up against me as her hips move to the rhythm, I feel a set of eyes on me. Searching around, I spot big blue eyes watching me from the other side of the dance floor.

Sutton.

It's been days since I saw her in the library, the day when her laser eyes damn near burned a hole in me. She hates me—that's a given.

She doesn't smile; instead, she narrows her eyes slightly as she continues to dance with whatever moron she's grinding against. Her long, dark hair is pulled into a sleek ponytail instead of a bun. And her white tank top glows against her tanned skin, low enough for me to see the sheer layer of sweat covering her skin like a blanket.

I have everything I've ever wanted in my arms. But, yeah, someone like Sutton Savage makes it hard to not at least look.

Her body moves effortlessly. Almost like it's easier for her to dance than it is for her to stand still. I want to look away. I *need* to look away. But, Christ, I'm entranced by this she-devil.

I'm a piece of shit for letting Paige grind her ass on me while I'm staring at Sutton. And there's no denying the weird fucking tension between us right now even though I know it's wrong.

After blinking a few times, she seems to snap back to reality, and her eyes are the first to break contact. Looking away from me, she pays attention solely to the man in front of her. She moves on him in a way that if they weren't wearing clothes, I'd suggest the day-after pill tomorrow morning.

Paige reaches her hand behind her back and runs her fingers over the hard lump through my jeans, and I swallow hard. Wanting to get her the hell off this dance floor and away from this crowd.

Because I know damn well that she's coming home with me tonight.

But now, I'm wondering why the fuck I keep asking myself who's going home with Sutton. Why do I care?

I don't. I definitely, fucking certainly don't.

# SUTTON

Sweaty and smelly, Ryann and I head into the house after a few hours of dancing and flirting.

I found a pretty good dance partner, but when he asked if I wanted to come over, I respectfully said hell to the no. It had been fun while it lasted, and we'd had some nice moments, but that was over, and there was no way in hell I was going home with him.

Hunter, on the other hand, walked out, looking extra cozy with Paige. I have to give it to her; I didn't know she could dance that dirty, and I found myself impressed. It's clear they have chemistry in the way they move and interact with each other. He's comfortable with her, and she basically owns him. It's also obvious that he's missing her. Only a fool wouldn't see that.

But it makes me feel bad for him, knowing that his parents ruined their relationship—almost. Then again, they did her a favor. Who would want to marry into a family like that?

There was a look in his eyes when he watched me dance. I'm not even sure what it was. All I know is, if I hadn't looked away, I'm not sure he would have. I felt his eyes on every inch of my body. I'll never say it out loud … but I didn't hate it. But I do hate that I didn't.

It's a weird feeling, knowing he and I are connected through hate. And enemies shouldn't look at each other like that. It's not normal.

After brushing my teeth, I wash my face and take my hair down. Tomorrow is a full day of classes and dance. Even though I know I need rest, when I lie down in bed, I can't help but wonder what Hunter and Paige are doing. And then, for some stupid reason, I feel the smallest bit annoyed, knowing damn well what that is.

*I've never given a shit before. Why now?*

# HUNTER

As Coach finishes explaining what he signed us up for, all the guys and I stare at him like he's lost his damn mind. Right now, I'm wondering if he has.

"So, the ten names I just said are the players I've chosen to do this." He tucks his clipboard under his arm. "I know this isn't your cup of tea. But it's for charity. And for that, I need you to just pretend for a few measly practices that you're Magic Mike." He pauses. "The uglier, non-stripper version, that is."

"Dancing? With ballerinas? Coach, you're shitting me," Link groans. "I'm sure Tate's going to love this."

"It's for charity, Sterns. And not just any charity. It's for the one Brody O'Brien started. And that boy is one of our own," Coach warns, shooting him a glare. "And you'll do it with a damn smile on your face, or you'll ride that bench so hard that your ass will be sore. You feel me?"

Link sighs, "Yes, sir."

I don't say anything because frankly, I am terrified of Coach. But deep down, my mind is reeling, and my back teeth are grinding together. I'm no fucking dancer. And I think it's bullshit that we have to do this and not the football team.

"With all due respect, Coach, what about our season? Seems sort of insane that we're going to fuck around with dancing when we need to be focused on winning games." I say what everyone else is thinking. "Not to mention risking an injury, twirling around in a tutu."

Coach nods slowly, pointing at me. "For that, I just might make you wear an actual tutu, Thompson." He holds his arms out, looking around. "It's a few hour-long practices a week, damnit. They have been told to keep it light and easy, to not put players at risk of an injury. This isn't going to be a big deal. You'll meet with your dancer when both of your schedules allow it. The two of you will come up with a plan. And then when the time comes, you'll dance. Likely look like a moron. And go about your life while kids in need get to play sports." He gives us a no-bullshit look. "To me, it's not hard to figure out. So, for the love of God, just shut up and do it."

"Yes, sir," we all say.

"Great. Now, I know you're all tired, but you've got the whole afternoon to recover. But guess what. Tonight at seven o'clock … you will go to the dance studio in the Finnigan building. You'll go there and do whatever the hell Jolene asks of you. Do we understand each other?"

We all nod, and he looks around, pleased with our answer.

"All right. Get on out of here, boys. I'll see you tomorrow."

The dance teacher … lady … instructor—whatever the hell she is—pinches the bridge of her nose, gazing at all of us. It's obvious we suck ass, and she's probably wondering what the hell she got herself into by agreeing to this. But in our defense, we're all still fucking wiped out after practice earlier.

"Well, we certainly have some work to do," she huffs. "Lucky for you all, I have some incredibly talented dancers. They could make even *you* clowns look good."

We showed up here, as requested by Coach LaConte. Did some stretching, had to show off our nonexistent dance moves. All in all, it was probably the most awkward I've ever felt in my life. I'm pretty sure the only one who didn't hate it was Cade, and that's just because I think he was half-drunk.

"All of you will receive an email sometime in the next few days. The email will state a date and time to come back here to find out who you'll be working with." Giving us a tight-lipped smile, she waves her hand. "You are all free to go."

"Thank God," someone mutters under their breath as we all waste no time filing out of the room.

"I don't know what y'all are sulking about. Do you know how wild dancers are in bed?" Cade grins as we head through the hallway and outside toward the parking lot. "That Poppy girl is hot as hell. I hope she's my partner. She's an absolute bitch, but I'd let her ride me until she had a big ol' smile on her face."

"Dude, shut up," Link groans, dragging a hand down his face. "I can't believe I have to do this shit."

"How'd Tate take it?" I grin.

He scowls. "She fucking laughed. Thought it was hilarious that I had to dance with a ballerina." He shakes his head. "I'd figured she'd be pissed. But, no, she said she's inviting everyone to my performance. Like I'm a fucking first grader or some shit."

"Look on the bright side," I say, trying to make him feel better. "She said it doesn't have to be a ballet dance. So, no tights for you, big guy. Unless you're into it."

"I'd wear 'em. I don't give a fuck." Cade shrugs, and I know he isn't kidding. He literally gives zero fucks. "I'd have to beat the women off of me once they saw my dong in them."

"Wow," Watson mutters. "Just … wow."

"I know I said I wanted Poppy, but now that I think about it, there's a chick with black hair that I saw on the steps of the dancers' house the other day. I was on my run, and if she hadn't been talking on her cell phone, I would have walked right over to her." He licks his finger, pretending it's sizzling. "Fucking. Hot. With an ass on her that I instantly got a half-chub for."

"I bet you're talking about Sutton Savage. That's Tennessee's Senator Savage's daughter," Watson says thoughtfully. "She's in my Business class. She and her friend Ryann Denver both are."

Grinning at Watson, Cade smacks him on the abdomen. "Gentry, if I didn't know better, I'd think you had a little crush on this Sutton girl."

Out of nowhere, I feel my jaw tense and my hand curl into a fist. I don't like these guys talking about Sutton. Though I have no idea why.

"No," Watson says quickly. "I mean, yeah, she's hot. Really hot. But her friend … she is too gorgeous."

"Watson's got a crush," Cade chimes in, annoying Watson to the point that his face reddens.

"Fuck off," Watson mutters. "Seriously, Huff."

"Sterns, want to go grab a beer?" I say, ignoring the other two morons.

"Fuck yes, I do. The old lady is off visiting her mom and sister tonight."

"And if she wasn't, you'd what … not go?" Cade cackles. "Does Tate just carry a tiny purse around with your cock in it? Since it probably doesn't have to be a big one."

"Huff, shut the fuck up, would you?" Link growls, his shoulders tensing. "Or go snort something up your nose or get drunk and piss yourself."

"I didn't piss myself. I pissed *on* myself while I was trying to piss," Cade corrects him, completely unfazed, though I'm sure Link mentioning snorting something probably doesn't sit right with him.

Cade's been to rehab before. And honestly, I'm surprised he even has a spot on the team. Especially since Coach LaConte runs a tight fucking ship.

"Whatever," Link mumbles.

I think we all know Cade is just being typical Cade. He isn't a bad dude. He just has a shit ton of demons. And I think the only way he can stand himself is by cracking jokes. Even if they are usually at others' expense. And as our captain, it's Link's job to keep his guys in line.

"Let's roll, Thompson." Link jerks his chin toward his truck. "After this shitstorm of an audition, I'm ready for a beer."

"Same." I nod, pulling his truck door open.

# 6

## SUTTON

We head into the studio. After receiving an email from Jolene late last night, we know the time has come to find out who we'll be matched up to dance with. I'm hoping for one of the dudes I've heard is nice. Watson Gentry has literally been labeled a golden retriever. He also isn't known to sleep around, which means he might actually have morals. Unlike most of the others. And in this situation—where I'll literally have to teach someone what to do—a golden retriever sounds pretty darn good. Besides, he's hot. Really hot.

"Let's get this over with, ladies," Ryann mutters, pulling the studio door open. "I really don't want Cade Huff. He's a whole fucking mess."

"He's so hot though," Lana gushes. "I love a bad boy. Remember bad-boy Brody O'Brien? The dude who started this charity? Well, before he grew a heart and fell in love, I got to ride that train." I swear her mouth waters as she says the words. "He had no clue who I was a few weeks later when we had a run-in at the coffee shop. But that one blissful half hour?" She fans herself. "I'm melting, just thinking about it. He. Was. Huge. But more than that, he surrrre knew how to use it."

I open my mouth to answer when I feel a body so close to mine that my skin prickles, sending a jolt creeping up my spine. Before I can crane my neck to look, Hunter's voice is in my ear.

"Nice sweatpants, Little Bird," he coos. "Oh, and the bun? Wow. Sexyyyy."

Whipping around, I shove his chest. "Piss off, Thompson."

"Oh, but I have to be here. In your little tiny-dancer world," he whispers, eyes narrowed on mine. "You'd better just hope they don't pair us up. Actually ... you're probably hoping they do."

I widen my eyes, tilting my head. "I'm surprised your girlfriend let you off that leash long enough to be here tonight."

His eyes darken with anger, but he keeps his composure. "And what girlfriend is that? Enlighten me."

"Why, Paige Sanders, obviously. The same girl you've been following around like a lost puppy dog for years now."

"She's not my girlfriend anymore," he growls.

"Yeah, that's what I've heard. But it sure looked like it last night." I tap my chin with my finger. "The crotch grab was what threw me off."

"Says the girl who had her ass dry-fucked by some random dude." He nods, putting his lips to my ear. "Don't worry, Little Bird. I saw you watching me and Paige, wishing it were you."

"Maybe in your dreams, preppy boy." I turn my head, peeking at him through my lashes. "You might think this campus is yours because you can push a puck around on the ice, but you're wrong. You're in my world now. And you'd better watch out."

Walking away from him, I don't miss at least ten of the girls in here staring at us. Some in awe, others confused. And then there's Ryann, who looks worried. Poppy just looks plain pissed off, likely not wanting the attention to be off of her for five seconds of her life.

And while we all anxiously wait for Jolene to break the news on who our partner is, I keep my eyes focused straight ahead. Yet, somehow, I still feel Hunter's smirk as he watches me, trying his best to get under my skin.

And even though I'm a tough bitch, it's working.

# HUNTER

On one hand, I really don't want my name to be said in the same sentence with Sutton's, signifying we're stuck working together. On the other, I don't want her to work with any of my horndog teammates either. Best case would be that she gets paired with Link or one of the other dudes who has a girlfriend. That would be my perfect scenario. Because not only would I not have to deal with her bitchy ass, but I also wouldn't have to think about someone like Cade putting his hands on her, charming her into bed with him, like he does every other chick at Brooks. Or Watson, who girls are obsessed with because he's actually fucking nice.

Jolene steps before us all, and next to her, surprisingly enough, is Coach LaConte. Even I can tell his grumpy ass thinks it's funny that he dragged us into this shit.

She clears her throat, smiling at the room before looking down at her clipboard.

"So, this wasn't exactly easy. But my assistant and I tried our best to match each player with a dancer we thought would complement him well." She snorts. "Which, like I said, wasn't easy. Because quite frankly, some of y'all are terrible."

After she has another laugh, she begins rattling off names. I'm only halfway paying attention until I hear her say the names of the guys I'm closest with and who they are partnered with.

"Cade Huff, you're going to be paired with Lindsey. Watson Gentry, you'll be with Ryann."

She says a few more, and I know we're getting close to the end. Link's already been chosen to work with Poppy.

*Lucky him.* That chick is bitchy.

Sutton's name hasn't been called yet, and I'm starting to fucking panic.

"Hunter Thompson," she says, looking up at me, "you struggled. Terribly, to say the least. But lucky for you, I have a secret weapon to make you look better." She swings her gaze across the room, and my heart sinks. "Sutton, work your magic on Thompson." Tucking the clipboard under her arm and clapping her hands together, she looks at Coach. "Thanks for lending me your men, Coach. This is going to be one hell of a fundraiser."

Coach sweeps his gaze to each of us. "Yep. I suppose it will."

I slowly move my eyes to where Sutton stands, and her face is as red as a tomato. Her eyes drift off into space as she stares straight ahead. It's bluntly obvious that she's just as annoyed with this as I am.

But for some reason, that makes it suck less. Knowing I'm under her skin.

When she finally dares to give me a glance, I smirk, narrowing my eyes. Which only causes her to roll her eyes. She pretends to scratch her cheek with her middle finger before looking away again.

*That's right, Little Bird. You're stuck with me.*

"Take the next hour or two to get to know your partner." She points her finger at us guys. "Don't even think about getting to know my girls *that* well. This needs to be about dancing and not sex."

A bunch of people laugh or shift uncomfortably on their feet. Me? I just continue to stare at the side of Sutton's head, infuriating her more. Because honestly, I've always thought she was kind of hot when she was pissed.

Which is a lot of the time.

# SUTTON

There're twenty people in this room—not including Coach LaConte, Jolene, and the assistant dance coach, Chasity. The hockey team selected ten of their most popular players, and Jolene chose ten of Brooks's best dancers.

And here we are, Hunter *fucking* Thompson and me, forced to work together.

Walking outside, I lean against the brick building and blow out every ounce of breath from my lungs. Even though I know I don't have a choice but to work with him, I'm hoping Hunter doesn't find me.

I take a puff from my inhaler and stuff it into my pocket. Squeezing my eyes shut, I lean my head upward toward the sun.

I feel someone next to me, but I don't even have to open my eyes to know it's Hunter. After smelling his scent in the library and again today when he came up from behind me, I would know it anywhere. And annoyingly enough, it's as delicious as he looks.

"Sutton Savage," he coos. "Just out of curiosity, are you going to wear those sweatpants during our performance? If so, we might get docked some points for looking homeless."

Popping my eyes open, I look at him. "Are you always this obnoxious? Also, I wouldn't worry yourself with my apparel when we're going to get docked points for the fact that—like Jolene said—you suck and can't dance."

"Oh, trust me, the judges will eat me up." He winks. "We can do this the easy way or the hard way. How it goes will depend on which one of the dozens of your personalities shows up at each practice."

"When you're around, I only have one personality." I bat my lashes. "I call it bitchy, and it sometimes makes me want to do things like cut your nuts off and serve them to you for dinner."

He yawns like he's bored. "Are you done?"

"Hardly," I scoff.

"Man, the apple didn't fall far from the tree, did it? Just. Like. Your. Mother," he says through gritted teeth. "Your heartless, backstabbing bitch of a mother."

Stepping around him, I walk away from him and toward the sidewalk. I know I can't get around that he's my partner. But I sure as hell don't want to listen to his mouth right now.

*I'm nothing like my mother. Nothing.*

"Come on, brat," he calls from behind me. "Cut the shit."

Ignoring him, I walk on.

"Fine," he yells again. "You win for today. I'm over this anyway."

And moments later, I hear a truck roar to life before it speeds past me.

Everything he is irks me. And when he's around, he turns me into someone even I can't stand. But last I checked, you can't escape yourself.

*Damn you, charity. Now, I'm stuck dealing with him.*

# SUTTON

The time has arrived. A dawn of a new day. The end of an era. That era? Me considering myself a good girl. Because now ... I'm a stripper.

I look at myself in the mirror. Wide eyes stare back at me, asking me what the hell I'm about to do. I wish I could say, but truthfully ... I have no idea. The moment when I need to dance at Peaches for the first time has been coming for weeks now. Now, it's here. And I'm terrified.

Out of all the outfits given to me by my boss, I went with a black bra with a matching lace thong for night one. I chose a simple black masquerade mask to pair with it and hot-pink pumps. The rest of the girls are already out there, doing what we're all here to do. Shake our asses. I've performed in hundreds of shows in my lifetime. Competing and winning countless times. But nothing has ever made me feel this nervous.

Wringing my shaky hands together, I pull in a deep breath, filling my lungs before slowly letting it out.

"I can do this," I whisper. "I'm Sutton fucking Savage."

Lifting my chin higher, I march toward the door and head out onto the stage.

It's lit enough for the pervs to watch the dancers, but it's still much darker than I anticipated. I've grown accustomed to bright lights on a stage. But this sexy mood lighting … it's different.

And for the first few minutes on the stage, I'm absolutely terrible.

I can't help but focus on the men and women below me, which makes it damn hard to get into a rhythm. At first, I just move around the pole slowly, not knowing really what to do with it even though Ryann gave me multiple lessons. But this right now seems so unnatural. Pole dancing isn't for the faint of heart. And, shit, it requires much more strength than I thought.

Slowly but surely, I get *it*—whatever it is that gives dancers the ability to deliver what the crowd is looking for. I feel that moment where it all shifts and my body becomes one with the music, giving the customers what they came to Peaches for to begin with. I hope so anyway.

It takes no time before I'm covered in sweat, and I have no doubt that on the nights I'm working, there's no way in hell I could get an extra workout in. Heck no. This right here will have to be my exercise.

I continue to dance, gripping the cool metal pole and wrapping my legs around it. Tossing my hair back. Hair that, for once during a performance, can be down. Freely flowing down my back and making me feel alive.

For the first time, there's no prize at the end of this night. And I don't have to kill myself to be perfect. I can play. Creating whatever the hell I feel like to pass the time. And I really, *really* like the thought of that.

Even if I do feel a little dirty right now.

# HUNTER

I sit on Sutton's porch steps, wondering where the hell she is. It's after one a.m. I got here at eight—right after practice got out. Two of her roommates have come out. Poppy told me she had no idea where she was and didn't care either. The other said she hadn't heard from her all night. I'm not worried. Yet something is keeping my ass planted here.

Headlights come into the driveway, and I squint, trying to make out who it is. As she steps out of the passenger side, taking in the sight of me, I frown as I look her up and down.

She's dressed in baggy sweats but has her eyes done up with makeup and her hair down in long black curls. I feel my heart stop when I notice how it looks. And when her friend steps out, she looks the exact same way.

Like they've both been with someone.

Like they were just thoroughly fucked.

"Hunter?" She frowns, standing before me. "What are you doing here?"

Ryann stops next to her. "You good? Or do you want me to stay?"

Sutton gives me a strange look before giving her a small nod. "I'm good. Go to bed. I'm coming in right behind you."

Once Ryann is gone, she turns her attention back to me.

"I got your number from the dance lady, Jolene. I've been trying to call you for hours."

I feel my body shiver when she sits next to me, her thigh touching mine. The smell of perfume assaults my nose. It smells good, but it doesn't smell like her. At the library and again at the dance studio, she was close enough for me to breathe her in. She smelled like a damn sugary cupcake. This is more like an expensive hooker, and that makes me uneasy.

"I was ... out. What's up?"

"Out where?"

She looks the slightest bit nervous as she shifts around. "Just out." Something inside of her snaps. "Why does it matter to you? And why would it be any of your business where I was?"

"It isn't, I guess," I mutter. "You've been avoiding me for almost a week. I don't want to do this dancing shit any more than you do. But if I don't? LaConte will have my balls. So, for the love of fuck, can you just grow up a little so we can get this shit over with?"

"Fine," she gripes. "When are you free?"

"Tomorrow night. We'll start then," I say bluntly.

"I ... have plans tomorrow night. Could we meet up in the morning? I just have one class first thing, but I'll be done by eleven thirty."

*She has plans.*

I shouldn't care. Hell, a week ago, I would have fucked Paige if she hadn't been so hammered. But she was drunk and passed out, and I had to carry her into her house. But that was a week ago. Before I suddenly gave a fuck what Sutton was doing with her free time.

But I do care. And that's really fucking annoying. She isn't mine to care who she has plans with. And I don't want her to be either. I want Paige. I *love* Paige.

"That should be fine." I nod stiffly, swallowing hard. "I have no idea how this whole thing is going to work. I don't dance."

I swear her lips turn up a tiny bit. The ice queen smiles—a little anyway.

"I think, for tomorrow, we could just meet up and brainstorm some ideas on what we're going to do. What vibe we're going for. And then after that, we can start actually practicing. If that's okay with you anyway."

"That's fine." I nod. "Meet at the coffee shop? Seems like a neutral place. Plus, if you murder me, enough witnesses will be around," I half-joke. "Noon?"

"You know what they say—the most obvious is the least obvious," she deadpans. "I'll be there."

As she stands up, dusting her hands off, I get a peek of what's under her zipped-up hoodie—a scrap of lace. Whatever she was out doing, she sure as hell wasn't doing it alone. An uneasy feeling settles in my soul. Knowing she was out being naughty for some random dude pisses me off.

"Have a good night," I say, clearing my throat. I stand awkwardly, unintentionally invading the fuck out of her space as I step past her and off the stairs. "I'll see you tomorrow."

"You too," she mutters, almost acting confused by me as she heads inside.

And that's okay. Because I'm confused as fuck too.

# HUNTER

After practice, I shower and drive to the coffee shop. Part of me wonders if she'll even show up today. But it almost seemed like we called a truce last night. Like, it clicked to her that we have to get this shit over with.

I wonder what she'll show up smelling like today. A cupcake or a fucking hooker. Then again, she said she had plans tonight, so maybe she's saving the hooker perfume for then.

I get there a few minutes early, so I head inside and get us a table while I wait. And at noon, on the dot, she strolls in.

Her black leggings are sculpted to her legs, hugging her ass in a way that makes every motherfucker in here take a peek—including me. Her hair is in two French braids instead of her normal bun or ponytail. But still, it's out of her face, and it makes me wonder if she just can't stand her hair being a mess.

She doesn't acknowledge that she sees me. Instead, she walks over and starts to pull out a seat. Before she has the chance, I stand, doing it for her.

She frowns, looking at me like I've grown two heads, but eventually, she sits down, and I push her in before taking my own seat.

"You showed up," I say. "Wasn't sure if you would."

"I said I'd be here, didn't I?" she tosses back before craning her neck to look at the board. "I'm starving though. So, do you mind if I grab something before we begin?"

"Yeah, I do actually," I answer before laughing. "I'm kidding. No, I don't give a fuck. What do you want? I'll go order it for you."

She looks shocked. Leaning forward a little, she gives me a funny look. "Are you going to poison me or something?"

"Would that stop you from eating whatever I bring back?"

"Honestly, no. I'm hungry enough to eat the ass off an elephant. So, I'll take my chances with a little poison."

"You *are* poison. So, maybe you'd be immune."

"Can you keep the dick-o-meter at a low today? I'm not in the mood to deal with you." She glares.

"It's hard to keep it on low when my dick is so big that it's always off the charts." I smirk before standing. "What do you want?"

"I'll take a toasted sesame bagel with cream cheese. And a cookie dough iced coffee with oat milk," she rattles off.

"Cookie dough iced coffee?" I rear my head back. "Huh. Never knew there was such a thing."

"There's, like, fifty flavors here." She laughs. "What are you, like, a *French vanilla* guy?"

"I'm a *no coffee* guy," I correct her. "Shit's nasty."

Her eyes widen. "Just when I thought you couldn't get weirder." Digging in her bag, she holds out some money. "This should cover it."

Ignoring her, I head to the counter and order our things. For some reason, an image of her plump lips wrapped around the straw as she drinks her coffee assaults my brain, sending an unwelcome jolt right to my cock.

I glance back at her as I wait for the dude to run my card. She's playing on her phone, the same scowl on her face she's had since she was a little kid. As if realizing she's doing it, she suddenly relaxes her face, and I practically hear her mother's voice inside my own brain, scolding her about wrinkles. Our families went on enough trips together that I heard it all.

"Uh ... sir?"

I faintly hear the kid's voice, and I snap back to reality, looking at him.

"What? Sorry," I mutter, rubbing the back of my neck.

"Your card," he grumbles, holding it out to me. "You can take a seat. We'll bring it out in just a few minutes."

"Thanks," I say before heading toward the girl with the angelic face and the devil's attitude.

50

# SUTTON

One last time, I go over the dance that I think will work. Three times later, and Hunter is still looking at me like I have three heads. Eventually, I shrug.

"It'll be fine. We'll keep it simple. And if we look like morons, it's for charity, right? I mean … fuck it."

He eyes me over, looking amused. "What would Helena Savage think about that filthy mouth?"

"Who cares?" I say bluntly. "Okay, so I think we're all set on this. Right? Do you have any questions for me? Like, for starters … maybe what's left and right?"

"Fuck off." He chuckles. "I'll apologize now for your poor feet. They are about to take a beating."

"It'll be fine." I stand, tossing my trash in the wastebasket. "You're not going to be worse than any of the other goons on your team. Well, other than Cade. That guy can move. It's sort of hot."

Hunter's body grows tense, and his smile fades. "He was probably drunk. Everyone moves better with a drink or two. Or ten." He shakes his head. "You'd be wise to stay away from Cade Huff."

Shocked from his sudden attitude, I scowl. "Umm … says the dude who is best friends with him."

As I reach for my tote bag, he grabs my wrist. "I don't have a pussy between my legs, Little Bird. He might be my friend, but he's a fucking mess. He also has a new chick in his bed every night of the week. Sometimes multiple." His angry eyes burn into mine. "Stay away from Huff, Sutton. Do you understand?"

"Fuck you," I hiss.

Looking down at my wrist, I pull myself from his hold and march toward the door. When I get outside, he's hot on my heels.

"Sutton," his deep voice growls behind me. "Stop being a bitch." He swings his gaze around. "Also, where the fuck is your car?"

"I walked here," I snarl before turning quickly and jabbing my finger into his chest. "And here's an idea for you. Why don't you stop being a little bitch, *asshole*? We're dance partners, and that's it. It's not any of your business what I do or who I do it with. Let's not forget that at the end of the day, we're still enemies. I hate you, and you hate me. So, save me the fake concern and don't try to pretend to care what I do with my life."

Stepping closer, so close that his chest almost touches my nose, he glares down at me. "Listen here, Little Bird. You don't have a fucking clue about the real world. You're naive. You've spent your life locked in that cage, and now, you think you're free? Guess what. Monsters lurk. Everywhere. So, smarten the fuck up."

His eyes float to my lips briefly, and I curse my stupid heart for sinking in my chest.

"Get away from me," I hiss. "You're mad that I think Cade is hot? What, scared he might like me more than you?" I can't stop myself, puffing my chest up. "He probably would. I could make him like me more than you."

"Shut. Up," he growls. "I'm not fucking around right now."

We continue our staredown. His chest heaves, though I have no freaking clue where this red-hot anger is coming from. We've never even had a friendship. Why the hell would Hunter care if I hung out with Cade or not?

"Hunter?"

A sweet, soft voice startles both of us. And I know he recognizes it instantly because he steps back, leaving my body cold once his anger isn't radiating against me.

Out of the corner of my eye, I see Paige. She's always been beautiful. And even though I can tell it kills her, she flashes me one of her signature smiles.

"Sutton."

"Hey, Paige," I say, holding up a hand.

Paige's eyes move from me to Hunter and back again. Her friends next to her look me up and down, not even trying to hide the distaste in their expressions.

"What are you guys doing?" Paige asks, now looking only at Hunter. "I called you last night. Where were you?"

"Sorry, I passed out early." He shrugs, clearly lying because when I got home from work … he was on my porch. "Did you need something?"

When Paige glances nervously at me, I hold my hand up. "I'll let y'all talk. Hunter, I'll talk to you later or something."

"I'm giving you a ride home," he tells me—not asking.

"I'll meet you at the truck then." Inhaling, I nod. "Nice to see you, Paige." I wave.

"You too," she says half-heartedly.

I walk away, feeling their stares on my back as I head to his truck. This is all bizarre. Every single part of it. Being partners with Hunter. His almost-jealous behavior before he's an ass the next moment. It's all weird.

But the weirdest, most unsettling thing is that right now, as I wait next to his truck … I wonder what he's talking about with Paige. And if he's running right back to her. And the thought makes my stomach knot.

# HUNTER

"So, it's finally happened, huh?" Paige's eyes darken, and by the way she's holding her mouth, I know she's mad. "All this time, you said you weren't attracted to her, and now, you're with Sutton?"

"I'm not dating her, P." I shake my head. "Coach is making some of the guys do this dance thing for a fundraiser. I got paired up with her." When I see how hurt she looks, I sigh. "Trust me, I'm pissed about it. She's a bitch."

I do think she's a bitch. But I also know I added that in because I hate seeing Paige upset. I don't hate being partnered up with Sutton nearly as much as I'm trying to make it look to everyone. Myself included.

She looks around, taking a small step closer. "Are you, like, sleeping together?" she whispers. "Because you and I still hook up sometimes, you know."

"No, we aren't sleeping together," I scoff. "But why do you ask, Paige? Are you having a change of heart? Do you want to be with me? Like, *really* be with me?" I say, calling her bluff.

Her shoulders sag a bit. "I can't. I'm sorry."

Staring at her, I narrow my eyes. "Yeah, that's just what I thought." I step around her. "I gotta go."

"Wait, Hunter," she says, touching my arm. "You know I love you, right? And I hope that if things change with you and *her* … you'll have the courtesy to tell me."

"Did you have the decency to tell me about the random dudes you've fucked since we split?" I say, turning around to face her. "No, you didn't. And, yeah, I know all about them." Running my hand down my face, I shrug my shoulders. "You need to figure out what the fuck you want. Because this shit isn't working for me anymore."

When she tries to grab my hand, I shrug her off.

"Hunter, stop."

"You've got two weeks to figure it the fuck out, Paige. After that, I'm done."

I walk off, not wanting to look at her anymore. But I realize something. Seeing me with Sutton got to her. And maybe that isn't a bad thing.

# SUTTON

I wait next to the truck. Shifting on my feet awkwardly, wondering what's happening with Hunter and Paige.

I could tell my presence wasn't wanted. And I don't blame her. His family always made her feel like she wasn't welcome. And before our family's feud, they voiced many times that they'd prefer him to be with me. The way I see it, she has every right to not want to see my face.

And while I understand why she finally reached her breaking point and left him, I also think it was the coward's way out. If she loved him the way she always claimed … her ass would be there, ready to fight for her spot next to him. Instead, she's settled for hooking up with him randomly, basically controlling his every move.

Seeing him walking toward me, I offer him a small, apologetic smile. "I hope I didn't get you in too much trouble. I know the last person you want upset with you is her."

He seems agitated as he fumbles in his pocket, retrieving his keys. Walking around to the passenger side, he opens it. "Didn't you say you had plans tonight? I'll drop you off so you can get to it." His tone is sharp, and everything about him is off right now.

But it's not my job to push for more details. So, swallowing my pride, I climb into the truck, buckling my seat belt before he reminds me to.

The ride to my place is quiet, and the dark energy from Hunter's body radiates throughout the entire cab of the truck. I have no idea what happened or why. All I know is, it wasn't good. Clearly.

When we pull in front of my place and he hasn't spoken a word, I push my own door open before he has the chance to get to my side. Climbing out, I brush past him as he makes his way around the front toward me.

"I was going to get the door," he grumbles.

"Don't bother," I mutter, walking toward my front steps.

"Sutton, wait," he calls lazily behind me. "Damn it, just stop, would you?"

I hear his voice grow closer, and when I turn around, my chest damn near bumps into his.

I glare up at him. "What?" I hold my arms out. "We just had a fifteen-minute ride where you didn't speak a word. Now, suddenly, I'm walking off, and you feel like it's a good time for a little convo?"

When I start to turn, he grabs my elbow, forcing me to face him.

"Stop," he growls, gritting his teeth.

"Remove your hand from my elbow, or I'm going to karate-chop your nuts so hard that you'll forever think of me as a nutcracker." I widen my eyes.

54

"And it won't be for my stellar ballet performance either. It'll be because your nuts are gone."

He pulls his hand away and puts it on his waist as he huffs out a breath. "I'm just … in a bad mood. Okay? Kind of like you are ninety percent of the fucking time."

"You lowballed it, babe. I'd say, when you're around, it's at least ninety-five." Folding my arms over my chest, I narrow my eyes. "I didn't ask for any of this. And while I truly am sorry for whatever happened with Paige back there, that's your problem, not mine. I wish more than anything that you could be with your sweet, perfect princess and I could be left the hell alone."

"That what you really want, brat?" he rasps, and I swear his eyes float to my lips. "For me to leave you alone?"

I stare up at him as our chest heave with anger. "Well, yeah. Obviously. But that's not really an option, is it?"

"You're so fucking impossible," he growls, looking at me like he wants to kill me before turning away. "Fuck!" He slaps his hand on the hood of his truck, making me flinch.

He drags his hand through his hair in complete and total agony. Whatever Paige said to him, it's clear it's put him in a mood. And I know I'm not helping the situation. But, goddamn, he annoys me.

As frustrated as we both are, it's probably for the best that he leaves. But as I watch him get in his truck and speed away, my heart sinks. And as I wait for brake lights to flash, which never do, I wring my hands together, wishing this night away.

Finally, he drives out of sight.

*And probably right back to Paige.*

And I'm both relieved that he left and sad that he's gone. And that makes no sense at all.

# HUNTER

"Hi, love," my mother's voice greets me on the other end of the phone. "How's your day going?"

"It's going," I breathe out. "Did you call earlier? I was at practice."

"I did," she says slowly. "I was reading the *Brooks U Informer*, and I saw something interesting. Something about the hockey players putting on some sort of show?" She pauses. "And I read that my son is coupled up with Sutton Savage. So, please, do tell me, is this true? Say it isn't."

*Damn online school newspaper.*

I never even gave it a thought that my mother would find out about this fundraiser. At least ... not for a while anyway.

"Hunter, are you going to speak or keep me wondering if this is true?"

"I didn't choose her as a partner," I begin to plead my case. "Trust me, she's the last person I wanted to be paired with. She's fucking impossible to deal with."

"Language," she hisses. "I just don't even know what to think. You know what her parents have done to us. And now, you are going to be, what? Besties with their daughter?" She sounds flustered. Just like I knew she would be. "I won't allow this, Hunter."

As tough as my parents are on me, Sutton's parents make my mom and dad look like saints. While my mother can be hard and often controlling, Sutton's parents are straight-up heartless. Hell, I don't think I've ever even seen Helena hug her daughter before. My father and I are like oil and water. But even he's a better man than Senator Savage will ever be.

"I don't exactly have a choice," I mutter. "And if I ask to switch, Coach will have my ass. And while I know you'd love to see me benched, I can't afford to be on his bad side this year."

"You need to be careful of her, Hunter," she warns. "She's pretty. Too pretty. And her last name is Savage. She's a snake. People like her will do whatever they need to in order to get to where they want to be."

"I get it," I snap. "But for now, I can't do a damn thing about it. So, just let me handle it and get it over with. Deal?"

"Fine," she huffs. "How are your classes going? I logged in to your account, and you got a seventy-nine on your test last week. That won't do, Hunter. Not if you're going to carry on your family's legacy. And, yes, I know that you want to play hockey. But I still don't see that as a feasible dream. I looked up the statistics of making it to the pros, and I have to tell you, it's daunting. I just want you to keep an open mind when it comes to carrying on the torch as a doctor. That's all. I'm concerned you're going to put all of your eggs in one basket and then things won't work out."

*Yep, I'm a junior in college, and my mother still logs in and checks my grades.* Talk about feeling like a fucking child.

In my mom's mind, she looks at hockey as this far-fetched dream I have that will never come true. Same with my dad. They've attended a handful of my games since I was a kid, and they just don't understand how I'll make it a lifelong career.

My father is a surgeon. And my mother is a scientist. Sports aren't exactly in their realm of thought.

"Yes, Mom, I know," I sigh. "Is that all? I have some homework to do."

"Haley arrives at the end of the week now that her dorm is finally ready. Try to check on her, will you?" Her voice changes, sounding concerned.

Haley spent the first few weeks of school attending online classes because there was an issue with her dorm. I know my mom worries about her. I do too. But I guess after what she's been through, that's expected. She not only had a stalker, but last spring, that stalker kidnapped her and physically assaulted her as well. It really changed her.

"You know I will," I promise her.

My parents aren't bad people, but they were absent a lot of the time while we were growing up. Their careers always came before being a parent. That left me worrying about my sister a lot. So, I don't need to be told to have her back. Mom should know that too.

Ending the call quickly, she doesn't give me time to respond. And that's fine because I'm not sure she'd like what I had to say. Because truthfully, something tells me Sutton isn't like her parents. And that maybe I've been reading her wrong all along.

# SUTTON

As much as I don't want to do it, I suppose it's my turn to show up at Hunter's and set up a time to practice. Despite that he was a bit of a dick a few days ago, I feel bad for him because I know Paige is stringing him along. And that's got to suck ass. I might be cold at times, but I'm still human, and I do have empathy for those in pain. It's pretty clear Hunter is.

Rounding the corner, I walk along the sidewalk at Brooks until I reach his road. I'm not sure if he'll even be home, but I guess there's only one way to find out.

I see his truck in the driveway, along with two others, and I swallow. I'm aware that this will probably look like I'm one of his puck bunnies, and that kind of annoys me. I'd be anyone else's bunny, but not Hunter's.

Spotting a doorbell, I press my finger to it and listen to the sound. Moments later, I hear feet heading toward me, and the door opens. A shirtless Cade Huff gives me a boyish grin, and he looks like he literally just rolled out of bed.

"Well, hello there, beautiful." He looks me over. "I'd better get my phone to let heaven know one of their angels got out, huh?"

Rolling my eyes, I scrunch my nose up. "Do those crappy pickup lines ever actually work?"

"Every. Single. Time," he says, as serious as a heart attack. "What can I do for you, sweet cheeks?"

"I'm looking for Hunter." I force the words out. Words that taste like acid. "Is he home?"

He smirks before opening the door wider. "Sure is. Come on in."

"No ... thanks." I shake my head. "I'll wait here. I don't want to catch chlamydia or something, walking in there."

"Suit yourself." He shrugs. "Thompson! You've got a visitor." He gives me a wink before sauntering away.

Hunter steps outside, looking surprised to see me. "Hey, what's up?"

I allow myself to look him over. When he's in his athletic shorts, backward hat, and no shirt on ... it's hard not to. And I fumble a little, trying to get my tongue to allow me to speak.

"Well, seeing as you showed up at my place last time, I figured it was my turn to put my big-girl pants on and come to yours." I pull in a breath. "If you're free tonight, we could practice our routine and finalize it."

"I was going to go to Club 83 to grab dinner with the guys—" he starts to say, but my pride cuts him off.

"That's fine. I have homework I can do anyway. No worries—"

"But I'll let them know I won't make it," he drawls slowly, and my damn eyes betray me, floating back to his abdomen. "Come in, and I'll get ready."

I look around, shifting on my feet. "Oh ... that's all right. I can wait here."

"Wasn't asking, Little Bird," he says sternly, holding the door open. "Come inside."

Folding my arms over my chest, I glare. "Fine. But just so you know, it's only because I don't want to be seen outside of the hockey house. It has nothing to do with the fact that you're basically forcing me to do it. Got it?"

"Whatever you say," he mumbles, grinning softly as I follow him through the house.

Cade is lying on the couch, looking completely lost.

Watson steps out of a side room. His eyes widen as he sees me, but he quickly holds his hand up and smiles. "Hey, Sutton."

"Hi, Watson." I wave. "Did you do that assignment yet for Business?"

"Hell no." He laughs before his face grows serious. "Wait, did you?"

I nod. "This morning actually. It wasn't nearly as bad as I'd suspected it would be. Though for just a few weeks into school, I didn't think the professors would already be such hard asses!"

Hunter clears his throat just as Watson opens his mouth. And when he looks at Hunter, they seem to exchange some secret message. Watson quickly says good-bye, and Hunter leads me into his bedroom.

I gaze around, not at all shocked by how insanely clean and organized it is in here. Growing up the way that Hunter did, there was no room for clutter.

I take a seat on the edge of his bed, looking at the posters on the walls and a few pictures of him and his teammates.

Taking his hat off, he tosses it on his desk before pulling a shirt out and yanking it down over his body. I'm not mad when he slides the hat back on his head, backward again. Something about it does things to me. Though I make sure to hide it from him.

"I'm sorry about the other day," he mutters, sitting next to me on the edge of the bed. He's so close that our legs brush against each other, and I feel my heart leap into my throat. "I just got pissed. But I shouldn't have been a dick to you. Especially since it wasn't your fault."

"It's okay," I whisper, swallowing back my nerves. "But just out of curiosity … why do you let Paige do that? Drag you along the way that she does?"

He's quiet for a minute, looking down.

"I guess because I love her. I don't know. And maybe … I just want someone who's normal. Who doesn't come from a mansion with a country-club membership." He shrugs. "And because I feel bad. My family was always so rotten to her. I would have done the same thing she did. I'm sure anyone would."

"Maybe," I say softly. "She certainly wasn't happy to see us together. That's for sure."

His head cranes toward mine, and his eyes float to my lips.

Everything inside of me is telling me to stand up. Yet my body won't do it. In fact … I feel myself subtly leaning closer.

Standing abruptly, he holds his hand out for me to grab. "Ready to go, tiny dancer?"

Staring up at him, I bob my head up and down. My cheeks heat with embarrassment. I hope he didn't catch that I almost kissed him.

"Yep. Let's go."

# HUNTER

In all the years I've known Sutton, I've never been this close to her. My hands are on her body, and I lift her up with ease, gripping her softly. After going over the routine, I realized there were certain things I clearly wasn't going to be able to do. But after over an hour of trying … slowly, I'm getting the hang of it. And the best part is, I haven't even broken her toes. Yet.

There's something sexy in the way that she moves her body. Despite ballet being this sophisticated way of dancing, it's different when it's Sutton's body doing the moving. It goes from being elegant and beautiful to sensual and downright entrancing.

When I set her down slowly, she coughs a few times before she holds up her finger, implying to give her a second. When she grabs her bag and walks into the hallway, I can't help but look through the window to see what she's doing.

When I see her take an inhaler out of her bag, giving herself a few puffs of medicine, a memory hits me of her doing the same thing when we were kids. I guess I forgot about it. But now, I'm a little worried.

After a few minutes, she walks back into the studio. "Sorry," she mumbles. "But the good news is, we got a lot done today. And I now pronounce that you're free to go for the night."

As she switches from her ballet slippers to her sandals, I run my hand down my neck nervously. "Do you have a lot of asthma flare-ups from dance?"

She looks embarrassed, seeming to shrink a little. "Sometimes. But I deal with it, and life goes on."

Another memory hits me, and I narrow my eyes thoughtfully at her. "When we were kids ... you were hospitalized from it, right?"

"Uh ... how many times?" she deadpans. "Yeah, uh, I guess you can say it's a fun thing to deal with sometimes."

I don't know a lot about asthma. But I know enough to know that I'm sure things like sports are dangerous for those who have it. And to dance to the standard she does? Impossible.

"Sutton," I say, taking a step toward her. "Is it even safe for you to dance?"

She looks annoyed as she steps back, walking toward the door. "Yes, Dr. Thompson. It's fine." She looks back at me. "You can text me when it works for you to practice again, and I'll see if I'm free too."

When she goes to pull the door open, I stop her by touching her lower back.

"Let me take you to get some dinner. I'm starving. You must be too."

When she looks back at me, I know the wheels are turning.

Slowly, she spins to face me, her eyebrows pinched together. "Why are you being nice to me, Hunter?"

"Because it's not your fault that your parents are snakes. And it's not my fault that mine have lost their minds." I shrug. "What do you say? I think after the patience you had with me the past hour or so ... you deserve a meal."

She continues to study me. Almost waiting for me to tell her I'm joking. And when I don't, she bites her lip. "Okay." She nods. "Yeah ... dinner would be great."

"Hell yeah, it will be." I smile. "Let's go."

"I guess I should have asked if you even liked barbeque." I cringe as I park in front of Bleecker's Barbeque. A place the guys and I tried a few weeks ago and loved. "If you don't, we can go somewhere else."

She chuckles. "Geesh, you really didn't pay attention to me at family functions, growing up, did you? I'd get seconds or even thirds on barbeque days." She gives me an amused look. "Your mom might be kind of bitchy, but the woman sure knows how to throw a party."

"Yeah, I guess she does," I grumble. "Well, anyway, the food here is fucking great. And the servings are huge."

Giving me a side-eye, she bobs her head. "And that's a selling point for ya, huh? Big servings for a big fella like yourself?"

"Are you calling me fat?" I glance over at her.

"No. But all of you puck boys are, like … ginormous. I'd hate to see y'all's grocery bill."

"Hey, working out and practicing at least five or six times a week takes a lot of calories." I laugh. "And have you ever seen some of the motherfuckers we're up against?" I pat my stomach. "It pays to have a little cushion when you get body-checked against Plexiglas."

"By cushion, you mean, lean, mean muscle?" She sighs. "Yeah, I suppose you do."

For our entire lives, we've avoided each other on all vacations, social functions, and everything in between. But without our parents around to analyze our every word, we can just talk.

And I'll admit … I don't hate it.

I'm warming up to Sutton. And I'm not sure that's a good thing.

# SUTTON

"I'm actually shook right now. But in, like, the best fucking way," Hunter says, staring at my plate. "I did *not* think you could actually eat all that when I bet you."

"If you hadn't bet me, I couldn't have done it—I never would have." I shrug. "I'm so competitive that I can hardly stand myself sometimes. So, when you said the word *bet*, I knew I was going to need to be rolled out of this place tonight from being full."

"I guess I should have known that without asking. I mean, fuck, when did you start dancing competitively? Age five?"

"Four," I say, correcting him. "Yeah, I don't like to lose. I highly recommend never bringing me to mini-golf or a bowling alley. I get mean. Might be a deal-breaker." My cheeks grow red. "Not that you ever would. But … you know what I meant."

Luckily, he doesn't pick up on my humiliation. Or if he does, he ignores it.

"We're bred this way though. Right?" He takes a sip from his water. "Why wouldn't we be fucked up and competitive?"

"Who said I was fucked up?" I raise an eyebrow, holding his stare for as long as I can before I laugh. "I'm kidding. I *know* I am."

"Do you ever want to just say fuck it?" He sighs. "Sometimes, seems like life would be so much easier if I were on my own."

"What about Haley?"

"Well, seeing as she's at Brooks now, I could never cut her off. I love my sister. She's normal. Sort of." The smallest, saddest laugh escapes his lips. "She tries her best, but her best will never be enough for our parents."

"I know the feeling," I mutter. "As for what you said before ... about being on your own, it is freeing—I'll say that much. But it's also scary, being in the real world."

Paying for my cell phone, groceries, books, and tuition—it was never anything I had to pay for before. Now, I fully feel the stress of making ends meet. Not to mention my inhaler. Or that I've been going through refills like crazy.

"What do you mean?" He narrows his eyes. "Your parents cut you off? Is that why you've been walking everywhere?"

Pulling my lips to the side, I sit back slightly. "Sure is. Every decision has a price, Hunter. I knew the price when I chose to come to Brooks. I did it anyway."

"Fuck," he utters. "I had no idea."

"It's all good," I say calmly. "I have a job to help me buy the things I need, and most of all, I'm no longer killing myself to be something that I'll likely never be."

"What's that?" he says curiously.

"Perfect," I whisper. "I don't even have to try to be that anymore."

He looks at me, as if seeing me as a real person for once. One with real feelings.

Eventually, he swallows. "And your job? What's that?"

I cough on my soda, wiping my lips and nose with my napkin. "Working at a restaurant off campus." I nod and am thankful as hell when the waitress drops the check on the table to distract him from asking anything else about my job.

Hunter quickly snatches it up, but I reach to grab it, but accidentally grab his hand.

"I can pay for my half," I tell him, trying to ignore that my hand is on his. "It isn't like we're on a date."

Shooting me an entertained look, he shakes his head and pulls his hand away from mine. Putting some cash with the bill, he shrugs. "Might not be a date, but you're still not paying."

He holds the cash and the receipt out to the waitress just as she walks by. "That's all set," he says.

"That looked like a huge tip," I whisper.

Making sure the waitress is gone, he leans closer. "Did you see her stomach? She's pregnant. And waiting tables can't be easy while lugging a watermelon around."

My heart does some weird fluttery thing, and I stare at him in shock.

"What?" he says, holding his hand out for me to take when I stand up. Like I'm a ninety-year-old woman. "Didn't think I could be nice, did ya?"

"Have you met your parents?" I deadpan.

That earns me a deep, loud chuckle just before we head out through the door.

"I suppose I can't argue with you there. We both know my parents are assholes." Nodding toward the river, he almost looks nervous. "Do you want to go for a walk?"

For a moment, I stand there, unable to form a thought. Much less a word. Because the guy I painted in my mind as an asshole is starting to prove me otherwise.

Finally, I give him a small smile. "Sure."

It's dangerous when Hunter does nice things. Because I know it'll end up with me wanting more. And I know him enough to know that his niceness … is going to run out.

# HUNTER

The walk starts off pretty silent. So much in fact that all I hear is the damn water rushing beside us as we trudge along lightly, her short legs trying their damnedest to keep up with mine.

Slowing a little, I grin. "Okay, so … let's see how competitive you really are, brat." I jerk my chin toward a black food truck at the end of the river. "Last one to the ice cream truck is buying dessert."

She pats her stomach. "Dessert? Do you know how much food is in my stomach right now?"

"Well, yeah. I watched you eat like it was your last meal back there." I nod my head toward her. "But what do you say? After all … it's a bet."

Her eyes flash with mischief for a moment before, suddenly, she rips off her flip-flops, bolting toward The Scoop. I've only been here one other time since I've been at Brooks, but they make their own products in their warehouse and then sell them out of this little food truck. And they are fucking incredible.

I take off behind her, impressed with how quick she is on her feet. But I'm a winger for the Wolves. Speed is what I'm trained for. I also refuse to lose. Even if I am enjoying the view of her ass bouncing as she runs.

Chasing her down is like being on the ice and heading toward the goal. I know what my plan is, and I will execute it.

I catch up to her quickly, but when she sees me passing her, she tries her best to get her lead back. But her little legs just can't carry her that fast.

"Ouch, my foot!" she screeches.

I turn toward her, slowing just enough for her to lunge toward me, yanking my shorts down halfway.

"Sucker!" she calls out, taking her lead back as I fumble to pull my shorts up.

She bolts away from me, laughing her ass off, and I shake my head, grinning like a fool.

She only makes it about twenty feet before I come up behind her. Before she can fight it, I lift her up into the air, tossing her on my shoulder as I continue to run.

"You play dirty, Little Bird!" I grip the back of her thigh, just under her asscheek.

Her leg is smooth and toned, and I will my brain not to think about raising my hand higher to palm her ass.

"Hey! Cut the shit!" she screeches, pounding my back and kicking her feet. "Put me down, butthead!"

"Butthead?" I snort. "Been a while since I've been called that. In fact, last time was probably at that fancy dinner at your family's lake house."

"Well, you were being one then, and you are being one now!" She tries to hide the laugh in her voice, but I hear it anyway.

We get closer to the truck, and I know I have to think of something to liven this so-called race up even more. As fast as she is, even if I set her down now, I know I could still beat her. I'm six foot three. She can't be more than five foot three, if that.

Heading down toward the bank, she pounds on me harder as she sees where we're headed. "Don't you dare throw me into the river, Hunter Thompson! I will chop your balls off! And then I will let you bleed to death!"

I pretend like I'm going to toss her into the river, but instead, I set her down gently, only ankle deep in the water, before I turn and head toward the truck, Sutton right on my heels.

"Now, my feet are nasty. You're so going to pay for that!" she squawks.

Picking up the pace, I almost make it to the counter before I slow up and wait a few seconds for her to catch up. If I lose, I get to buy her ice cream. And I'm sure as hell not letting her buy mine.

Passing me, she touches the counter before turning toward me. "You let me win, jerk!"

"Did not. I got a leg cramp and had to slow down." I shrug. "Guess I'm buying your ice cream tonight."

Rolling her eyes, she smiles. "Real smooth, Thompson. *Real* smooth."

"What?" I play dumb.

Taking a step toward me, she looks up, tilting her head to the side. "If you wanted to buy me ice cream … all you had to do was ask."

I lean a little closer, and the corners of my lips turn up the slightest bit. "I don't know what you're talking about."

"Sure you don't," she teases before turning toward the menu. "I know what I'm getting." Smiling at the girl in the window, she looks at the board one last time. "Pumpkin, please. One scoop on a sugar cone."

"Pumpkin ice cream?" I scoff. "That's gross."

"Excuse me, jerk. It's September. Which means it's PSL season." When I stare at her blankly, she throws her arms up. "Pumpkin spice latte. Duhhhh."

"Yeah … I don't drink coffee. Or lattes. Or any of that crap. And I sure as hell don't eat pumpkin pie."

Stepping back, she widens her eyes. "Psychopath."

The girl hands her the cone and takes my order.

And when I go with plain chocolate, Sutton tilts her chin up and down. "Feeling super adventurous, huh?"

"I know what I like," I say, resting my hand on my hip lazily. "And it ain't pumpkin."

My eyes move downward, staying fixated on her mouth as her tongue pokes out, swiping across the ice cream before licking her own lips as she shuts her eyes.

"Mmm. So. Freaking. Good."

A jolt of electricity goes directly to my dick as I watch her lap the creamy substance again. With each lick her tongue takes, my eyes glaze over more. Unable to look away even though I know I need to in order to not look like a complete fucking pervert. Breathing becomes harder as I imagine her on her knees, submitting to me as she uses that same enthusiasm on my cock.

After the girl hands me my own and I pay, we start walking back toward the restaurant, where my truck is parked.

"This is so good," she coos. "Seriously, you should try it."

"You must be warming up to me, huh? Offering to let me lick your ice cream."

Glancing up at me, she narrows her eyes and smiles. "You make it sound dirty. It's ice cream. *Pumpkin* ice cream. Literally tastes just like pumpkin pie." She stops walking and holds it up to me.

I frown. "I really hate pumpkin pie. But I feel like you're not going to leave me alone till I try it. So, fine, here I go." Taking a lick, I shrug. "It's not terrible, I guess. But it's no chocolate. That's for sure." I nod toward hers when she pulls it away. "But I'm glad you like it."

"It's the bomb. Now, if it were a little colder, I could pretend I was in New York again and that fall weather was actually coming."

The way she says it, it is clear as day that she loves New York. I know she was out there for school for a year, and it surprised the hell out of me when I ran into her in the library. Literally.

"You liked New York?"

"Loved it," she says quickly.

"Why did you leave?" I ask, watching her every move, looking for some sort of tell.

"Some things just aren't meant to be. Even if you wish they were." She shrugs. "And I've reached a point in my life where I no longer feel like killing myself to try to be what everyone else wants me to be."

I stare at her, completely entranced in every word she's saying. And wanting more.

"Why Brooks?"

She pulls in a breath. "I really, *really* can't believe I'm telling you this. But the conditions in New York—the climate in the winter months and the air quality—it was hard on my lungs. Couple that with how incredibly strenuous Juilliard was, I guess you could say I just couldn't hang anymore."

"Fuck," I mutter. "I'm sorry, Sutton."

I can't imagine wanting to play hockey as hard as I do, but physically not being able to. She has the heart to achieve all of her goals—she loves dancing that much. And yet she can't do it. She's been cut short of her abilities.

"And your parents?" I slow as she stops, looking at the river. "How have they been through all of this? Before they cut you off, I mean."

"They've always been aware that I was pushing my body beyond what it was likely capable of. Still, they ignored doctors—even paid off some to get a note saying that I was healthy enough to dance competitively." She continues to watch the rushing water. "And when I finally told them I'd had enough, that I was transferring to a program that wasn't nearly as vigorous ... they weren't very happy. To put it lightly. And now ... well, I haven't actually spoken to them in months."

"So, they really did cut you off just for transferring here?" I grumble. "Just when I thought I couldn't hate them more."

"Yeah. But if I'm being honest ... it hasn't been all that bad. Like I said, my mom's expectations were so heavy. I mean, I had to attend an all-girls school for as long as I can remember. Not a fun one either. There was zero fun to be had at this school. No prom. No dances. No being a kid. And my dance schedule?" She cringes. "Oof, don't even get me started on that. If I kept going the way I was, I was bound to break. It's a blessing really," she says, trying to sound unbothered but I can tell it's an act. "Anyway, I should probably get going. I have some homework to catch up on."

"No prom? That kind of sucks." I frown.

She smirks, giving me an amused look. "Let me guess, lover boy. You wore a white tux?"

My lips go into a straight line as I roll my eyes. "Shut up. We're not going to talk about that." I shake my head, trying not to grin. "I'll give you a ride home, but I have to know, if you don't have a car, that means you walked to my place earlier?"

"Yep, I did. I know; I know. Welcome to the front-row seat to the demise of Sutton Savage. No car. No money. No family." She gives me a small shrug. "You can laugh, if you want. I know my family screwed yours over. And for a long time, you thought of me as a brat—maybe you still do. But if it makes you feel better … I'd love to think of a way to get them back for throwing me away like I was garbage. I'm just as angry with them as your parents are."

I can't help but stare at her in awe. She's completely on her own, away from her parents. She's sick, and they fucking abandoned her for needing to take time away from *their* dreams for her own health. *Fuck them.*

"We'll think of something to pay those fuckers back," I say, nodding toward my truck. "Let's go."

I don't want to press her for any more information tonight. I'm sure she's tired of sharing for one day. As I open the truck door and she climbs in, flashing me a true smile … I can't help but give her one back. Because tonight didn't suck. And I'm beginning to think she isn't at all who I thought she was all along.

*Or who I convinced myself she was.*

I'm no longer seeing her with devil horns and a resting bitch face. And I'm not sure if that's a blessing or a curse.

# SUTTON

The ride home is filled with chatter—luckily nothing too deep. I think I shared enough for one lifetime just on our walk around the river. I don't even know what came over me. I'm usually such a private person. Yet there I was, just rattling on about my issues like Hunter was a dang shrink.

As we pull in front of my house, I reach for the door, but his hand on my arm stops me.

"Wait."

Looking at him, I frown. "What?"

"Okay, so this is going to sound nuts. And it is probably crazy. But hear me out." He pauses. "You want to find a way to get back at your family for cutting you off. And I ... well, I just want to get it through Paige's head that I'm moving on and that she doesn't have forever." He swallows, his Adam's apple bobbing. "How pissed would your parents be if you and I got together? Not only got together, but also started showing up at fancy events that they used to be invited to?"

"Really pissed," I whisper. "I'm sorry, but I don't really understand where this is going. Especially when it comes to Paige."

"Say we fake date. It'll piss your parents off, and it might get Paige to finally smarten up."

"Or it'll do the opposite and make her hate you," I deadpan. "You could lose her altogether. Come on, bro. You can't possibly think that would work."

"Don't call me bro," he says quickly. "And since we broke up, we've had an agreement that we can do what we want. I've just never flaunted who I've been with in her face. But when she saw us together, something shifted. I guess because it's you, and she's always been insecure when it comes to you, Sutton. And since then, she's been texting and calling me a whole lot more."

His words cause an ache deep in my gut as I imagine her calling and texting him and them meeting up. Of course, that's what they are doing. And it's none of my business.

*So, why do I feel like it is?*

"Just think about it, okay?" He gives me a small smile. "I mean, what the hell do we have to lose, right?"

"I will," I say before my eyes widen. "Wait ... what about your parents?"

He flashes me a boyish grin. "You just leave them to me, okay?"

"All right," I say slowly. "This night just got really weird."

"No kidding." He laughs before pushing his door open and coming around to my side to open mine. "I'll text you tomorrow to plan our next practice. Until then, at least think about what I said, okay?"

As I get down from his truck, looking at him, I almost feel like we're supposed to hug good-bye or something. But that would be awkward. So, instead, I stuff my hands into my pockets and bob my head up and down. "Will do. Night. Thanks for dinner and the ice cream. Even if you did try to drown me."

"First off, you're welcome. Remind me to never bet against you again because I'd probably be a broke fucker by the time we went out to eat a few times. Second, you were ankle deep, brat." He laughs. "Good night, Sutton."

"Good night, Hunter." I turn away from him and head inside, hiding the stupid-ass grin on my face.

Fake dating isn't something that happens in real life—is it? And even if it is, it has disaster written all over it. But still, I'm considering taking him up on his offer.

And a part of me knows it has nothing to do with getting back at my parents and everything to do with spending more time with someone I hated a few weeks ago.

# 10

## HUNTER

I finish gearing up for practice and check my phone, seeing a message from Haley, thanking me. Earlier today, my sister's dorm flooded, and she showed up on my doorstep with her bags. The last place I wanted my baby sister was in a house with my two best friends, but she had nowhere else to go. Replying with a short message, saying that it's no problem, I tuck my phone away and get ready to head out of the locker room.

"I still think it's so cool that the foundation we are raising money for is O'Brien's. Kinda makes it suck less that we have to do this dancing shit on top of class and hockey." Watson looks shocked while he talks. "Honestly, I only just learned he'd started the foundation a few months ago. But I think it's so fucking awesome of him."

"Hell yeah, it is. That's O'Brien for you, making lemonade out of lemons—or however the fuck you say it," I answer. "You know, he took the small amount of money his grandmother had left him and the money from selling her house and started One Wish," I say, bragging up my friend.

I can't even be mad that his foundation is what landed me in the position to work with Sutton because it's an incredible thing he's doing. From what I've heard, his upbringing was awful. And I guess this is his way of healing himself—by helping other kids who are in similar situations as he once was.

"That's sick," Watson mutters thoughtfully. "Already knew he was a badass dude, but this proves it even more."

"A *crazy* badass," Link adds, laughing.

He, Cam, and Brody are best friends. And I don't think anyone who's ever skated on the ice with Brody O'Brien would disagree that he's a tad mad at times. But he's a good dude. I know we all on the team miss the hell out of him.

We get done lacing our skates up just as Coach strolls in, looking around the room.

"We've only got a little over a week until opening game, boys. And our first game, as you know, is against South Carolina, and from what I've heard, they are stacked. We're looking better all the time, but we've still got a few kinks to work out, both offensively and defensively. So, for the next week, we're going hard. You hear me?"

When we all say yes, he nods, leaning against a set of lockers.

"Good. Now, those of you participating in the One Wish fundraiser, thanks for not being crybabies about it. I know it's not ideal to be a fucking ballerina during the season, but as stated before, it's for a good cause." He smiles—well, as much of a smile as he's capable of.

"Like I said before, this is our very own Brody O'Brien's fundraiser. One he started himself, which he holds very near and dear to his heart. O'Brien is not only an incredible athlete, but also one of the best men I've ever coached on and off the ice. So, when this opportunity came up, we couldn't say no. And I know I'm hard on you all, but I do appreciate you doing this."

Standing up straight, he hits his hand lightly on a metal locker. "All right, let's get to work!"

"Yes, sir!" we chant, following him out of the locker room.

"Hey, Thompson," Cade says from behind me. "How long is your sister going to be staying anyway?"

"Why?" I grunt. "And like I said before, don't fuck with her. Matter of fact, don't even look at her. She's been through enough the past few years. She doesn't need Hurricane Cade ripping through her life."

"Whoa, whoa, whoa. First off, I consider myself more of a tsunami really," he drawls, and even without looking at him, I can hear the smirk in his voice. "Second, I was simply asking—that's all." As we skate onto the ice, he hits my arm. "Damn, Thompson. Look at you, always thinking the worst of me."

"No, I don't. But she's my sister, and as much as I love you, man, I don't love you for my sister. So, do us both a favor and stay away from her."

"I'll think about it." He grins before skating away.

"Nope. More like you will fucking do it!" I yell after him, grinding my back teeth together. "I'm serious, Cade. Fuck around and find out!"

The thing about Cade Huff, as good of a guy as he is, he's got some serious issues. He's also a bit of a womanizer. And while I usually turn a blind eye, I can't do that when it comes to Haley. Especially since I know that she's not in the best headspace right now.

Speaking of Haley … if Sutton agrees to be my fake girlfriend, I'll have to explain it to my sister. *Perfect.*

# SUTTON

The pole is cool against my flesh as I wrap my limbs around it, tipping my head back seductively. The music moves at a slow tempo. In ballet, I always feel self-conscious on the stage. My mother's eyes were somewhere in the stands as she judged my every move. So were hundreds of others. But when I'm dancing at Peaches, I don't feel that same gut-wrenching feeling. Maybe it's the mask, allowing me to just dance, feeling a sense of weightlessness. Because at the end of the day, this doesn't really matter. It's just a paycheck and not my future.

Or maybe it's because the audience isn't picky. All I have to do is literally shake my ass, and they are happy. Either way, sometimes, I feel like I'm a rock star, headlining a show. Other times, not so much. But one thing I don't feel is desired. In fact, I feel a little yucky at times. Which is why I've made it a point to avoid looking directly at the audience. When you see balding, middle-aged men watching you, knowing they're likely sporting a boner, it's demoralizing. It also makes my stomach churn.

But Ryann wasn't lying; it's good money. And that's something I need right now for the first time in my life since I have no safety net.

My lungs begin to burn, and I know I need a hit from my inhaler. The smoky atmosphere in here isn't good for my condition, but so far, I've been able to make it work.

The tightness in my chest gets worse, and I try to hide my wheezing, though I know the music is covering it for me. And when I get my signal from my boss that it's time for my break, I waste no time rushing down the stairs and back to my purse.

Grabbing my inhaler, I take a puff and then another, pulling the medicine into my lungs. I collapse into a plush chair, throwing my head back and shutting my eyes. My mind instantly traveling to my new dance partner.

*Hunter.*

I texted with him earlier, and we are supposed to meet for practice tomorrow morning. Our messages were brief—and he never mentioned the deal he'd tried to make with me. But I'm sure it'll come up when we see each other.

It would be pretty sweet to send a big *fuck you* to my parents by hanging out with the enemy. Not just because of all they've done to me, but also because I truly believe that when they had their falling-out with the Thompsons, it was my family's fault.

But there's something else I want—something deeper that I don't have the money or resources for. The past few weeks, it's hit me how little I know about my own mother. I have no idea where she grew up, and I know nothing about her family. It genuinely seems like she got dropped off at my father's doorstep and they started a family.

I want to hire a private investigator to find out more about her. Because I have this feeling in my gut that she's hiding something, and I just need to know what it is. I know having the information—whatever it might be—won't change anything. But there's a hunger in me that wants to know anyway.

Hunter could help me with that. He has the funds. Revenge on my parents isn't enough to make me pretend to be his girlfriend. Because not only do I feel like it's degrading, but I also don't want Paige to look at me like I'm a snake. Then again, she's sort of choosing her own fate, I suppose.

I guess it's true what my father has always said. Everyone has a price. And Hunter Thompson is about to know mine.

# HUNTER

"So … it's a little hard to perfect this dance when she hasn't chosen our song yet," Sutton says, stretching her arms before pulling one leg behind her, giving it a stretch. "But I know we have a slow song because she did tell the dancers that much—which ones had a more upbeat tempo versus slow. So, we're on the right track, and if we need to tweak a few things once we get the music, so be it."

"Sounds good. You're the expert." I nod. "But there's an elephant in the room. And that motherfucker's so big that he's taking up half of the place."

I raise my eyebrows.

"Have you thought about what I said?"

"That pumpkin ice cream is gross? No, not really," she deadpans before exhaling. "Yes, I have. And I think I'm interested in taking you up on it, but I have some conditions."

"Okay, shoot." I grin. I can't wait to hear this.

"Number one, you have to respect me. I'm not just some toy to make your ex jealous. Don't treat me like that. You aren't my boss. We are equals." She points her finger. "Number two, no sex. I understand to fake this thing, we will need to show some public affection, but it ends there. Are we clear?"

"Crystal."

"Good. Number three, you will tell your sister about this deal so that she knows. She already hates me. I want her to know this was your idea and not mine." She swallows. "And the last thing … you're going to help me find out some information on my mother. Don't ask why. Just help me out."

I frown, completely confused. "I won't ask, but I really don't get why you need information about the woman you lived with for the first eighteen years of your life. You know her."

"I don't," she answers quickly. "And I feel like she's hiding something. And I want to figure out what that something is."

"Done." I shrug. "I have conditions too, just so you know."

"Go on," she says coolly, arching an eyebrow. "Let's hear 'em."

"Number one, you can't try to touch my dick." I wiggle my eyebrows. "I know I'm sort of irresistible, but let's keep it professional."

"That'll be easy," she coos, "since I find you slightly repulsive."

Unlike her typical leotard, she's wearing a sports bra, paired with black shorts that hug her ass in a way that even I can't ignore. Her asscheeks are barely covered, and it's going to be really fucking hard not to sneak a grab during practice.

"Sure you do. Anyway, two, aside from Haley, we can't tell anyone about this. And at the end of it, we'll just say it fizzled out."

"Fine." She folds her arms over her chest, and I catch a glimpse of a small tattoo on the side of her ribs, just under her bra line. It's tiny and almost too hard to make out. But when I squint, I see *5 … 6 … 7 … 8* tattooed there.

"And three, you cannot, by any means, fall madly in love with me." I wave my hand down my body, feigning a frown. "I know it's hard. But just keep it together."

Holding up her middle finger, she rolls her eyes. "Yeah … I don't think that's going to be a problem. For starters, your last name is Thompson. That right there is enough to shut down any feelings that could potentially bubble out of my cold, dead soul. And another thing." She stops, scrunching her nose up. "It's just never going to happen. So, rest peacefully, knowing I will *never* fall in love with you, Hunter Thompson. In fact, I'm simply tolerating you right now."

Giving me a sickly-sweet smile, she hits play on the remote, prompting the music to start. "Now, shall we? Because I just can't wait for you to step on my toes some more."

Holding my hand out, I wink. "Let's do it, Little Bird. Or should I say … *girlfriend?*"

And that girl pretends to fucking gag.

# SUTTON

As much as I hate to stop our practice to use my inhaler, I know my body well enough to know that I need to. After all, taking a few puffs of medicine is a helluva lot less humiliating than having a full-blown asthma attack and being taken to the hospital.

Stopping my movements, I suck in a shallow breath before holding my finger up to Hunter. "Just give me a second," I squeak, heading for my bag, trying to hold back the wheezes coming from my chest.

Bolting around me, he runs to the corner of the room, snatching my bag up before bringing it back to me. "Here," he says softly. "Need me to get your inhaler?"

I shake my head, grabbing it out of the side pocket. Turning away from him, I push my thumb down on the top, dragging a few hits into my lungs. We've talked about my asthma, so it's no secret. But I had no idea he'd know when I needed my inhaler. He's observant—I'll give him that.

Crouching down, I drag in a few shaky breaths. I'm determined to not only dance this school year, but to also be damn good at it. But I need to come to terms with the fact that my asthma attacks are becoming more frequent. And dancing likely isn't my future.

Coming in front of me, he squats down to my level. "You good? Is there anything I can do?"

I shake my head lightly, my cheeks on fire with embarrassment because nothing kills me more than being seen as frail. I'm not frail. My lungs are, but that's it.

"How did you know I needed my inhaler?" I whisper, looking up at him. "Obviously, you know I have asthma, but … how'd you know that's where I was headed when I needed my bag?"

"Because for thirty seconds before that, I watched you try to fight off that breathing was becoming harder," he answers honestly. "I know you don't want me to look at you like you're a beaten puppy dog. And guess what. It's your lucky day because that isn't what I think about you." His gaze holds mine before he reaches his palm out to rub my back in small, soothing circles. "But, Sutton, you've got to be honest with me when you're struggling. I need to know in case things get bad and you need medical help."

I'm met with eyes filled with kindness. There isn't a speck of anything else in them. Not judgment or humor. In fact, he looks worried. And that scares me. Because my whole life, I've known everyone's intentions almost instantly. But I don't know his. And it's terrifying. He's being nice to me. But why?

"Don't worry; for our performance, I'll be fine. This is just a struggle because we've been at it for almost two hours straight." I give him a small smile. "A five-minute dance? That I could do in my sleep. No inhaler needed. We've just been practicing a lot."

"I have no doubt that you could," he answers instantly. "What you see as your weakness, I see it as a strength. I don't know many—no, I don't know anyone who would go this hard without letting their condition slow them down." His hand moves from my back to lightly slap my shoulder. "Be proud, Little Bird. You're a badass."

My eyes float from his to the ground, and I sigh. "Thanks."

"But I did some research, and I learned about something called a rescue inhaler," he says, completely serious. "Do you have one of those?"

Slowly, I nod. "Uh … yes."

"Where do you keep it?" he asks, nodding toward my bag. "And how do I tell it apart from your regular one? I want to make sure I know what to do to help you if you ever have an asthma attack when I'm around."

Completely dumbfounded, I fumble around in my bag, and eventually, I pull out my second inhaler and show it to him.

"This one with the red? This is my rescue inhaler. If I'm *really* struggling, I'll use this one." Holding up the other one, I nod toward it. "This is my maintenance inhaler. I use this every day, no excuses."

Looking at them, he eventually bobs his head up and down a few times. "Got it." Giving me a small grin, he shrugs. "I don't know what your schedule looks like, but I don't have class till this afternoon," he says, his voice low. "Want to go grab a coffee? I'll even buy you another one of those nasty sesame bagels you like so much."

"I have class at one. You know, you don't actually have to buy me food. After all, we're not really dating." I raise an eyebrow. "You could save yourself some money and just do the bare minimum, like every other dude would do in this situation."

"Fake or not, technically, right now, I'm your boyfriend. So, that means I'll keep you fed and caffeinated with those nasty coffees and all the carbs. Deal?" A boyish grin spreads across his face. "Never in a million years did I think I'd be saying this, but, Sutton Savage, you're my girlfriend now. Deal?"

I pull my lips to the side, narrowing my eyes. "Never thought I'd give you this answer, preppy boy. But … sure. Now, how about that coffee and bagel?"

In true Hunter form, he holds his hand out and helps me up. And all seems like it might be okay.

# SUTTON

"I want to know about that tattoo of yours," Hunter says, wiggling his eyebrows.

"It's nothing." I look down, shaking my head. "It's stupid really."

"I get that it's for dance. The whole counting thing." He nods. "But what made you want that?"

I chew my lip, wondering if I should really tell him. But when I look up to find his soft eyes and boyish grin, I can't help but want to open up.

"I've been dancing so long that even in stressful situations that have absolutely nothing to do with dance or ballet, I count in my head before I react. To calm myself down." I shrug. "It might sound dumb, but I just take a breath, and silently count the numbers. Five … six … seven … eight. And then I deal with whatever the problem is."

He stares at me for a minute, almost rearing his head back, like he's surprised. "Wow. I have to tell you, I like the tattoo a lot more now." He nods slowly, like he actually understands my reasoning. "*A lot* more. I thought it was strictly for your love of dance."

"Dance is the only thing I've had for most of my life," I utter. "And I guess I've had to incorporate it into my day-to-day living." I reach across the table, smacking his arm lightly. "What about you? Any ink?" I raise an eyebrow, taking a sip of my iced coffee. "Or piercings? Are you a secret freak, Hunter Thompson, country-club member?"

He cringes. "If you're asking if my dick has a metal rod through it, fuck no." He continues to scowl. "The thought of that makes me want to cry."

I shrug playfully. "Paige might be into it. Spices things up, Thompson."

His eyes narrow. "You've been with someone who had their dong pierced?" He shakes his head. "Guess I didn't realize that was what you were into."

"That's because you don't know me," I say sweetly.

He's seemingly annoyed, and I actually love it. No, I've never been with someone who had his dick pierced. But I would if the right guy came along. Besides, messing with Hunter right now is too funny.

"Enough about my weird kinks." I sigh. "Tell me about hockey. Is the plan still to go pro? Or are you going to medical school and then working for your dad?"

"Fuck no," he scoffs. "I'm going pro, or I'm going to die trying. Fuck medical school."

"Geesh, tell me how you really feel, why don't ya?"

He leans back in his chair. "Not many people get it. The pressure. The hunger to be the best." He nods his chin down. "You get it, Sutton. Your parents have pushed you to the point of breaking. I've seen it firsthand. And I ... we're not all that different."

I blink a few times, tilting my head to the side. "And be honest ... did you ever think you'd be saying those words to me?"

"Fuck no." He laughs once. "Not in a million years."

# HUNTER

I hold the door open for Sutton after we finish our drinks and bagels at the coffee shop. I never knew she even had a sense of humor. I knew she was a sarcastic chick, but it always came off as her being bitchy. But, fuck, the girl had me laughing my ass off for a while there. The icing on the cake was when she did an impression of both of our parents. And she nailed it.

"I'll give you a ride home to get your stuff for class, and then we can just ride to campus together," I tell her when we get closer to my truck. Walking to the passenger door, I open it, waiting for her to climb her little legs up inside. "I'm headed that way after."

"You know, I can walk back to my place," she says, holding her hand over her eyes to block the sunlight. Her eyes squint as she tries to look at me. "Just because we're 'dating' doesn't mean I expect you to chauffeur me around."

Actually, I sort of like giving her rides. I like feeling needed for once in my life. But I'm not going to tell her that. She might get the wrong idea. So, instead, I think of a white lie that might have a little truth in it.

"Well, a big part of this deal is to make a certain someone jealous, right? If we're going to make it credible, I can't have my chick walking everywhere." I wink. "Anyone who knows me would know that'd be bullshit if they saw my girl having to walk. You might think of me as a conceited prick, but when I'm with someone, I'm *all* in." I shrug. "Even if it isn't real."

She looks down, picking at her fingernails before, finally, she gets into the truck. "Good point." Her eyes widen as she looks in front of the truck. Then, she gives me a small smirk, holding her hand up, waving me closer. "Speaking of credible ... it's go time."

I start to turn my head to follow her stare, but her hands land on my shoulders, pulling me closer. She spreads her legs, tugging me between them. She giggles the sort of sound I've never heard come from her—ever.

She puts her lips to my ear. "Just play along, Thompson. After all, this was your idea."

"Paige?" I mutter.

"Yep. And let's just say … she isn't alone."

Feeling a pang of jealousy, quickly replaced by anger, I bury my face into Sutton's neck. I expect her to push me away. Or at the very least, tense up. But she doesn't. Instead, it's like the most natural interaction there ever was. And when my lips run along her flesh, kissing her skin until I reach her chin, I swear her body melts into mine. And then I hear a small moan, and my dick can't help but harden.

I don't kiss her on the lips, but I'm tempted to. She smells so sweet, and I wonder what her mouth tastes like.

*I wonder what between her thighs tastes like too.*

Suddenly, she stiffens before pulling back. "They're gone," she says, clearing her throat. "They, uh … they left."

"Oh," I murmur. Because for a second there, I forgot they were there. Because for a moment, as much as I hate to admit it, there was only Sutton and me.

Scooching back in the seat, she gives me a small smile before buckling her seat belt. "I think we sold it. Guess we'd better get going." She speaks softly. "Class and all."

I close my eyes, willing myself out of whatever trance the sweet smell of her delicate skin against my lips just put me in. Exhaling, I open them back up and plaster on a fake grin. We have conditions. Ones that don't include my cock being rock hard, like it is right now.

"Good thinking, Little Bird. Let's roll."

# SUTTON

I don't think my heart has stopped pounding since Hunter's body was between my legs and he was kissing my neck. It's all part of it—this fake dating thing. But, dang, it's hard to draw a line when we're no longer being watched. Because even when Paige, the guy she was with, and her friends walked off … I wasn't ready for it to end. In fact, I had to force the words out, letting him know they were gone.

"I'll drop you off at the door, and then I'll drive to my class," Hunter says thoughtfully as he pulls into the parking lot of the building where my classes are located. "When do you get out?"

"Three thirty," I answer softly.

"Same." He nods. "I'll be back to get you to give you a ride back to your place."

"Are you sure?"

"Yes, ma'am." Pulling into a parking spot, he puts the car in park and jumps out of the driver's side.

By now, I've come to realize that he really, *really* likes to open the door for his women. It's going to take me some time to get used to, but I respect him for it.

Opening the door, he takes my bag and holds it while I climb down. As he starts heading toward the building, taking my hand and tugging me gently behind him, I frown.

"What are you doing?"

"Walking you to class like a good boyfriend would do. *Obviously.*" He grins, opening the building door as we walk the short distance to my classroom.

Handing me my bag, he leans in, kissing my forehead. "Have a good class, Sutton. See ya soon."

Stepping away, he holds his hand up and waves before heading outside.

And here I stand with a goofy-ass smile on my face, unable to wipe it off.

I'm learning that fake boyfriends are kind of fun after all.

# HUNTER

I watched Holden look out at the rocky coast of Maine in awe. In all our years of vacationing, we'd never come to New England. But when a brilliant doctor had offered to meet with Holden if we came to him … we had gotten on a plane the next day.

None of us kids cared. We loved to travel, but not for something like this. But in a way, I was happy that my brother got to see something he'd always wanted to. Seals in their natural habitat.

Holden wheezed a few times. He was on the trip mentally, but physically … he was shutting down. We were running out of time with him, and I knew it. I think Haley did too. But she was young and refused to think that way. My dad was a doctor. And both my mom and dad were impossibly smart people. If they had gone by what they knew, they'd see that Holden was dying. And that there was nothing anyone could do to save him. But my parents were in denial. They had been ever since Holden was diagnosed with cancer years prior. Since hearing the news, they'd spent every waking second trying to fix him. He couldn't rest because he was being dragged across the country as they urgently searched for something, anything, to make it better. Because miracles in medicine did happen. They happened a lot.

But my brother had given up. He was tired, and I couldn't blame him for the simple fact that he was over being poked and prodded. He was over the treatments that made him ill, and he was mostly sick of not being able to be a normal kid. And I guessed that was *why he and I had become closer toward the end of it. Because with me, he didn't have to put on a happy face and pretend that he was going to be okay. I let him be him. Even if that really fucking sucked.*

*Seagulls squawked in the distance as we sat out on those rocks, looking out at the horizon. I didn't know if I'd ever seen anything as beautiful as the ocean there. Maine was the perfect combination of trees and wooded area and water. Even the way it sounded was soothing. Almost like a fizzy drink with carbonation. The waves hit the rocks, creating a melody of some sort.*

*"Hey, Hunt," Holden said softly, never taking his eyes off the ocean. "Can I ask you something?"*

*"Depends. If you're going to ask to steal my PlayStation, then no way," I joked before adding, "Go ahead. Ask away."*

*"Why do you pretend to hate Sutton so much?"*

*"I'm not pretending anything," I scoffed. "She's bitchy. Stuck-up. And spoiled."*

*At thirteen years old, I probably shouldn't have been using the word* bitchy, *but, hey, it was how I felt.*

*"She's not," he muttered. "She's just really sad."*

*My brother had always had this weird thing for Sutton for as long as I could remember. She was three years younger than him though and never gave anyone, besides Haley, the time of day.*

*"Why don't you just tell her you like her?" I nudged his side gently, not wanting to hurt him. "Maybe that would make her a nicer person if she thought someone in the world actually liked her."*

*He breathed out one sad, lonely laugh before shaking his head. "If I got my cure, I would. Trust me on that. But I'm not going to. Besides, she's never looked at me the way she does you, Hunter. Even if I wish she did." He looked at me again. "If, one day, you finally see her the way I do, I give you my permission to go for it, little brother." He smiled, his lips dry and cracked. "I mean, she's out of your league, but you have my permission to try. If it meant she had a smile on her broken face ... I'd be more than okay with it."*

*"She doesn't look at me like anything, you crazy bastard. Well, besides with that bitchy look that's permanently on her face." I scowled.*

*"She does. Before you started being a dick to her all the time," he grumbled. "You've made her act the way she does toward you."*

*"What the hell are the meds Mom and Dad are giving you these days?" I stared at him for a minute before my eyes narrowed, and I threw my head back. "You're crazy. You know that, right?"*

*"Maybe I am. But either way, if I had to choose who would love the girl I will never get to have ... I'd pick my other favorite person." He elbowed me. "I'd choose you." He narrowed his eyes. "That is, when you finally grow up and stop being an immature dick to her."*

86

I rub my eyes, making myself snap out of my daydream. I'm supposed to be typing a paper, but here I am, not doing a damn thing besides thinking about the past—shit that I can't change.

I remember that day so clearly. We met with the doctor *again*. He reviewed Holden's records and had some new scans done, only to determine there was nothing he could do. Because at that point, the cancer was in every major organ and his body was shutting down. He asked if we could go on a boat to explore the ocean some more to cheer him up. He wanted to see a lighthouse, so my parents chartered a boat to take us around Mount Desert Island, where we got to see the Bass Harbor lighthouse. It was beautiful. And so strange to look at it from the water instead of land.

When we got back on land, my mom began making other plans on what doctor or hospital we'd go see next. Dad got on his phone and began to make arrangements, and that was when Holden snapped. I'd never seen him that upset. For all of his life, he'd always been so respectful and easygoing. But his time on earth was limited, and he knew that. He didn't want to be carted to more doctors, only to hear the same thing again. He wanted to actually live even if it was only for a little bit longer. I can so easily recall the sadness on my parents' faces when he said he didn't want to travel anywhere else unless it was for fun. And I remember the fear in Holden's eyes because I recall thinking how fucking horrible it would be to know your days were limited, yet he handled it with such bravery. And that's why my brother will always be my hero.

He died seven weeks later. But up until the day he did, my parents hadn't given up hope. They still spent most of their time researching and trying to find someone to help him.

But he had gotten to see that damn lighthouse that day. And he smiled, a sense of peace coming over him that I had never seen before. And then … he'd told me that he'd choose me to be with Sutton fucking Savage since it couldn't be him.

I've thought about that day hundreds of times. I remember the stupid shit, like him feeding the seagulls and looking at seals. But until recently, I've never really thought much about him being in love with Sutton since he was seven years old. Or that he gave me permission to date her. I haven't thought about it because I was never interested in her. It didn't matter that I had his blessing because I didn't look at her that way.

*So, why the fuck am I thinking about that conversation now?*

We're fake dating. She's still a bitch, and I'm still an asshole. Except something between us has changed. And that something is that I can't get her off my mind when we're apart. And when we're together, I'm never ready for it to end. And now, I'm guilt-stricken because despite him saying he'd be okay with it, I'm thinking about a girl that my dead brother secretly loved. A girl he never got the chance to tell how he felt because he figured, *What's the fucking point?*

And that makes me a shitty brother.

I don't want her. I want Paige. Paige might be complicating my life right now, but once she comes back to me, things will be simple. She's not a pain in the ass like Sutton is because she wasn't raised the way Sutton and I were. And that's what I love about her. I just need to keep remembering that. Even when I'm dancing with Sutton and my fingertips graze her body and she looks up at me, sad eyes burning into mine, searching for whatever the fuck she's trying to find. It's in those moments I need to remember that she and I are too alike. It would never work because we would constantly butt heads.

Whatever she's looking for, I can't be the guy to give it to her. No matter what my dead brother once said.

She's beautiful, and she's talented and wildly enchanting. But she's not my girl. Not my real one anyway.

My phone rings, and I look down to see my father's name on the screen. Closing my laptop, I sigh.

*I'm not doing a damn thing on this paper. Might as well answer.*

"Hello?"

"Hunter, there's the guy who's going to make it possible for me to retire," he jokes. "How's school?"

He doesn't completely mean what he said. While he wants me to be a doctor and work with him, he isn't going to retire anytime soon. Everyone knows that. In fact, I don't know if he'll stop being a doctor until someone pries his license to practice medicine out of his hands. And I don't foresee that happening anytime soon.

"As good as school can be," I toss back, leaning back in my chair. "How's work?"

"Busy," he says instantly. "We're booked out as far as the eye can see. And a day off? Pfft, forget it." I can hear the exhaustion in his voice. "But I can't complain. So, look, your mother and I have a business meeting in Georgia on Thursday. It's only about forty-five minutes from Brooks. Care to meet for dinner?"

I run my hand up the back of my neck. I have practice on Thursday but will be out with plenty of time to eat dinner with them. The question is, do I want to?

"I can probably make it work," is all I give him. "I'll check my schedule and shoot you a text tomorrow."

"All right," he mutters. "What's this I hear about you dancing with Sutton in a fundraiser?"

"I didn't choose to work with her," I say, trying to think if this is a good time to drop the fake-dating bomb or not. "It just sort of happened."

"I liked Sutton," he says softly. "I've *always* liked Sutton. But I worry that she'll follow in her parents' footsteps and try to screw you over the way they did us." He sighs into the phone. "You know, I really thought they were going to help us with Holden's research center. They knew it was for a good cause—a new research center in honor of your brother—and they didn't care. They sold the land to some big corporation instead. For hardly any more money than we were offering." There's a short pause. "Just be careful. I know your mom and I are hard on you, but the Savages … they are on a whole other level."

It might not be my place for me to tell him the truth about Sutton and her family's falling-out. But, damn it, I want the world to know how truly fucked up her parents are.

"Dad, Sutton doesn't even talk to them anymore. When she left Juilliard, they completely cut ties with her. She's on her own. And honestly, she's not like them. I know she isn't."

"Shit," he utters so low that I barely hear it. "Sons of bitches, they are. Is she doing all right?"

"Well, yeah. But remember how she's always had asthma? Well, it isn't great." I cringe, knowing I shouldn't say anything else, but my big fucking mouth can't help it. "I think that's why she left New York to begin with. It was too much." I swallow. "There's something else I need to tell you."

"What?"

"Well, it happened fast. *Really* fast. But … we're kind of dating." I squirm around in my seat nervously. "Sutton and I—"

"Holy fuck," he grumbles. "Your mother is going to love this. Y'all couldn't just date someone who wasn't your family's enemy?"

"S-sorry. But look on the bright side. Her family is going to be even more pissed than you are." I shrug. "That's got to count for something."

He chuckles. "Yeah, I suppose it does. I'd do anything to get back at those motherfuckers. Does this mean she's coming to dinner too?"

"Is she allowed?" I half-joke.

Even though I can't see him, I know he's running his hand down his face, probably stressed out.

"Bring her. It's not her fault her parents suck," he says quickly. "Don't worry about your mom. I'll talk to her."

"Thanks. I gotta run. I've got practice in twenty-five minutes." I pull in a breath. "Thank you, Dad. For, uh, being cool with this."

"I'll be watching her like a hawk. Know that," he warns. "Have a good week, Hunter."

"You too," I say, ending the call.

*Well, that went much better than I'd thought it would.* Which sort of scares me. Because if it went that easy, then what the hell is my dad up to?

There's a small knock at the door, and my sister slowly pushes the door open, covering her eyes. "You're not naked in here, are you?"

"I hope not. That would be weird since I was just talking to Dad." I laugh. "Nah, I'm good. Come in."

Walking in, she sits at the end of my bed, gazing around at my walls. "Word around campus is … you're dating Sutton. Sutton *freaking* Savage."

I inhale, blowing it out. I planned to tell my sister about the arrangement. I just haven't had a chance. I guess now is as good of a time as ever.

"Yeah, so … kind of." I nod. "By kind of, I mean, not really, but yes."

"What the hell are you talking about?" She narrows her eyes. "Seriously? What's going on?"

"Strictly between us, we're fake dating."

She doesn't hide the look of shock on her face. "Why? That makes no sense."

I look up at the ceiling, figuring out how the hell to explain this fucked up situation I've found myself in.

"Paige is stringing me along. She's trying to dictate my life while also living hers. I've had it." I shrug. "But I love her. And I know she loves me too. This will show her I'm not to be fucked with anymore." I swallow. "Sutton's parents cut her off for transferring to Brooks. And this right here, well, it'll piss them off when they find out she's with me. Plus, she needs my help with finding out some dirt on her mom. She just … thinks her mom's hiding something."

"You know this is going to get difficult, right? If you think you can just fake date someone like *Sutton Savage* and not walk out of it an unchanged man, you're more of an idiot than I already thought." She stares at me, eyes wide. "You're going to fall for her, Hunter. And then what will you do when this deal is over?"

"No." I shake my head quickly. "No, I won't. Is she gorgeous? Yes. Do I like hanging out with her? Surprisingly … yes. But, no, I'm not going to fall in love. This is just something I need to do."

"So, you really want Paige to come back to you strictly out of jealousy?" She looks ashamed. "Come on, Hunter. You're better than this. I like Paige, but she isn't the person you've always painted her to be. You have to know that by now."

"She can't be another thing Mom and Dad take from me." I shrug. "She just can't."

Pointing at me, she tilts her head to the side, eyes wide. "So, that's what this is about. Wow."

"No, it's fucking not," I snap. "That isn't the only reason. Either way, when Sutton is around, I expect you to not be a dick to her."

"Why would I be a dick to her?" She throws her arms out. "She and I were actually friends, dickwad. You were always an ass to her."

"Yeah, well, things have changed. And now, as far as this world is concerned, she's my girlfriend."

"Jesus," she mutters before flopping back on the bed and staring up at the ceiling. "Well … shit."

*Yeah, tell me about it.*

# SUTTON

The walls in this doctor's office are completely bare. Making it look as sterile as it smells in here. With the stench of bleach in the air, at least I don't have to worry about germs.

The past few years, I've had to bounce around between a few different doctors. When I was a kid, Hunter's uncle—who is a pulmonologist—was the doctor I'd see for checkups on my asthma. But after the falling-out with Hunter's family, my parents quickly found me someone new. And then there was the debatably insane doctor in New York, who closed her eyes when she spoke to me, breathing loudly through her nose, making me almost as batshit crazy as she was.

But now, I'm on my own, no longer having parents to do things like schedule checkups and all of that adulting crap. So, here I am, at my initial visit with the doctor I found online. I put this off for as long as I could, but the medication I've been on for years seems to be less effective. And I'm willing to try anything to not have flare-ups as often as I have been lately.

On the way here today, I went to a nearby soup kitchen and volunteered to help with lunch. It's something I did in New York every now and then, and it somehow gave me joy. I've never told a soul I do it because, honestly, it's not about trying to impress people or to sound kind. And as messed up as it might sound, I think it's always sobering to see how much worse things in life could really be. And if spending a few hours of my day helps get more people fed, I'll do it in a heartbeat. In fact, I can't wait to go back again.

A knock on the door is followed by the doctor pushing it open, stepping inside. I've never understood the knock all doctors do because they don't leave enough time—from when their fist touches the door to the second they open it—to actually give a warning. But whatever. I'm sure it's just the law, and they are obeying that. Still, it's annoying.

"Miss Savage." He smiles, holding his hand out. "I'm Dr. Kramp. How are you today?"

"Good." I nod, releasing his hand. "I'm good."

For an older man, he isn't bad-looking. I mean, he's no DILF, but he's attractive for someone who's got to be pushing mid-fifties. His hair is mostly white, though some black still peeks through, but not much. And his skin looks like he's worn sunscreen every day of his life, never letting the sun damage it. And those eyes ... wow, eyes as blue as his I'm certain got him in trouble when he was a younger man.

Sitting down on the stool in front of the computer, he hits a few keys before pulling his glasses down onto his nose, reading through the notes the medical assistant left for him.

"So, I see you're here to talk about your asthma." He directs his attention to me. "Are there any other concerns?"

"No." I shake my head. "Just my shitty lungs—that's all."

He gives me a small, sympathetic smile and wheels the chair a little closer. "Well, I'll ask you some more questions to figure out a plan and then do a short exam. Sound good?"

"Yep." I nod. "Sounds good."

"How often are you using your inhaler?" He rolls back to the computer, typing as I begin answering his questions.

"Two times a day, no matter what." I pause. "That's more of like an upkeep type of thing, you know. But using it because I need it? I'd say two to three times."

"And what are you typically doing when you need your inhaler?"

"Dancing," I say, but instantly want to add more. "I'm a ballet dancer, and sometimes, depending on what kind of routine I'm doing and how long I'm dancing for, I need an extra puff. Or two."

I'm going to leave it at that because I'm not about to tell this man that, these days, I've taken up wrapping my body around a pole and shaking my ass for money. Something tells me he doesn't want to know that.

"Would you say your asthma is stopping you from doing the things you enjoy?" He looks at the computer screen. "Is it limiting what you can do when you're dancing?"

Part of me wants to lie and tell him it doesn't. But he's not my dance instructor. And he isn't one of my fellow dancers either. At the end of the day, I'm just a number that he's seeing today.

Shrugging, I bob my head nonchalantly. "I mean, I'd say yes. A little bit."

Raising an eyebrow, he narrows his eyes. "A little, Miss Savage? Or a lot?"

"In the middle?" I say, sounding more like a question than an answer. "But giving up dancing isn't an option. I need it."

*It's all I have left.*

He doesn't sound convinced. But eventually, he moves on to more questions. Ones that, luckily, can be answered with a simple yes or no.

And like always, when he brings out the spirometer, followed by having me take deep breaths, I just have to pray my body does good enough for me to get some actual good news today.

I wait for my Uber outside the doctor's office. It's a long enough walk back to Brooks that I need to get a ride back.

The doctor visit ended with a warning. The same one I'd gotten countless times before.

*"If you continue to dance, you could end up in the hospital."*

In New York, my physicals were ignored for the simple fact that my parents made a large donation to the school as hush money. Because, God forbid, their daughter couldn't continue to dance. But here at Brooks, I don't have that option. And at my next visit, if my numbers aren't better and I'm not having less asthma flare-ups … Dr. Kramp won't sign off on the clean bill of health I need to continue on. He even made a point to tell me that.

But I'm hopeful that with all the medication switch-ups, along with some other things he suggested I try, I'll prove to him and myself that my lungs can handle dancing. After all, if I don't have dance … what the heck will I have?

I wouldn't even have Hunter to hang out with, seeing as he's my dance partner.

Hunter calls me just as my Uber pulls up, and I head toward it. Hitting Ignore, I make a mental note to call him when I get back home. Not that I need a mental note—I'm sure I won't forget.

Which is stupid.

# HUNTER

Just like not long ago, I sit on the same steps outside of Sutton's house. This time, no one comes out to greet me.

After trying to both call and text her and getting no answer, I decided to just show up. This seems to be becoming a regular occurrence for us. Her ignoring me. Me acting like a caveman, rolling in, unannounced. But I really don't give a fuck how it looks, to be honest.

When a small car pulls into the driveway, I hold my hand over my head and squint to see who it is. And, thank fuck, out comes Sutton from the backseat. Seconds later, the car backs out, pulling away as she heads toward me.

"Hey," she says, sounding off, almost like she's bummed out about something. "I was going to call you back. I was getting in the Uber when you called. And then my phone died."

"Your phone died," I deadpan. "While in a fucking Uber. Christ almighty, Sutton. You should have asked to use my truck. I had practice anyway. I could have gotten a ride with one of the guys after." I stand, stepping toward her. "My girlfriend shouldn't have to Uber anywhere. And she certainly wouldn't do it with no phone to use in case the driver ended up being a serial killer or some shit."

Looking toward the house to make sure no one is by the door, she narrows her eyes, crossing her arms over her chest, and I know she's about to get sassy. And that's okay because, to be honest, my cock loves it when she is.

"Yeah, except like I told you before, I'm not actually your girlfriend, Thompson," she whispers, hissing like a damn feral cat. "So, an Uber works just fine, thanks."

When she starts to walk past me, I step in front of her, blocking her from passing.

She glares up at me. "What?! What do you want, Hunter?"

"What I want is for you to actually pretend to be my fucking girl, Little Bird. That's what I want." I drop my mouth a little lower to hers, looking down. "Are you going to start acting like it or not?"

Her eyes dart around me, and I know someone's watching us.

"Poppy," she mutters, clearly annoyed. "Nosy bitch is watching us like we're a freaking Bravo reality show."

"Then, let's make it worth her time. I've watched enough of that shit with my sister to know it's a hell of a show," I coo before leaning my head down and gripping her chin.

"What are you doing, Hunter?" she whispers, looking at me, completely scared.

"Kissing my girlfriend," I growl, bringing my lips to hers and kissing her like she's actually mine. My hand slides to her neck, and there's no mistaking her body folding against mine.

She tastes like sweet, minty gum, and she kisses me back like her life depends on this fucking act we're putting on for her roommate. My cock hardens, and I curse myself for wearing sweatpants over here.

I pull her bottom lip between my teeth before I finally pull back, resting my forehead on hers. "If she was questioning it before, I'd say she's fucking convinced we're together now," I grumble. "Good job, Little Bird. Now, you're finally acting like you belong to me."

"I don't belong to you," she mutters. "But, sure, I'll play."

When I release her and she stumbles back, she looks at the house. "She's gone." Her eyes move to mine, her cheeks hot and her face flushed. "So, what are you doing here?"

"My parents want to go to dinner with me on Thursday. I'd like you to come with me."

Her eyes widen before narrowing, and she rears her head back, a look of disgust on her face. "What? No way, Hunter."

"A deal is a deal, *babe*. If you're going to be my fake girlfriend, you're going to need to go to this kind of shit with me. And I'll do the same for you. And don't worry; I broke the news to my dad that we're together."

"And?" She bites her lip. "How mad was he?"

"He wasn't mad." I shrug, telling the truth. "He thinks it's pretty fucked up your parents cut you off. And despite what they've done to my family … he likes you. Always has."

"But I *am* my family," she whispers, barely audible. "I share their blood."

"Guess he doesn't look at it that way. He looks at it as a way to piss off your folks—that's a win in his book." I smirk. "So, that means you're going with me to dinner because that's what a good little girl would do."

"Who said I'm a good girl?" she says, raising an eyebrow, and fuck if my cock doesn't stiffen to a level of discomfort.

Reaching for her chin, I tilt it upward. "Something tells me you will be, Little Bird." Stepping back, I wink. "Oh, and next time I catch you in an Uber, it won't be good."

Climbing into my truck, I blow her a kiss before backing out of the driveway and driving away.

Still thinking about that fucking kiss and still tasting her mouth on mine.

## Hunter

Dinner is going better than I thought it would. Right off the bat, Sutton cleared the air with my parents, telling them both that she has no idea what transpired to make her parents do what they did, but that it isn't her fight and that she would like to be thought of as her own person. After a round of questions, my mother seemed to have left the past in the past. Well, as far as Sutton is concerned.

"How's hockey been going, Hunter?" my dad asks, sipping his old-fashioned. "Y'all lost a few big players. How's that affecting things this season so far?"

"We did. We lost our center, Cam Hardy, who was our team captain, and we lost a key defenseman, Brody O'Brien. But it's going all right. I think we'll do just fine with our new lineup."

"Just one more season of hockey after this," my mother says, finishing her glass of wine. "And then it's onto medical school."

I don't bother to say anything back. It's useless, and no matter how many times I've explained to her and my father that I'm good enough to make it to the pros, they don't believe it. So, instead, I just ignore it.

"His opening game is tomorrow," Sutton says, surprising the fuck out of me because I didn't know she even knew that it was. She looks at my parents.

"Y'all plan on staying in town for that? Should be a good game." She looks at me, giving me a small grin. "At least, that's the buzz around campus."

"Oh, no. We have to get back," my mom says, shaking her head. "Work never ends, you know."

I watch Sutton swing her gaze to my dad, who gives her an odd look. "Sylvie is right. We'd love to watch him play, but we have lots of work to get back to. One day, you kids will understand."

"What about you, Sutton?" My mother's eyes burn into Sutton's. "Are *you* watching his game?"

It's all a test. Every second of this dinner is a test for them to dissect if her intentions are good. I hate it, but I guess it's expected.

What I don't expect is for Sutton to reach up, brushing her hand across my face sweetly. "Of course. I wouldn't miss it. He's the talk of Brooks, you know?"

My parents watch cautiously before my dad smiles. "I'm sure he is. That's great, Sutton."

When Sutton's eyes meet mine, I stare at her in complete shock. Maybe this is all for show. She probably doesn't actually give a shit if my parents watch me play hockey and doesn't care if I'm the talk of Brooks or not. And she sure as hell isn't really coming to my game. But something about this, even the way her fingers feel on my skin … feels real.

And it also feels good.

We watch my parents get into their SUV and drive away. We stand there, hand in hand, until they are out of sight. And once they are, she drops her hand down and pokes my chest.

"Well, I think we sold that shit, if you ask me. Give me the Oscar already, folks. I'm *that* good," she jokes sarcastically before taking a bow.

"You were all right, I suppose." I shrug, teasing her. When she sticks her tongue out, I wrap my arms around her, pulling her to my chest. "I'm kidding, Little Bird. You did great. Thank you for being here with me."

She did good, I'll admit. Better than I did anyway. I knew we were going to walk into this today and pretend we liked each other, but I had no idea she was going to be that friendly to me. I give her major props just for staying through the damn dinner because I'm sure it wasn't easy after my parents voiced how much they hated her mom and dad. But she was good.

She was fucking perfect, to be honest.

"Whoa there, Thompson. Your 'rents are gone. No need to pretend to like me."

She smiles, but I can tell she feels uncomfortable. When I don't release her, she stiffly moves her hands awkwardly to my sides before she eventually hugs me back, looking up at me. The moisture in the air makes her hair curl at the back of her neck, and for some reason, I think it's adorable.

"I don't think I ever actually hated you, Sutton. I hated what you stood for." I swallow. "Or what I *thought* you stood for."

"Which was?" she whispers.

"I thought you were like your parents. Shallow and all about money and clout." I look down at her, tilting her chin up. "I guess I thought all you cared about was following their rules, making them happy. But you, Sutton Savage, are your own person." I pause, inhaling. "I also thought you were weak. Like a little bird stuck in a cage, but not willing to fight your way out. But, shit, I was so wrong. Because here you are. Free."

She sucks in a breath. "Thank you, Hunter." She smiles. "That means ... a lot."

"You're still a little bird. But you sure as hell are not in any cage." I grin down at her.

I know she likely won't be coming to my game and that it was just all for show, but a small part of me is just hoping she might anyway. I kind of like the idea of her in the stands, cheering me on. Even more, I like the idea of her watching me play, wearing my number on her back.

*What the fuck is happening to me?*

# SUTTON

I walk inside my house, sighing as I replay the past few hours. I know one thing to be true. When Hunter holds me in his arms the way he did after his parents left, I know ... I'm in trouble.

*Shit.*

And even though it hasn't been easy, escaping that world has been almost like a blessing. Hunter will be living in that world, no matter what happens with hockey.

If he makes it to the pros, he'll be living in the limelight. Rich and famous, adored by millions. And if he doesn't play for the NHL, he'll likely return to Tennessee and take over his father's practice. Which comes with power, money, and a whole lot of stipulations, I'm sure.

I want to live my life for me. Because for most of my life, I haven't gotten to. I know I love to dance, but then I wonder, do I really love to dance? Or

HANNAH GRAY

is it just all I know? I've always been über-competitive, pushing my own limits to an unhealthy place. But if I took dance out of my life ... what would I even have? I mean, shit, I don't even have a cat to keep me company.

I wrap my arms around myself, and I swear I can still feel the effects left by Hunter's touch earlier. When I close my eyes, reliving the moment, my stomach whirls, butterflies the size of bats flying around. Every part of my body feels him when he's near. Even though I wish it didn't.

"So, you and Hunter, huh?" Poppy's voice startles me, and I open my eyes, looking to where the voice came from. "I saw you guys on the porch the other day."

I give her a once-over and shrug. "Yep. Me and Hunter. Hunter and I."

Standing outside her door, she holds a small, round laundry basket in her arms. "Last I knew, he was still trying to make things work with Paige. You do realize she and I are friends, right?"

"I wasn't aware of that," I say, shrugging. "And to the best of my recollection, she dumped him. Close to *two* years ago. So, I'm not sure where you're headed with this."

"They are going to get back together." She says the words so surely, her eyes narrowing. "After college, when he's in the pros, they'll get married and have kids." The smallest smirk creeps up. "And you will be long forgotten. So, do yourself a favor. Stop being a home-wrecker. It's not really a good look."

"They would have to have a home to wreck for me to be a home-wrecker, Poppy." I stand taller, not backing down to her and her mean-girl energy. "And word on the street is, she's certainly not waiting around for him either. What I've heard is ... she might be more into football players these days."

The words roll from my lips because it is something I've not only heard, but I also saw it the other day when we were leaving the coffee shop. I didn't tell him who she was with because, frankly, I didn't want to hurt him more than he'd already been hurt.

"He wants her, not you, Sutton. You're a mere distraction. A body to fill the void," she mutters. "Give it up."

' Walking into her room, she closes the door behind her. And suddenly, every ounce of the electricity I felt on my lips moments prior ... is gone.

Because she's right.

I'm a pawn. Something for him to use to make his ex jealous. And I have no reason to be upset because that's exactly what I agreed to. But it seemed so much easier before he kissed me.

23

# HUNTER

I wave to Sutton as she sits in the stands. Her friends, Ryann and Lana, are next to her. Lana is smiling so big that it looks like it hurts. Ryann ... looks like she wants to murder someone.

I blow Sutton a kiss because that's what a good boyfriend would do. But instead of blowing one back, she stiffens before holding her hand up and waving. She forces a smile, but something is off with her—I just don't know what it is.

She's never minded the pretending with me before. But right now, she seems like she wants no part of it. Maybe I took it too far, kissing her the other night. Truthfully, I did some of that for selfish reasons. I needed to taste her lips. The trouble is, now that I have ... I want more. The floodgates of dirty thoughts have opened, and I can't make them stop.

Now, even in the stands, she seems like she's a thousand miles away from me. But still, she's here. And that counts for something.

I can't believe she actually came to watch me. Not wanting to pressure her, I hadn't brought it up since dinner with my parents. But she showed up. All on her own.

*For a fake girlfriend, she's doing pretty damn good.*

I skate off, heading to warm up. This is our opening game, and we need to look our best. It will set the tone for the season. It'll show the other teams that we aren't to be underestimated. If we instill fear now, it'll carry through much of the season. We need that.

Yesterday, I contacted Jake, my dad's friend who happens to be a private investigator, and he agreed to look into Sutton's family for me. I was sort of shocked my family hadn't already done it after the falling-out. But he told me to give him a few days and he'd have all he could find on Helena. Personally, I don't think there's anything worth looking for. She's just a shallow, materialistic, coldhearted woman who isn't qualified to be a mother. But I'm holding up my end of the deal. And I want to help Sutton find what she's looking for.

I sneak glances at her every now and then, making a mental note that she should be wearing my jersey. That's what a good girlfriend would do, and if we want to sell this, she needs to have my number on her back.

*Maybe after the game too. With nothing else under it.*

Images of her in heels, wearing nothing but my jersey on and nothing underneath it, assault my brain. Holy fuck, I have no idea where these thoughts are coming from. It's not appropriate. I mean, I'm trying to get Paige back, for fuck's sake. That's what this entire thing with Sutton is meant for—to make Paige jealous.

So, why the hell does it suddenly seem like it's not about Paige and it's more about Sutton now?

Or worse, more about me.

# SUTTON

I watch Hunter play, and suddenly, I'm seeing him differently. As an athlete myself, it's not hard to notice the drive he has while he's on the ice. And to be honest, I respect him even more right now because I recognize the hunger he has when he plays. And it's the same when I dance.

I can tell myself dancing has always been for my parents, but deep down, I know I love it too. Every cell in my body has been touched from dancing. And maybe I've been trying to convince myself that I don't love it as a coping mechanism since I know that my career is going to be cut short because my lungs hate me.

Hunter moves on the ice so flawlessly. He isn't fatigued. He doesn't need to stop and take a puff of an inhaler to keep himself from spiraling out of control. I'm envious of him because for him, the sky is the limit.

"I'm going to get a soda. Anyone else want anything?" Lana says, standing up.

"Can you grab me a Coke?" Ryann tosses back.

"I wouldn't pass up a Kit Kat bar." I give her a sweet smile, handing her some cash. "You rock."

Once she's gone, Ryann looks at me. "Okay, spill it. Spill. The. Fucking. Tea."

Giving her a side-eye, I feel my chest tighten. "Uh … what do you mean?"

"Homegirl, I know you didn't go from hating Hunter Thompson to exchanging saliva outside my bedroom window the other night." She nudges my side. "What the hell is going on? Did you see his dick and it was huge and you couldn't resist?"

I don't want to lie to Ryann. I really like her. I like Lana too. But if I tell Ryann, I'd be betraying Hunter in a way because he and I made this arrangement together.

"I guess I just … started seeing him differently," I tell her, looking at the ice again.

A part of me knows that the words I just said aren't complete bullshit. I am seeing him differently. Slowly, I'm feeling things that I know I shouldn't be feeling.

"Mmhmm," she drawls. "Sure you did." She pokes her finger into my arm. "Something is fishy here, and I'm going to figure it out."

Hunter flies down the ice, keeping the puck safe. No one seems to be capable of catching him. And with one move, he hits it in, sending it into the goal just before his teammates swarm around him.

I glance over to where Paige stands, cheering as she jumps up and down.

And in that moment, Hunter looks up, giving a smile as he holds his stick up.

And that smile … isn't at his ex-girlfriend, who he's trying to win back.

It's at me. And only me. And that makes my heart pound in my chest.

# HUNTER

I finish up with interviews, still high from the win of our opening game. The buzz in the locker room has been off the charts, and I know everyone is equally as hyped up as I am.

We know we have a good team. But after losing some of the best players to ever grace Brooks's ice … we were all a little uneasy, going into this season. Now that we've proven to ourselves that we can and will work well together, it's like a weight has been lifted.

Heading toward the exit, I pull out my phone. Before heading out to meet with the press, I sent Sutton a quick message, thanking her for coming to my game, and a bit ago, I briefly saw the text notification when she answered. But before I can read her reply, I'm distracted when arms wrap around me from behind.

I smile, immediately thinking it's Sutton. But when I turn, I find red hair instead of black. And green eyes instead of blue.

"Good job, baby." Paige beams up at me. "Let's go celebrate."

I stare down at her, not sure what to do.

*This is what I wanted.* This was the goal.

Yet here I stand, unable to form a thought. The only thought that flashes through my mind is … it's no longer Paige who I want to see at the end of a game.

It's Sutton.

"I love you, Hunter. I was scared, okay? I needed space. And, you know … everything with your parents and just knowing that they don't like me. It all got to be too much." She looks up at me, eyebrows pulled together. "Say something. Anything."

"Paige … I don't—fuck, what do you want me to say?"

"That you love me too. That I'm yours and you're mine. That we will leave here and go celebrate. Together." Her hands move to my abdomen, sliding lower. "That you've missed me the way I've missed you."

Before I can respond, she throws her arms around my neck and crashes her lips to mine. Lips that I always loved the taste of suddenly don't seem so sweet.

And when I pull back, I'm completely fucking speechless. And that's when I see her, waiting outside the arena doors, watching the entire exchange between Paige and me.

Sutton.

And when her eyes connect with mine, she turns quickly. And then … she runs.

# SUTTON

I run. I run because it's the only thing my brain could think of doing. It's dramatic and embarrassing, and within minutes, my lungs are cursing me as I walk between two buildings.

I can't face Hunter. I just can't. A lump forms in my throat, and coming from someone who hasn't cried since I was ten years old, I don't know how to handle these feelings.

I need to convince Hunter I ran because I wanted to play it off that I'd caught him cheating and wanted to pretend I was upset. In reality, I felt like I had seen something I wasn't supposed to see. And I couldn't handle seeing it unfold. Also, watching him kiss her made it feel as though my heart was being ripped into a million pieces. Something that was so foreign for me to feel.

They kissed. And he didn't push her away. Why would he though? He loves her. He wants her.

I continue walking in the darkness until I feel like I'm a far enough distance away that I can slow, giving my lungs a rest.

"Jesus fucking Christ, Sutton!" Hunter says, charging around the corner. "You run into dark alleys at night now?"

"Sorry." I shrug, trying to sound normal. "I told the girls I'd meet them at Club 83. Figured I'd take a shortcut."

"And running away? What the fuck was that about?" he growls, stepping closer. Close enough that his scent fills my brain when I inhale.

"Sorry. I was just trying to act like a real girlfriend in case anyone was watching me." I swallow. "I figured that would entail either charging up to you and yelling or running away. I chose the latter."

"Is that really it, Sutton?" Even in the darkness, I see his eyes narrow. "That's really all that was?"

"Yes," I whisper.

Energy burns between us as his chest heaves. Finally, he grabs my hand, pulling me toward him. "Did you run away because you were trying to be a good fake girlfriend, or did you run away because you hated seeing her kiss me, Little Bird?"

I stare up at him, feeling so confused that I can't even organize all the thoughts in my brain. The truth is, it had nothing to do with acting and everything to do with the very reason that I don't want him kissing anyone else. And in another life, maybe I could be the only girl he kissed. But that is insane, and besides, there's too much history between him and Paige. I don't need to complicate things further by inserting myself in the middle of all of that.

"I don't know, Hunter," I whisper, my voice barely audible. "I really, really don't know."

His eyes burn into mine, and he leans down the slightest bit. "Don't fucking take off at night, Sutton. Do you understand?" he growls. "It's not safe."

"Yes." I nod, not knowing why I'm so quick to submit to him.

"Let's go," he grumbles. "I'll take you to Club 83."

"You don't have to give me a ride, Hunter," I say, my voice small. "If you need to go back to Paige, I understand." I offer him a small smile even though it's forced. "The point was to get her back, right? It looks like ... it looks like maybe we succeeded."

He looks down at me. "Fuck Paige, Sutton. I'm done with that whole mess."

"Wh—why?"

"Because I don't think it was ever about my parents. I think it was and has always been about her." He stops. "But a deal is a deal. And if you're up to it, I'm still game for pissing off your parents. As for your mom, I have someone on that. We should know something in a week or two."

"You don't have to, you know." My cheeks heat, and I'm thankful he can't see them in the darkness. "It's okay if you want to back out. We can just dance together and call it a day."

"No," he says bluntly. "I'm not going anywhere. Now, let's go."

As he begins to walk, my legs are shaky as I walk behind him, his hand tugging me along.

"Okay."

When he glances over at me, I vaguely see his smirk in the darkness.

"Next game of mine you come to, I want you in my jersey. Got it?"

I chew the inside of my cheek before shrugging. "I mean ... I *guess* I could do that."

"No, you will do it." He winks, squeezing my hand.

And there goes my heart again, doing that squeezing thing it does when he looks at me like that. Because Hunter Thompson's damn smirk makes it impossible for my heart *not* to do that.

Club 83 is packed, bodies filling the dance floor. Everyone is celebrating Brooks's victory, and the energy is palpable, but for Hunter and me, the tension is so thick that I could cut it with a damn knife.

"Snooze" by SZA plays through the speakers as my body rocks against Hunter's slowly. I don't know what we're doing or why we're doing it. He says things are done between him and Paige, but I have no idea why he's holding me this close. All I know is … I don't want him to let go. But I'm too scared of rejection to admit that out loud.

His hands hold my body in a protective way. And I find myself in a trance, breathing him in. Sex would blur the line to a point we couldn't come back from. So, maybe I'll just dance on the edge of this imaginary line, pushing just enough without going too far.

"Why did you really run off back at the arena, Sutton?" he murmurs against my ear before pulling back and looking down at me. "No bullshit. Just be honest."

My breath catches, and my entire body tenses as I try to look away from him. But before I can, his fingers catch my chin, and he forces me to look at him.

"I don't know," I squeak. "If I did, I'd tell you. But I don't."

His eyes burn into mine, daring me to say the truth.

Instead, I narrow my eyes. "Why did you chase me?"

I watch him swallow, his throat bobbing softly as he drops his fingertips from my chin. "I have no idea." He pauses. "All I know is, I couldn't *not* chase you, Sutton. My body wouldn't let me not chase you." He swallows. "That's a fact."

After a staredown for a few seconds, I put my head back against his body, and we continue to sway as the song switches to "Monster" by Justin Bieber and Shawn Mendes. Even with the pulsing of the speakers, I can feel his heartbeat against my cheek.

His lips move to my ear. "Next Sunday, my family is having a fundraiser on a yacht. It's only about twenty minutes from Savannah. They're expecting you to come with me."

Pulling back, I tilt my chin up. "And you? What do you expect?"

"I don't expect anything." He stops. "But I want you there. Next to me." He says the words so surely. Like there's no question. "And it will be fun, I promise. My parents are only coming out for the dinner event. Other than that, the boat is ours. After they leave, we'll have the night to be alone."

A shiver runs up my spine as I imagine being alone with Hunter … on a yacht.

"I'll go," I say.

The corner of his mouth turns up in a crooked grin, and he nods his head. "Good."

## SUTTON

After a few weeks of practicing, Jolene gave each couple a time slot to show up at the studio and show her what we'd been working on. The past few times we've practiced, I can tell Hunter is tired. And although I want us to do well in our performance, having him in tip-top shape for hockey obviously should—and does—take priority.

"I'm fucking nervous," Hunter mutters. "I've got sweat dripping down the crack of my ass. She's scary."

"She is not." I giggle. "She's just … intense. Kind of like you on the ice."

Jolene looks toward us and tips her chin up. "All right, you two. Let's see what you've been working on." She looks sideways. "Good luck with those toes, Sutton."

I cover my mouth to hide my smile before nudging a frowning Hunter. "She's kidding. You'll do great. And my toes are fine. I bandaged them for extra protection this morning."

That gets his attention. "Really?"

"No!" I shake my head. "But it'll be fine. I'm strong. Now, let's go."

"Just run through the first thirty seconds or so of your routine, and then I'll add music for the next run," Jolene says, eyes on us as we head to the center of the floor.

I give Hunter a reassuring smile and mouth, *It's okay*.

And then it's go time.

He's not perfect, but why would he be? He's a hockey player and not a dancer. But he's far from bad. In fact … I'd even say he's pretty good. I can tell every move he makes, he's overthinking, worried that he'll mess up in front of Jolene. He plants his hands on my sides as I dance in front of him. Turning to look at him, I cup his cheek. It's all part of the routine. Something I added once I could actually tolerate him.

When I think it's been long enough, I stop moving. Looking at Jolene for any sort of criticism, I chew my bottom lip anxiously.

For a few seconds, she just stares at us. But eventually, she claps her hands. "You two have been working hard—that's for sure." Walking toward where her phone is plugged into the speaker, she hits the screen a few times before glancing at us. "This is it. This is the one. Take your places, please. Show me your entire routine. And this time, slow it down just a little. Really savor it. Savor each other."

At her words, I snort but cover it as best as I can. Holding my hand out for Hunter to take, I inhale. And then … it's showtime.

I'm instantly taken aback by her song choice. But I shake it off, getting my head right.

"All of Me" by John Legend plays through the studio. His heartbreaking voice fills every crevice of the room, and I become one with the words, feeling them deep in my soul even though they don't apply to Hunter and me.

It's just him and me, and the rest of the world melts away. It's crazy to think that this man has become the closest thing to family I have these days. I trust him more than I trust anyone else in my life.

With music, somehow, his touch feels different. Our movements are slower and more in sync. A lot of the routine is me dancing while also incorporating him into it. But during a few parts, he has his own moves. And as we near the end, I leap into his arms, praying he'll catch me. He does. And he lifts me higher into the air, looking up at me as the music stops.

Both of our chests rise and fall in a perfect rhythm. I know I need a puff from my inhaler, but I'm on such a high in this moment while he holds me in the air, like I'm as light as a feather. And right now … I feel weightless.

It isn't until Jolene claps her hands together in applause that we're both pulled from our trance. I shake my head, trying to wake myself up as he sets me down on my feet.

Reaching in his pocket, Hunter hands me my inhaler. But when I narrow my eyes, questioning how he got it, he nudges it toward me.

Putting it to my lips, I inhale before I turn to face her. I straighten myself out, holding my chin high.

"Well done, Sutton. Well done, Hunter." She looks at both of us, eyes wide and smiling. "You two can thank chemistry for how far you've come because … wow." She bobs her head up and down. "The pair of you certainly have it. I was expecting something comical. What I got was Beauty and the Beast. And I loved every second of it." She nods toward the door. "You're both free to go."

"Thank you, Jolene," I say softly.

"Thanks for not telling me I suck." Hunter waves. "But I just gotta know, am I Beauty or the Beast?"

"Obviously Beauty," I mutter.

"Obviously," Jolene agrees. "See you two next time."

Glancing nervously at Hunter as we both grab our things and head out the door, I can't stop the grin spreading across my face even if I tried.

But at the same time, things keep shifting between us. Little by little, inch by inch. And I'm not sure how far to let it go before I put my guard up and stop it from escalating. After all, he's a Thompson. And his life is always going to be anything but ordinary.

I kind of like the thought of just ordinary.

# HUNTER

I jog to the passenger side of the truck and open the door. Finally, Sutton has learned to just let me open the damn door. It's just something that my grandfather taught me as a young kid. He might have been a workaholic as a surgeon himself, but the man knew how to treat my grandmother.

He always said, "Keep your woman well fed, open the door, and when in doubt … just bring home flowers or treats."

She steps down, and we walk toward the house.

"I'll wait out here while you get your things," I tell her, nodding toward the porch swing.

"Okay." She smiles, walking into the house, looking over her shoulder. "I'll be right back."

"Take your time."

I sit on the swing, looking out toward the road.

After I had hockey practice this morning—and chugged a Red Bull—we had to show Jolene our routine. She was impressed. And that made me feel much fucking better about the whole thing. Because honestly, I'm not used to sucking at something. Even if it is dancing.

The door creaks open, and I'm just about to stand and tell Sutton how fast she was at getting her shit together. But when Poppy steps out, full resting bitch face and all … I give her a tight nod.

"Poppy."

"Hunter," she says, sounding grouchier than ever. "I heard Ryann and Sutton talking. Going away for the night, I take it?"

"Yep," is all I give her. Because honestly, it's not her business.

"You know, you're more of an idiot than I thought for being with *Sutton* when you could be with someone like Paige." She checks her nails over, frowning. "Paige is kind. Smart. Going into one of the most compassionate fields of work one can choose—nursing." She points toward the house. "And you're throwing all of that away to be with someone like Sutton Savage, who only cares about her own hopes and dreams. That girl doesn't have a sweet bone in her body."

"Oh, Poppy. Poppy, Poppy, Poppy." I shake my head, smirking. "First off, your friend is the one who dragged me along for nearly two fucking years. Claiming my parents scared her away when we all know that's bullshit. She wanted to have her cake and eat it too. And I can't blame her." I wave my hand at myself. "I'm pretty good fucking cake." I stand. "Second, you don't know jack shit about Sutton. So, don't act like you do and kindly piss off."

"Sutton's going nowhere, Hunter. Her lungs are shot. Last I checked, professional dancers don't need to have an inhaler in their hand twenty-four/seven." She shrugs. "And if you think she'll stick by you when you go pro … think again. She'll be long gone." Holding her hand up, she wiggles her fingers. "Now, if you'll excuse me, I have a dinner date with a *real* woman. Named Paige. Later."

I watch her strut away, getting into her car. I don't know how the other women in this house stand to live here with her. Maybe she's only mean to Sutton. Who the hell knows? And everyone knows what her problem is with Sutton. Sutton has more talent. Before she arrived here, Poppy was at the top. Now, that's been taken from her. Crappy lungs or not, Sutton was made to dance. And if she really wants it for her future, I know she'll figure it out.

"I'm ready!" Sutton chimes in, stepping onto the porch. "Let's do this."

I take her bag from her, and she follows me to my truck and climbs in.

Grinning up at her, I narrow one eye. "So, on a scale of one to ten, how much are you dreading this dinner tonight?"

"Honestly … I'm not dreading it at all. Everyone knows shit like this has *the* best food at it." She shrugs her slender shoulders. "I've been on a budget since my parents gave me the ol' boot. Which means … no high-end food." Holding both hands up, she moves her head up and down. "I say bring. It. On."

I laugh before closing the door. *I guess that's one way to look at it. Shitty company, but damn good food.*

Besides, I'll have her at my side. How bad could it be?

# SUTTON

I watch the slide show, trying to hold in my yawn. It's nearly nine o'clock at night, and for the past hour and a half, Dr. Thompson has been talking nonstop about the future plans for the newest foundation he and his wife started.

A foundation that promises to provide travel care to those children whose families might not be able to afford it. From the sounds of it, the money won't go toward making the kids' last bit of time on earth more comfortable, but rather to get them to appointments and try to get cured.

One thing I have known since Holden passed away is that his parents will never stop fighting. Even though he's gone, they are still desperately trying to fight this bear of a disease that took him away from them. They have two beautiful children still here, but they are so blinded by their grief and sorrow that I don't think they can shut their minds off from Holden. Nor should they. But I also feel bad for Haley and Hunter because I know they probably miss how things were before he got terribly ill and died. I remember how different his parents were before Holden got cancer. Sure, they still worked a lot back then. And their careers were the most important things. But they also made sure to make time for their children. Even if it meant bringing a nanny along on family vacations—much like my own parents did.

Dinner was incredible, just like I had known it would be. Lobster from New England waters. Steak from the best butcher shop. And the most delicious mashed potatoes I'd ever had in my mouth. Literally. Chef's kiss on those.

And then there was dessert. Which didn't include the fancy, dried-out cupcakes that Hunter's mother likes so much from the overpriced bakery in the city. But instead, a flourless chocolate cake with whipped cream. But I have to say, the pieces were a little small, and I definitely could have had a second.

Glancing down at how snug my dress is, I sigh. I guess it isn't like I need a second one—that's for sure.

Reaching over, Hunter splays his hand on my thigh, and when I glance at him, he gives me a look, as if telling me he's sorry and that it's almost over. Maybe the second part is wishful thinking because my ass is starting to fall asleep.

As his hand lingers on my flesh, a million butterflies fill my stomach, flapping around, causing a whole dang tornado in there. I have to tell myself not to squirm from his touch—even if I want to because it renders me breathless.

A fake boyfriend's touch isn't supposed to make your skin catch on fire. Yet here I am, waiting for the fire department to show up, hose me down, and put me out.

I wonder if his sister is seeing him touch my leg this way when no one is looking. She knows it's not real. Or isn't real to her brother. Tonight, she's been a little cold to me. She isn't rude, but she's not her warm, fuzzy, usual self that she was back before everything changed.

His parents rented this huge-ass yacht for the night and aren't even staying here. Apparently, the second this is over, they and the other dozen people are leaving. Which is nice because Hunter and I get to spend the night and hang out until noon tomorrow before we head back to Brooks for practice—my dance and his hockey. But I plan to make the most of it. Having the private chef make me a delicious breakfast, jumping off the boat, soaking in the hot tub that overlooks the ocean. I'm going to pack as much luxury into this night as I can.

Finally, the presentation ends, and everyone begins to move around a bit.

"Be right back. Haley is headed out to go visit some friends who live nearby," Hunter says, kissing the top of my head, and I remind my heart it's only for show and to beat in its normal rhythm.

Watching him walk over to his sister, I smile because they've always been so close. Hunter has always been so protective of her too.

Before she leaves, her eyes find mine, and she holds her hand up and waves good-bye. It's not much, but she flashes me the smallest smile that gives me hope that, one day, maybe we'll get back to how we used to be. Maybe.

A man in his mid-thirties, who I used to have a crush on, steps in front of me. "Sutton Savage? Wow, I haven't seen you in years. You've grown up." He holds his hand out, raking his eyes down the entire length of my body. "Elliot Klavert. You probably don't remember me, but I used to come to some of your family's events."

I do recognize him. How could I not when Haley and I always thought he was so hot? Heck, every girl who came across him thought so.

"I recognize you." I smile, shaking his hand before he releases mine.

"I haven't seen your parents in quite some time. How are they doing?"

"They are good, thanks," I lie, not wanting to explain anything to him. "How have you been?"

"Better now," he coos, winking. "I know I already told you this, but, wow ... you've really grown up. How old are you now?"

"Nineteen. I'll be twenty in a few months."

His eyes twinkle with mischief as he leans closer to my ear. "Would you look at that? You're legal now."

"Yep." I nod. "Scratch-offs and cigs. Can't beat it."

"Oh, I can think of much more fun things than that, beautiful," he utters before reaching in his pocket and handing me a business card. "You should call me sometime, and we'll hang out. Unless you're free tonight?"

I frown. Opening my mouth to speak, I'm cut off by Hunter kissing my cheek as his arm goes around my waist.

"Sorry, babe. I just needed to talk to my old man," he says before looking at Elliot. "Keeping my girl company, are you, Elliot?"

His energy is different than it was when his hand was on my leg. His hand holds my waist in an almost-protective way. And I watch him look at the man who was just hitting on me. And honestly, Hunter looks angry.

"Yes, I, uh ... hadn't seen her in quite some time." Elliot clears his throat. "She's all grown up."

Stepping closer, Hunter holds out his free hand, extending it to Elliot. But when he takes it, Hunter grips it tightly. "Let your eyes look up and down her body again, I fucking dare you," he growls. "I know you saw her sitting next to me. Stay away from my girl. Got it?"

Elliot pulls back, his face reddening. "I didn't realize she was yours." He glances at both of us. "Lucky man."

"Yes. Yes, I sure am. Now, do yourself a favor and don't even fucking look at her," Hunter says coolly. "After all, we're on a boat. And the sharks are probably hungry tonight."

First, Elliot looks confused. And then ... shocked. And as he struts away, I look at Hunter, narrowing my eyes.

"You son of a bitch," I hiss, low enough for only him to hear. "What the fuck was that about?"

"He's a creep," he growls against my ear. "Everyone knows that."

"And you're a psychopath, apparently." I hold his eyes, matching his dark energy, and my nostrils flare. "Careful, Thompson. It almost seems like you care."

Backing away slowly, I start to walk away. Needing a second to breathe. But as soon as I get around the corner and out of sight from the crowd, his hand grabs me, spinning me around and pushing me against the wall.

"Maybe I do care, Little Bird," he mutters, his lips hovering over mine. "What if I do?"

I open my mouth to speak, and that's when his dad calls to him before rounding the corner.

Backing away from me, he looks at his dad. "Dad."

"There you are. Got a minute to talk?" His stare hardens at his son. "Now."

They walk around the corner, leaving me alone.

I can still feel the buzz of his lips almost touching mine. And the weight of his words that he cares.

A whole lot.

# HUNTER

"I don't know what that little thing with you and Elliot was, but he's donating a pretty big chunk of change into this thing," my dad says once everyone else has left. "I don't need you convincing him otherwise."

I look around the sky lounge, taking note of all the details on this yacht. "Yes, well, he should try to be a little less creepy. Don't ya think?"

"He's harmless," he scoffs. "And if this is over Sutton, that means she's already causing issues. I like her. She's a beautiful girl, but please, keep your head on straight." He looks at my mother as she walks into the room. "Ready, darling?"

My mom nods, placing her hand on his chest. "You did great, sweetheart." Turning to me, she hugs me. "Thanks for coming. Enjoy the boat, but be careful. And please, for the love of all things, don't break anything."

"Wouldn't dream of it," I say as she releases me. "Safe travels."

Looking around, she frowns. "Where is Sutton? I didn't get a chance to say good-bye. And to thank her for coming." She cringes. "Can't be easy, you know. Being here when her family hates us."

"At least the feeling's mutual, right?" I shrug. "Y'all have a good night."

"No truer words have ever been spoken." She snorts. "Bye, honey."

Waving, they head toward the exit.

And as soon as they are out of sight, I waste no time going to find my girl.

My *fake* girl.

# SUTTON

I lie on the outdoor sofa, looking up at the sky. There must be a zillion stars out tonight, all shining bright, demanding to be seen.

It's weird, being on this boat with all these rich people. I used to fit in—sort of. Now, I'm a damn stripper, trying to earn money for food and medication.

Out of the corner of my eye, I see Hunter strut closer before leaning against the bar. But quickly, I turn my attention back up at the stars, ignoring him.

"You're mad," he says. His deep voice sounds much louder in the quiet night air.

I inhale through my nose, filling my lungs as I contemplate what to say.

"You acted like a caveman," I mutter. "And it was a little uncalled for." Turning my head against the cushion, I stare at him. "And truthfully, it was too over the top. We might be trying to fool a few people in this world that we're together, but come on, Hunter. We all know it doesn't matter. And another thing, it's *Elliot Klavert*. Every girl's wet dream."

"Yeah, and what do you want, Sutton? Want me to wait till he's slipped you a date rape drug next time before I step in?" He glares at me. "Use your fucking brain. He's a creep. And if he so much as looks at you again, I'll make sure he spends the next few months eating his meals from a straw."

Taking a few steps toward me, he leaves me speechless when he reaches into the small pocket of my dress and slides his hand in. His fingers graze me through the fabric, making me suck in a breath. But just when I think he might actually go further, he pulls Elliot's business card out, holding it in front of my face. He tears it into pieces, his eyes narrowed to slits.

"Guess you won't be calling him now, will you? Fuck Elliot Klavert."

"No, fuck *you*," I hiss.

I start to push myself up, but his hands anchor me to the cushions.

His face moves closer to mine, and his lips are a mere inch away from my own. He radiates with unmistakable anger.

"You make me fucking crazy, Little Bird," he growls. "I've never been a jealous man a day in my life. Yet here I am, losing my fucking mind."

"Yeah?" I whisper. "Well, what are you going to do about it then?"

When he moves his mouth closer, my eyes flutter shut with anticipation of his kiss. But just as his lips graze mine, his mother's voice startles both of us. For the second time tonight, his parents have stopped us from taking something too far.

"Hunter? Is that you?"

Standing up straight, he looks past the bar, where she must be standing. "Hey, I thought you'd left."

"Just forgot my phone," she calls back, her voice moving closer as she comes around in front of us. "Oh good. I wanted a chance to thank you for coming, Sutton."

She smiles at me, but I can read her like a book. She doesn't trust me as far as she can throw me. Why should she though?

"Thank you so much, and y'all have fun."

"Thank you, Sylvie." I give her a sweet smile. "Have a nice night."

"Night, sweetie," she says to Hunter before leaving.

And I don't know if I should thank her for saving us from whatever we were about to do or curse her for it.

"I'm, uh ..." he says, dragging his hand through his hair. "Look, I don't even fucking know what we're doing anymore. I'm sorry that I'm acting like a jealous prick, but, fuck, you turn me into a monster," he grumbles before turning away and walking behind the bar. "You want a drink? Seems like we could both use one. Or ten."

"Yes," I huff out. "Yes, I do."

"What would you like?" he drawls, pouring himself a shot of Jameson and downing it, only to do it again. Slapping his shot glass on the bar, he looks at me.

Getting up, I saunter over to him, taking a seat on the other side of the bar. "I'll have what you're having, big guy."

His eyes twinkle with something as he takes a second shot glass from under the bar and slides it to me, filling mine and his own.

Holding mine to his, I smirk. "To getting way too drunk and probably acting like morons."

"Cheers, you absolute pain in my ass," he mutters, clinking his against my own.

The second the liquor is down our throats, he's pouring us another. And with the way my head starts to buzz after a few minutes and the way he's looking at me ... something tells me we're about to do something very, very dumb.

# HUNTER

My head spins as we collapse on the couch next to each other. She's so close that her smooth leg brushes against my own in my shorts. And she smells like some kind of mix between perfume and sweetness. I know I'll regret all of these shots tomorrow morning, but something about this feels needed.

Maybe it's to break the ice between us. Maybe it's to loosen her up. I don't really know. All I know is, I'm drunk, and she's looking really, really sexy.

"Truth or dare?" she blurts out, giggling, her cheeks a deep shade of pink from the Jameson. "Or are you too scaaarrrred, big guy?"

"Keep calling me big guy, and you'll find out how big I really am," I say, serious as a heart attack.

"You're too much of a gentleman to take advantage of a drunk girl. Truth or dare?"

"Truth."

"Ooh, what a baby," she teases, poking my arm. "Were you and Paige actually in love? Like, hopelessly, wildly in love?"

I sit there, stunned. Because honestly, I don't know. I have nothing to compare what Paige and I had to anything. I had hookups, but no other girlfriends. Well, until Sutton. And she doesn't even count because it's fake.

"Yes," I finally say with little to no emotion in my voice, but not on purpose.

She eyes me over, her eyes narrowing the slightest, subtlest bit. "You know what I think? I think you were bored with Paige. But she was the safe choice, and you loved that your parents hated her because, secretly, you like to be the black sheep."

Even in my drunken stupor, my jaw tenses. "That's not true. I loved her."

"So, you're saying you don't now?" she says, tilting her head to the side.

"What? No." I run my hands through my hair. "That's not what I'm saying. I don't know what I feel for her now." My head spins, and I laugh. "Truth or dare?"

"Dare," she coos. "I'm no little bitch, like soooommme people on the boat."

"I dare you to call your parents and tell them you're with me now."

She holds her hand out. "I'll do you one better. I'll call them from your phone."

Placing my phone in her hand, I lean back on the couch and watch her dial their number. It's late. Hell, it must be eleven at night. But she hits a few more numbers and puts the call on speakerphone.

After a few rings, her father's groggy voice answers. "Hello? Hunter, this had better be good if you're calling me. You no-good sack—"

"Actually, it's me," she says smoothly. "Hunter let me use his phone, like the good boyfriend he is, and you're on speakerphone."

"Sutton?" Her father seems to wake up, knowing it's his daughter on the line. "What the fuck do you mean, your boyfriend? This must be a joke."

"It's not a joke. We're together and in love." She grins. "Isn't that right, Hunter?"

"Sure is," I say. "Hey, Sam."

Before he can respond, Sutton speaks again. "I just had the best dinner with the entire Thompson family. They've excused me for the fact that my parents fucked them out of the land they were going to get."

"So, let me get this straight, years ago, we mentioned you dating Hunter, and you were appalled. Now that we're at war with the Thompsons, suddenly, you're in love with him?" He laughs bitterly. "You really are something else, Sutton." He pauses. "Oh, and, Hunter, your brother was twice the person you'll ever be. Remember—"

Before he finishes his sentence, she ends the call. She suddenly looks sober, though I know she isn't.

"He's a dick," she says nonchalantly, relaxing back on the couch. "Sorry."

"Nah, it's all right." I shake my head and give her a half-assed grin. "He speaks the truth. We all know that Holden was the better person. And he would have been a way better man."

Her dad would have been crazy to not think my brother was the better person. Everyone knew that he was. He didn't have to work at being a good kid. He just was one. He planned to dedicate his life to finding cures and fixing people. And even though he was way too young to decide on a lifelong career, I have no doubt that he would have followed right in my parents' footsteps to medical school.

"Truth or dare?" I say, and she rears her head back.

"You just had your turn, jerk."

"Truth or dare?" I repeat.

"Truth." She scrunches her nose up. "The last dare didn't turn out all that great."

I inhale, looking at her before I look up at the stars. "You knew my brother loved you. Even though you were young, you knew."

In that moment, while I wait for her to answer, all I can hear is the sound of the ocean beneath us. And I'm not sure what the hell is going to come out of her pretty lips next.

"He didn't love me, Hunter. He was just a kid."

"He did though." I nod. "He was infatuated with you." I cringe. "And now, I'm fake fucking dating you. Kissing you for show when someone's watching. And wanting to kiss you when they aren't." I drag my hand down my face. "Fuck, Sutton. Why'd we think this was a good idea?"

We're both quiet as she relaxes next to me, resting her head on my shoulder.

"Even when he was alive, it was never Holden I was looking at. He was kind and sweet, sure. But the one I was looking at spent most of his time hating me. Eventually, the feeling became mutual."

"What? What do you mean?"

"You know what I mean, Hunter. You had to have seen how I looked at you when I was a kid. But you saw me as a brat, an entitled girl who wanted for nothing, and it showed because you were a complete ass to me." She snuggles into my side. "And that made me hate you. And I suppose that's when it all began. This ... hatred we have."

"I couldn't hate you right now if my life depended on it," I rasp. "You have to know that by now."

I sit there in utter shock, unsure of what else to say. I guess I just always assumed the feeling of hate was mutual. Then again, I know why I acted the way I did. And it wasn't because I actually couldn't stand her. It was because when I first started noticing her—*really* noticing her—it was the same time Holden did. And I just figured if I hated her—or acted like it—I could fool everyone. Including myself. He might have been the family's favorite, but when it came to popularity, I won every time. I guess I wanted him to just have that. He was terminally ill and deserved that much.

Still, he chose me to pursue her after he died. He gave me his blessing.

"Truth or dare," she murmurs before looking up at me.

Slowly, she climbs onto my lap, straddling me. My dick instantly begins to harden as her dress hikes up her thighs. I know I should tell her to get off of me, but I can't.

"Dare."

"I dare you to go to bed," she whispers, her eyes floating to my lips. "I dare you to push me off of you right now and go in your room. Alone."

"Is that what you want, Little Bird?" I say, my voice sounding pathetic. "What you really, *really* want? To go to bed, all alone?"

"I don't know what I want," she says, giving me a small shake of her head. "But neither do you."

I slide my palms up her smooth thighs. "I do know one thing."

"And what is that?" she says, her eyes narrowed slightly as she tilts her head to the side.

"That I don't want to go to bed alone."

# SUTTON

I stare down at Hunter, unsure of what magic was in the liquor that gave me the courage to be in his lap right now. His erection grows below me, making me tingle between my legs and suck in a shaky breath.

He looks so hot right now. His hair tousled. His eyes that same intense, possessive look he sometimes gets when he looks at me. It should scare me. Instead, it turns me on.

Slowly, he reaches up, taking my hair out from its holder.

"Let your hair down, Little Bird. Let me see you undone."

My hair falls over my shoulders, hanging forward, and he reaches up, fisting his hand through one side.

"You're beautiful, Sutton."

"You're drunk," I whisper. "We poured too many shots down our throats. This is silly."

"I've always thought you were beautiful," his voice says low. He drags his finger to my throat and presses against my skin softly. "And if I'm being honest ... I've also thought about pouring something else down your throat besides liquor."

I swallow thickly, my heart stopping in my chest. "Y you have?"

"Anytime you shot me a glare or mouthed off, I'd imagine pushing you onto your knees, telling you to open up these plump, pouty lips, and giving you a mouthful of my cock," he says as his eyes glaze over. "Something told me that no matter how bitchy you acted, you'd be a good girl for me if I asked you. Something told me you'd even swallow me down."

My head spins the smallest bit, but I know it's not from the alcohol; it's from his words and the ache between my thighs that's spreading through my stomach.

Brushing his thumb across my bottom lip, he tilts his head to the side. "Would you, Little Bird? Would you be a good girl and suck my dick the way I know you want to? The way, deep down, you've *always* wanted to?"

Tipping my chin up to show boldness, I inhale. Knowing I'm about to say words I never imagined would come from my mouth. But not wanting to stop them from coming out.

"That depends. What are you going to do for me?" I narrow my eyes. "I have needs too, you know."

"Oh, the things I'd do to you," he rasps. "I'd eat you until the sun came up, brat. And then I'd go ahead and eat some more."

His words cause such a deep ache within me. Desperation fills every single part of my body, and I know there's only one cure. And it's one I'll regret in the morning, but I'm desperate enough to do it anyway. And drunk enough too.

Resting my hands on his thighs, I slowly move to the floor. And to my surprise, he lets me off his lap. Slowly, I unbutton his jeans, but pause.

"Fake girlfriends probably shouldn't do this, right?" I whisper, hearing my heart pounding in my ears. "It would make things ... complicated."

"Fake or not, if it includes my cock down your throat ... I don't really give a fuck," he growls low. "Take what you want from me, Sutton. And if what you want is a mouthful of my dick or my tongue between your legs ... I'll gladly give it to you."

"It doesn't have to mean anything," I say, my voice shaky.

122

"It won't mean anything," he answers, suddenly zero emotion in his voice. "But I know you're wet; in fact, I'd bet my life that you're dripping. So, go on. Show me what those mouthy lips can do."

I tug his shorts and then boxers down, and his cock springs free, instantly begging for me to give it the attention I so desperately want to. But when I inch my head forward, he grabs my wrist, lifting me to my feet. Reaching between my legs, he pulls my thong down, sliding it to my feet. And when I step out of it, he grabs it in his hand.

"Soaked. Fucking soaked. Just like I knew you would be." Tossing my thong to the side, he smirks up at me. "Change of plans, baby. I need to eat right now too."

Pulling me toward him, he lies flat on the couch and maneuvers me until I'm on top of him, facing his cock. Pushing the fabric of my dress up, he lifts my hips higher and higher until his face is between my thighs. I lean forward, and he jerks his hips upward, grazing his cock against my lips.

His tongue dives inside of me, sending a jolt right through my body with each lick and flick he delivers.

Wrapping my mouth around his length, I take as much of him as I can before I embarrassingly … gag. But something that's humiliating for me makes him groan against me.

"Gag on me like that again, Little Bird, and I'll blow my load down your throat right now," he hisses. "Jesus. Fucking. Christ," he murmurs before his tongue dives inside me again.

His tongue. His words. Having him inside of my mouth while he uses his own mouth on me … it's too much. And as I involuntarily start to rock against him, he grips my ass and forces me to move faster against his mouth.

Everything tingles, and the buildup between my legs is enough to make me feel like I'm going to black out. My head spins—a combination of his magical mouth and the alcohol, I'm sure. And as my release finally surfaces, his hips thrust against my face as I continue taking him as deep into my throat as I can.

When I come back down to earth, he growls against me, "Fuck, feeling you squeeze my tongue like that was hot. If you don't want my load down your throat … you'd better stop now."

After what he just gave me, no way am I stopping. Continuing to let him slide in and out of my mouth, I gag again when he hits the back of my throat. And that gag is all it takes for him to lose it. Because within seconds … he's pouring himself into my mouth and down my throat. His hips jerk, and his body trembles until every last drop of him is released. And I take all of it, swallowing him down without hesitation. And when I climb down from him, I adjust my dress and laugh awkwardly.

Because I just sixty-nined the hottest guy on the planet on a yacht. And after the high I just felt that's making my legs still shake, I think he might have just won the Best Fake Boyfriend of All Time award.

"Well ... night, I guess?" I yawn, lying on the bed as I stare at the ceiling with the fanciest molding I've ever seen. "Are you sure you don't want me to go in the other bedroom? I don't mind. After all, this was your parents' event. So, you should get to choose which room you want without me crashing."

I've sobered up, but my brain still isn't functioning at one hundred percent. And for that, I'm kind of glad. Otherwise, things would feel even more awkward than they already do.

"Stay," he says, folding his hands behind his head. "Could be a bogeyman on board—ya never know. I need someone to keep me safe."

"And you think I'm the right choice for that?" I all but snort.

"Yep. If it's a dance battle, you'd definitely have that shit in the bag." He smirks, giving me some sort of smoldering look. "Plus, you'd have me on your team, and we all know I'm the talent."

I punch him lightly, shaking my head. "You're annoying. Is there a way to make you stop talking?"

"Put something on my mouth. That'll quiet me right down." He winks. "But you already learned that, didn't you, Little Bird?"

I tense up, chewing my bottom lip. "As long as you're sure, I'll stay. But if you're drunk and you'll forget I'm here, leaving you to wake up in the morning and think I'm trying to take advantage of you, I should leave now." I half-laugh. "We all know your ego is big enough. I'm not sure it could handle inflating even more if you forgot about this night and woke up thinking I was trying to get with you."

"Trust me, I'm not drunk enough to forget you're next to me." His eyes burn into mine, leaving me feeling so raw and exposed. "I've probably forgotten a lot of shit in my life. But what we just did tonight? Burying my face between your thighs while you choked on my cock?" He shakes his head once. "Well, let's just say that's not going to be one of them." He gives me a small, sly grin. "Come on, Little Bird. Rest."

"You can't tell me what to do," I whisper, narrowing my eyes while fighting a smile. But with his sweet, lopsided grin ... it's hard to do.

It takes me a second to oblige. But when I do, lying close enough to smell his scent and feel his presence, I don't think I've ever fallen asleep so fast in my life.

# 16

## HUNTER

Physically, sure, I'm here at practice while Coach has us run over the same play for what could be the twentieth time. I'm sweating my nuts off while last night's Jameson seeps through my pores. Mentally … I'm on that yacht with my face buried between Sutton's thighs as she rides my mouth like it's her damn job.

And if it were her job … she'd deserve a bonus. A *big*, fat bonus.

Not long after, we stumbled back to the master suite, and even though it took a little convincing on my part, we went to bed together. She started on the other side of the king-size bed, but ten minutes after she dozed off … she was nuzzled against me, wrapping her leg around mine. But when we woke up and the alcohol had worn off, it was a little fucking awkward between us. Ignoring the elephant in the room, both of us avoided what had happened just hours before—that I had blown my load down her throat just after I ate her until she came so hard that I thought her pussy might actually squeeze my tongue off. But, hell, if it had, at least it would have gone on to live a damn good life, stuck inside of the sweetest place I'd ever tasted.

We acted like it hadn't happened. Even though we both know it sure as hell did.

*I'm ready for it to happen again too.* But it can't. Or it shouldn't. I'm in no position to jump back into anything with anyone.

"Thompson, are you here, or are you thinking about your mother's fucking titty milk?" Coach screams. "Get your fucking head on this ice, or we'll stay here all night. Don't believe me? Then, keep fucking up and find out."

"Sorry, Coach," I say quickly, telling my brain to stop thinking about Sutton's luscious asscheeks resting on my forehead while I drove my tongue inside of her sweet heat. That doesn't help my daydreaming much, but when I look at Coach and see his face is beet red, I snap back to focus.

After running over the play a few more times, along with some conditioning drills, I'm relieved when Coach tells us to hit the showers and get out of his face. Like a jackass, I drank too much last night, and I'm in desperate need of a nap.

Heading into the locker room, Cade taps the back of my leg with his stick and cackles. "Late night, Hunter boy?"

"You could say that," I mutter, pulling my jersey off and tossing it into my bag.

"What you need, my man, is three Motrin, one Tylenol, a Big Mac with a large fry. Oh, and an ice-cold Coca-Cola."

I frown at him, narrowing my eyes. "I mean, I get the first two items. But the last three? Why the hell would I want that when I feel like dog shit?"

"I'm tellin' ya, big dawg. McD's is where it's at when you're hungover." He laughs. "In high school, my local one knew my order by heart."

"I'm not sure if I'd be bragging about that," Watson chimes in. "Actually, I know I wouldn't."

"That's because you're a good little boy, Gentry." Cade shrugs. "And that's why I get more ass than you ever will."

"Don't count Gentry out," I say, pointing to Watson. "He gets his fair share of women. And he does it without being a dick."

"Gotta be a dick to give 'em the dick. Otherwise, they wanna sleep over and have breakfast." Cade smirks. "Ladies love a bad boy. They love an asshole too." Nodding his chin at me, he leans against his locker. "Go on and tell us what you were up to last night. I'm intrigued. Was a bit of a slow weekend for me."

"Says the dude who had three girls on our couch when I got home," Watson mutters. "Couldn't be any more interesting than your night, Huff."

"This is true. I don't know why I said that," Cade agrees. "But Thompson looks like ass wrapped in shit paper, tied with a piss-covered bow. Now, I knew you had some fundraiser thing, but I also know that no way did your parents stay on the boat last night too. So, I wanna know, did you have company?"

126

"Nope," I grumble with the shake of my head. "Now, kindly piss off. I'm tired."

I walk toward the shower, and Cade takes the shower next to mine.

"Be ready in ten, Thompson. We're headed to Mickey D's! Gonna fix you right up."

I say nothing because, let's face it, Cade Huff doesn't take no for an answer. Besides, maybe hanging out with his loud ass will distract me from filthy thoughts of Sutton.

*Yeah, right.*

# SUTTON

I lie on my back, staring at the ceiling. My head hurts. My body hurts. My *brain* hurts. Number one, why did I drink so much? Number two, why did I drink so much and decide it would be a good idea to literally sit on Hunter's face? Thong-less.

With the few others I'd romantically been with, I never came *that* hard. Sure, they gave me pleasure, and I enjoyed myself. But Hunter was a whole other ball game.

I'm feeling things I shouldn't be feeling for him. But even though he and Paige have been formally split up for two years, they still have something there. At least, they did until just recently. I don't want to be a rebound. And with Hunter, that's exactly what I would be.

But maybe … we could use each other to get over our shit. He's sulking over the rejection of his ex, and I'm getting over getting the boot from my parents. Sex could be helpful. In fact, I think we both deserve it, to be honest.

The door squeaks open, and Ryann peeks through the crack before pushing it open the rest of the way. Taking a few steps, she leaps onto my bed, landing next to me.

"Okay, so … tell me everything and don't leave anything out," she says, eyes wide. "Ya girl is getting no dick. You have that *I just got some dick* look on your face. Do tell."

"I do not!" I smack her lightly. "And I did not!"

A few days ago, after asking Hunter if it was okay, I told her the arrangement was fake. And that we were just pretending to date, but there were no feelings involved. Somehow, I knew I could trust her, so it felt good to tell her the truth, no matter how messed up it is.

"Hmm …" She taps her fingers to her chin. "Well, I know that look. So, unless you just stashed your vibrator before I walked in here … you had one hell of a release earlier. And since you were with Hunter last night, my money is on that sexy motherfucker."

Putting my pillow over my face, I feel my cheeks heat to the point of melting. "I'm not telling you shit!"

She tickles me, and I peek out from the pillow.

"Please, I'm not ticklish. You have to have actual feelings to be ticklish. My soul is dead."

"Wow, you really are like a zombie." She shrugs. "That's okay. I'll just ask him next time we see him, I suppose!"

When she starts to stand, I grab her hand, pulling her back down. "Okay! Fine!" Putting the pillow back over my face, I exhale. "We did something on the yacht. Something … that is a certain number."

"A number?" she mutters. "Oh! Oh! Ohhh! Shit! You guys did the ol' sixty-nine?" She hits me, tearing the pillow from my face and chucking it on the floor. "On a yacht? Holy shit! That's hot."

I'm somewhere between laughing and dying as I cover my face with my hands. "It was dumb! I was drunk. He was drunk. And I guess we just—"

"Decided to put your mouths on each other's genitals?" She laughs. "I love it. I mean, I don't love him. Because, you know … athletes. *But* truthfully, girl, you've been a bit uptight. Glad to see he loosened you up a bit." She winks.

"It's actually gross when you say it like that." I groan. "It can't happen again. It shouldn't. He's probably still in love with Paige. His parents tolerate me, but deep down, I'm sure they don't like the idea of me being around. And let's not forget that he's probably going pro."

She eyes me over. "Sounds like you're trying to convince yourself not to fall in love with him, Savage."

"That's *so* not it." I shake my head. "It's just … hooking up makes things complicated. We need to just get through this dancing ordeal and go our separate ways. Deep down, we still can't stand each other."

"Mmhmm … I always sit on the faces of those I hate too," she deadpans before her eyes widen. "Does he know you're dancing at Peaches?"

"No." I shake my head. "I've played it off like I just work in a restaurant off campus. And when he asks for more information, I just change the subject." I cringe. "I hate lying to people, so I guess I'm just, well, avoiding it?"

"Are you embarrassed?" she asks, but there's not an ounce of annoyance in her voice. Just curiosity.

"No! Well, maybe a little." I shrug. "I don't know. I guess I feel awkward, saying it out loud. Because guess what? Whether you want to call it this or not … we're strippers. And we both know there's a stigma around that word."

"Sure is. But guess what. Every one of us doing it has our reasons why we're there." She sighs before she gives me a nervous look. "When it comes to Hunter, whatever you do, just be careful. It's easy to act like a coldhearted bitch now, but the deeper you get into it … the harder it's going to be to let go. And maybe you'll be the girl in the fairy tale. Maybe, just maybe, you'll get that happily ever after that everyone likes to fantasize about. But if not, just know I'll be here for ya, homie."

"Thanks. But if I was smart … I'd just turn off the idea of any sort of physical or emotional relationship." I clear my throat. "And I am smart. Sort of." I crane my neck to look at her. "What about you and Watson? How has working with him been going?"

Her body tenses, and she inhales, making her nostrils flare. "It's fine. He's nice. *Too* nice. But he's not fooling me. They are all the same."

I laugh. "I wouldn't be so sure. I hear he is genuinely nice."

"Whatever," she mutters, scooching to the side of the bed. "I'm headed to the gym. Wanna join?"

"Hell no. I'm taking myself a damn nap."

When she stands, heading toward the door, I smile. "Ryann?"

"Yeah?"

"Thanks. For being you. I'm happy to have you."

"Backatcha, babe." She winks before strutting off.

When she leaves, I let my mind wander. To a place where maybe Hunter and I never hated each other—or pretended to hate each other. Where his ill brother didn't love me and Hunter wouldn't feel obligated to keep me at arm's length. Maybe then things would have been different between us.

When we were kids, he was the boy at events and family get-togethers who would tease me, making fun of anything from my dress to my hair. As much as I wanted to hate his guts, whenever I caught him smiling, my heart would do a flip. The older we got, the more he pretended like I didn't exist. And that pissed me off. I was far from perfect, but I wasn't awful enough to be treated like an invisible piece of dirt. All along, I guess both of us were using a messed up defense mechanism of ours. He didn't want to risk falling for the girl his brother wanted. And I wasn't about to look like a fool by showing my cards to the boy who made it a point to hurt my feelings.

Such a shame really. But perhaps it means those rare occasions when I could almost swear Hunter was watching me, growing up, maybe I wasn't crazy after all.

A yawn rips through me, and I close my eyes. Drifting off to a land far away. Where Hunter Thompson's hands are back on my body and his lips are on my own.

# HUNTER

I take the long way home after the team dinner, driving by Sutton's place. I have no fucking clue if I'll stop or not. But I haven't been able to talk to her much this week with hockey season being in full swing, and I really miss that girl.

But the problem is, when I do see her, I worry I won't be able to keep my hands to myself. The past week since we got back from our mini getaway—where she, hands down, gave me the best blow job of my life—we haven't really talked about what happened. And it sort of feels like she's avoiding me a bit. Then again, I've been insanely busy, and I haven't been able to make much time for her either. But maybe I'll change that tonight. And maybe, if I'm lucky, she'll let me.

I don't want to declare us happily ever after. But one time of tasting her wasn't anywhere near enough.

She's a complicated creature. And I'm dying to find out everything about her.

# SUTTON

I zip my hoodie up a little higher when I feel a shiver run through my bones. I'm not sure if it's because with fall arriving, it's brought some cooler temperatures this week. Or if it's because I'm walking home in the dark from the studio and I'm secretly afraid of Bigfoot. Or bears. Or really anything that might be lurking.

Needing to practice my solo routine, which is the week after the charity, I looked at the studio's schedule and saw that late nights were really the only time it was free. Ryann is working, Lana is with her boyfriend, and I sure as hell wasn't about to ask Poppy for a ride, which is my reasoning for being out here on a pitch-black night.

Hunter would have let me use his truck. Or he would have figured out some way to make sure I had a ride. But I felt too guilty to ask. Between hockey practices, games, and now getting ready for our dance routine, the man has a lot on his plate. And tonight, he had a team dinner after practice, and I didn't want to bother him with needing his truck.

Headlights flash behind me, and I inhale a breath. Reminding myself that this is a safe campus and that if I take off running, I could, one, have an asthma attack and the killer would catch me anyway. He'd probably see my lungs were shit, and I wouldn't be worth anything to him, so he'd leave me alone. Or, two, I'd draw attention to myself when it was a perfectly sane person behind me.

When the vehicle stops beside me, rolling the window down, I know it's neither option.

Hunter might not be a serial killer. But judging by the look in his eyes as he sees me walking at night … he's not exactly sane either.

Holding my hand up, I gulp. "Hey." I smile. "Fancy seeing you here. I was just, uh … well, you see—"

He growls as he jumps out of the truck and walks quickly to the passenger door. "Get in." Opening it up, he points to the seat. "*Now.*"

Stuffing my hands in my hoodie pockets, I start toward the truck. "Nice to see you too," I attempt a joke, but he only shoots me a harsher glare. "You look nice. Real nice."

"Shut up. I'll deal with you when we get home."

Like a little kid, I climb in, but not before sticking my tongue out at him and scrunching my face up like I'm five years old. Actually, I'll give five-year-olds more credit. I'm acting more like I'm three right now.

Pulling into my driveway, he wastes no time in getting out. And within a moment, he's on my heels, following me inside.

When I walk into my room, he shuts the door behind him, turning the lock.

"Walking at night isn't safe. First of all, there're a lot of bad people, Little Bird. Wake the fuck up. You're not safe in a cage anymore. Second, you're wearing all black clothes!" He waves his hand at me. "Not one fucking reflective piece. And, third, what would you do if you had an asthma attack on the side of the road? Huh? What the fuck would you do, Sutton?"

He walks toward me, crowding me against my desk. He's mad. No, he's irate. Yet he's so incredibly hot right now that my face heats.

"I'm sorry. I just—"

"No," he snarls, pushing his finger to my lips and holding it there. "Don't speak, Little Bird," he growls before gripping my chin. "The only sound I want to hear you make right now is you gagging on my cock or choking on my cum." His eyes darken. "Understood?"

An aching sensation twirls between my legs, making me squeeze my thighs together. Nodding slowly, I lick my lips before I slowly sink to my knees before him voluntarily. Reaching up, I run my hand over the growing bulge in his sweatpants. A hiss escapes his throat, and he blinks slowly.

Pulling his sweatpants down, I unleash his growing erection, palming it in my hand. As I stroke him, slow at first but becoming faster, he pulls back, gripping himself. When he slowly presses his cock to my lips, I eagerly open wide, letting my tongue greet the tip.

"Fuck, Little Bird. That fucking mouth," he hisses just as his hips jerk toward my face. "Christ, I need to fuck your mouth. Or your pussy. Or maybe your ass."

Deep down, I know he just worries. But I'm also learning that when it comes to me, he feels the need to be in control. And truthfully … I like him this way too. Though I never imagined I'd be saying that.

Wrapping my lips around him tighter, I bob my head back and forth. Gazing upward at him, I cup my tongue, continuing to suck.

His hand tangles in my hair, giving it a pull, which only has me picking up my pace on him. Something about knowing that I have him on edge right now makes me ache inside. I love that it's me who's bringing him to this place.

"Good girl," he grunts out, throwing his back against the wall. "Just like I knew you were, baby."

Doing that thing I know drives him crazy, I go deep enough for him to hit the back of my throat, gagging instantly as my eyes water the smallest bit. Going right back to pleasuring him, I moan against him, gazing up through my lashes just as he tips his head forward.

"Gonna … come down … your throat, Little Bird," he growls out, struggling to get the words out. "Open wide."

Seconds later, liquid is hitting the back of my throat, and I never break eye contact with him while I swallow him down. His hips buck against my head slightly, and his body trembles before finally stilling as he pulls back.

Running his hand through my hair, he exhales slowly before dragging his fingertips down my face, over my lips, and to my chin. "You make it damn hard to stay mad when you look at me like that with a mouthful of my cock, Sutton." His lips turn up the tiniest bit. "Don't walk at nighttime anymore."

"Okay," I whisper, pushing to my feet.

"Tell me you won't do it," he snaps. "Say it."

"I won't," I tell him, looking him in the eye. "I promise."

He looks only partially satisfied with my answer, but points to my pants. "Take these off, panties too."

I wring my hands together, cheeks heated. "It's okay. You don't have to ... ya know. I wanted to do that for you."

"Take them off, Little Bird. You were a good girl, dropping to your knees and sucking my dick the way you did. Good girls get to have their pussy eaten by their fake boyfriend." His gaze sweeps over me, heating my entire body. "I've been craving you since you rode my face that night. Besides, between your legs is my new favorite flavor."

When I hesitate, he steps toward me, burying his face in my neck as he drags his tongue along my flesh before sucking and biting my skin.

"Hey!" I yelp. "That's going to leave a hickey!"

"Good," he murmurs against my skin. "That way, when everyone looks at you, they'll see you're taken."

He reaches down, effortlessly tugging my leggings and panties to the floor. Looping his arm around my waist, he tosses me onto the bed and hooks his forearms around my thighs, pulling me to the edge of the bed and against his mouth.

"Ahh," I cry out, gripping his hair as my thighs squeeze around his neck harder.

His tongue dives inside of me as he pushes a finger in at the same time. Taking one hand, I grip the sheets and watch him, though my eyes threaten to roll back in pleasure.

When he widens his tongue, working it over every part of me and making me feel it everywhere ... I lose it. An orgasm hits me like a freight train, and I come all at once instead of a slow build.

I scream, lifting my hips against his face.

Reaching up, he puts a hand over my mouth to silence me as I slowly rock back and forth against his mouth, completely and utterly gone— mentally and physically—to the magic that comes from Hunter Thompson's tongue.

Scooching my body up on the bed, I collapse on my back and drag in a few shaky breaths. My legs quiver, and my skin is covered in a layer of cold sweat. I didn't fall to my knees, expecting anything in return. But I'm sure glad he decided to return the favor anyway.

Enjoying oral sex or having someone go down there with their mouth has never been a thing to me. It's always seemed awkward and kind of forced. But with Hunter? It's absolutely mind-blowing. It's like dying and going to heaven. Only heaven probably doesn't include things like that.

Lying down beside me, he pulls me into his side. "What the fuck are you doing to me?" His deep voice rattles against me. "I've never been this crazy over another human being in my life. With you, I can't even try to control it."

How he reacted to not only me walking home late at night, but also Elliot hitting on me makes me realize that shit is going to hit the fan when he learns what my job really is. He's jealous. And overprotective. But even though I know I should tell him ... I can't. He might not look at me the same when I do, and that scares me. Because I really, *really* like the way he's been looking at me lately.

"Does it have anything to do with what happened to Haley?" I murmur against his side. "I could understand why that would make you worry."

His body stiffens a little. "You know about that?"

I nod my chin against him. "I heard enough to get the gist of it," I whisper, feeling like shit that I never reached out when I heard. But I figured I was the last person she'd want to hear from. "Is she okay now? I mean ... I saw her briefly on the yacht, but we didn't really talk."

"She's scared all the time even though she won't admit it." He sighs. "But it's not just that I worry about you, Sutton. The thought of another man even looking at you makes me fucking wild. I could have easily thrown Elliot off the boat and not thought twice about it." His hand grips me, squeezing me against him harder. "You're turning me into a monster, Little Bird. But I can't walk away from you."

Pressing my lips to his chest, I gaze up at him. "What are we even doing anymore, Hunter?" I whisper.

"Fuck if I know," he mutters back. "But I don't want to stop."

I place my hand on his chest, feeling his heartbeat against my palm. "Me neither."

*And I really, really mean those two words.*

My whole life, I've felt like no one truly gets me. He does. And he doesn't even need to say it.

"Can I take you somewhere tomorrow night?" he asks softly. "I promise you'll love it. I think so anyway."

I nod against him, yawning. "I'd love that."

We've already passed the point of complicated. Why turn back now?

# HUNTER

Sutton walks in front of me. Even in loose-fitting, light-colored jeans and a white crop top with no makeup and her wet haired pulled back into a bun, she is the most beautiful woman I've ever seen.

She grins up at the sign, pointing to it. "Blind Rage? We're going to a rage room?"

I take a few steps toward her, stopping as I rest my hand on her side. "Yep, we are."

"We're going to break shit?" she whispers, her eyes widening and a smile spreading across her lips.

Leaning down, I kiss her. "We're going to break shit."

She bounces up and down, clapping her hands together. "I've always wanted to try this!" She stills, raising an eyebrow. "But I'll warn you, if we make it into a *who can break more* competition, you're going down!"

"Oh, I already figured that much." I chuckle, looping my finger in one of her belt loops and tugging her closer. "All that rage inside of you when it comes to your parents or your asthma ... let it out." I kiss her forehead. "You'll feel a lot better once you do."

Resting her hands on my sides, she nods slowly, looking up at me. "What about you? What are you here for?"

I think about it for a second. Bringing her here was mostly for her, but it was for me too. I've never come to a place like this. I mentioned it to Paige a few years ago. I had heard Brody and some of the guys came here to try it out. She thought it sounded like the dumbest thing and didn't feel like she had anything in her life to be upset enough to break something over. I never mentioned it again.

In Sutton, I see the same frustrations, pressures, and feelings of not being enough that I see in myself. I figured that maybe something like this could help us. Who the heck knows?

"Losing my brother and not being able to help him. The constant pressure from my parents to become a doctor. The fear of never making it to the NHL and being trapped in my father's shadow. Everything that happened with Haley." I stop. "Your parents abandoning you and the hate I feel for them for that. I wish I could fix them so that they were better to you."

"Most of the things you listed are not really your battle to fight, Hunter," she answers softly. "But the last one, that's *definitely* not your fight. You don't need to feel bad for me." She gives me a small, sad smile.

"If it includes you, Little Bird, it's my fight now," I tell her, and I mean it.

Jerking my head toward the door, I grin. "Let's go fuck some shit up."

"Hell yeah." She smiles back at me. "But remember, you're going down."

# SUTTON

I'm decked out in my goggles, coveralls, and all this other ugly protective gear.

Hunter smirks at me. "You're so fucking cute right now."

"You won't think so in a minute," I warn him. "You'll remember not to piss me off when you see me tear this place apart."

I don't know what to expect, to be honest. Will it be fun? Will it be emotional? Will it be awkward? I really have no idea. But just knowing that Hunter brought me here ... I'm truly blown away by his thoughtfulness.

Standing behind the safety wall, he points inside the room, where anything from old computers to dinner plates and everything in between is spread out. "Go on. Do your worst."

"You go first," I say. Stepping behind him, I wrap my arms around him and nuzzle my cheek against his back. "Thank you, Hunter. This is really cool."

His hands rest on mine, and slowly, he turns around. Bending down, he kisses me. "Anything for you," he utters, smiling at me. "This is a good look on you. Hell, that kiss just made your glasses fog up."

Pulling off the safety glasses, I wipe them against my pants. "Shut up! It's hot in here."

"Yeah, because of me." He winks. "You sure you don't want to go first?"

"No, you go ahead." I lean against the wall. "Show me how it's done, big guy."

Grabbing a bat, he shrugs. "All right, here I go."

Taking a glass bottle from the floor, he sets it on the metal table and hits it with the baseball bat. An insanely satisfying noise of crackling glass fills the room before he moves on to something else. He lifts up an old computer from the dinosaur age and tosses it like it weighs nothing before grabbing the bat again. He rains blows to countless items in the room, smashing them to the point of no return.

After a few more minutes of raging, he walks toward me, passing me the bat, his chest heaving as he grins.

"Okay, you're up."

Taking the bat, I stand on my tippy-toes and kiss him this time. He seems surprised, but quickly deepens it, reaching to my ass and giving it a squeeze. Even through protective suits, after a little bit longer of kissing … I feel him harden against me.

Pulling back, I smack him lightly. "Behave, you horndog. Would ya?" Shaking my head, I start to walk into the rage room.

Unsure of what to even do at first, I look around, as if trying to decide what my first item should be. I see a stack of glass plates in the corner of the room, and I head toward them, needing to hear the same breaking glass sound as Hunter breaking the bottle.

I bring the bat way up before using all my strength to bring it down onto the glass. And when it does, the glass shatters, and I don't waste any time moving to the next item—an old TV.

When I see an old window lying on the floor in the corner, I attack it. The trim of it reminds me of the one in my reading room from when I was a kid, and when I start hitting it … I can't stop.

I land blow after blow on that damn window. It broke long ago, but I keep going. My chest burns, and I know I'll need to use my inhaler shortly, but I continue to smash the same spot on the floor where the glass window once was. And then I realize, for the first time in years … I'm crying.

I'm crying, and I can't freaking stop. I wheeze a few times before sinking to the floor, bringing my knees to my chest.

I feel Hunter next to me, pulling me against him, but I can't hear if he's saying anything. All I see is my inhaler being pushed in front of my face, and he gives me a shot of air before I bury my face against his chest.

Emotions I've kept in for as long as I can remember are coming out right now. I should be embarrassed. I should try to stuff them back in. But I can't. So, with Hunter rubbing circles on my back, I just let them out. And he never lets me go.

# HUNTER

We walk outside, Sutton's face blotchy and red as she holds on to my hand tightly.

After what was probably a half hour of her breaking down in my arms, she finally looked up, gave me a small smile, and whispered, "Thank you."

For as long as I can remember, that girl never showed emotion. For years, she was on autopilot, just following commands from her parents without thinking twice. Her family left her. She had to leave a city she loved to be here. And then she had me proposition her to make my ex jealous.

The girl had every right to break down. But after she did, it was almost like a weight had been lifted from her shoulders. And eventually, sometime soon, I'm going to tell her how I really feel.

Leading her past the parking lot where my truck is, I point down the road. "We can walk to our next stop," I tell her, heading toward the boardwalk that goes around a small pond. "If you feel up to it, that is."

"I do." She nods. "And despite crying like a baby, I really did enjoy myself. I'd never done anything like that. I hadn't realized how … moving it would feel."

"I know not to piss you off," I say, raising my eyebrows. "I'm a little scared, to be honest."

She shoves me, giggling. "Told you I'd win. I definitely did more damage than you did."

"Yeah … I'm not even going to try to argue with that." I shake my head at her.

She looks exhausted after all of that crying.

Stopping in front of her, I kneel down. "Because I caused you so much emotional distress today, I'll offer you a piggyback ride." I crane my neck at her. "Deal?"

Her eyes light up, and she climbs on my back. "Hell yes. Deal. This is better than walking."

Standing up, I continue to walk along the boardwalk. She rests her chin on my back and holds on to me tightly.

"I was so mad when Jolene paired us up." She sighs. "Turns out … you aren't all that bad after all. In fact, you're nothing like the guy you spent so much time making yourself out to be."

"I'm not that great of a person, Little Bird," I admit. "I fuck up a lot. I'm selfish. And my temper sometimes gets me in trouble."

"You're better than you give yourself credit for, Hunter Thompson." She's quiet for a moment. "You don't have to be a doctor or cure a rare illness to be a good person."

"Thanks," I whisper. "Here we are." I nod toward the hot dog stand. "I know it's probably nothing like the infamous hot dog stands I hear about in New York City. But a hot dog is a hot dog, right?"

As I set her down lightly, she looks from me to the stand, her eyebrows pulling together. "You brought me to a hot dog stand?"

"Uh … yeah? Is that okay?"

Throwing herself at me, she wraps her arms around my neck and kisses me a bunch of times. "You are the furthest thing from an asshole, Hunter Thompson. Thank you!"

"Uh … thanks?" I frown. "It's good to not be an asshole, I guess?"

"It's *very* good." She nods quickly, kissing me one last time. "Let's go!"

I don't think I'll ever tire of doing things that make her smile. It's becoming an addiction.

# HUNTER

I look up in the stands, bummed that I don't see Sutton sitting there, just like last night's game. I knew from her text earlier that there was a good chance she wasn't coming because she said she wasn't sure if she could get her shift covered. I've asked her for the name of the restaurant she works at numerous times, and she always changes the subject. It's fucking weird.

Since things changed on that yacht, we've grown closer. Acting like a couple, even when no one is around. But we haven't had sex yet, though there's been plenty of other shit that is equally awesome. But I can't wait to sink inside of her, to be honest.

Jake sent me everything he had on Helena this morning, and I want to pass it off to Sutton. Something about having it all day and not telling her has already left me feeling dirty. My plan is to call her after the game and go to her right away.

I didn't want to know anything about what the files consisted of. It isn't my business. But right after sending them to me, he called me. And before I could stop him, he rattled off that when Sutton's father met her mother, she was a prostitute. One whose name was actually Helen, not Helena. And somehow, Sutton's father turned her into a housewife.

"You good, Thompson?" Link skates next to me, stopping enough to throw some ice with his skates. "You seem a little off today."

Turning my attention from the empty chairs to him, I nod, plastering on a grin. "I'm good. Ready to pick up another W—that's all. Think we can do that?"

He eyes me over before hitting my shoulder. "Fucking right, we can."

I'm not the only one who seems off. Cade has been spiraling, and I'm worried he might be doing shit he isn't supposed to again. It's not unlike him to drink or smoke pot if he thinks he can get away with it. But the way he's been acting lately isn't normal, and I'm beginning to wonder if Watson and I need to step in and help him.

On the ice, he's been doing great. His temper is worse than ever, and oftentimes, that gets him in trouble. But as a defenseman, that sort of goes with the territory. Cade was great at his position last year, but when we lost Brody, we really needed him to step it up. And in the arena, sure, he does. But it's not just about the games. It's about showing up for your team all the time. And lately, he just hasn't been doing it.

Just before the puck drops, I skate next to Cade.

"Everything all right, man?" I tip my chin up at him. "Ready to do the damn thing?"

He simply smirks, giving me his usually cocky nod. "You know I am, Thompson. You know I am."

And I just have to hope to hell he means it. Because without him, we're fucked.

Game six, and we've already got a loss under our belt. And it doesn't feel good either. It feels really fucking shitty. After winning against this team last night, I think some of us came into this game way too cocky.

And by some … I'll go ahead and add my dumbass into the equation.

Last year, we were undefeated. To be coming into the season so early with this loss feels like a swift kick to the nuts.

The locker room is somber. Some of us toss shit around while others just move through the room like zombies, dressing and packing up our shit.

"I get it; you're pissed," Coach says, standing before us all. "I'm pissed too. You all know I don't like to lose. But what I like even less is to lose in the way we just did." He looks down before lifting his eyes again. "I don't know where the fuck a few of your heads were, but it sure as shit wasn't on the ice."

It's so quiet in the locker room that I'm pretty sure I could hear Watson's stomach growling if I listened hard enough. Because that motherfucker is always hungry.

"I need you to come to Monday's practice ready to work because after the shit I saw tonight, I'll have you crying for your mother by the time you leave here." He points to the door. "Take tomorrow off from reviewing game tape or anything hockey-related. And if you think I'm being nice, I'm not. I simply can't stand the thought of looking at your faces."

Turning, he heads into his office. Leaving us all to look and feel like morons.

"According to Cade, some of the team's going to Peaches after this," Walker James says, walking up next to me. "You in?"

Walker James took Cam's spot as the starting center. As a freshman, he has big shoes to fill, but he's been doing pretty good so far. I wouldn't wish the position of being the next Cam Hardy on anyone. Because truthfully, it's impossible.

"A strip joint?" I frown. "That's not really my scene, man."

"Gentry said the same thing. You guys are boring as fuck," he scoffs. "You're all acting like a bunch of old men. No, I take that back. Even old fucks like strip clubs."

"Hell yeah, they do," Cade chimes in. "Come out with us, Thompson."

"It's not likely, fellas."

I need to see Sutton. I need to give her the information that Jake found on her mother. And for selfish reasons, I guess I kind of want to see her too.

# SUTTON

The music is a slow enough beat that dancing isn't overly strenuous, and I don't find myself needing my inhaler nearly as much as some other shifts. Truthfully, since switching my meds up, I've been doing much better lately.

The smell of perfume in this room is strong. And even though one of them requested Ryann and me for a private performance in the back room, I declined. And lucky for me, our boss lets us choose what we're comfortable with and what we're not.

And being alone with a bunch of horny men in a back room ... yeah, hard pass.

I continue dancing, rolling my hips as I wrap my fingers around the cold metal. My outfit tonight might be my sexiest yet. But with a bunch of medication refills needed, I need to make some cash. And Lord knows the sexier you look, the better the tips when it comes to the horndogs in this place.

Guilt strikes me. I wish I could have been there at Hunter's game tonight. As a friend, of course. And if I didn't have to work, I probably would have gone. It's late enough that if the game isn't over, it should be very soon. I hope Brooks won. The boys on that team give it their all, and they deserve a good season.

After a bit longer, I'm signaled that it's time for my break, and I slowly work my way to the back.

I'm just sitting down, taking a drink of my water and having a few crackers when my phone rings. Hunter's name is displayed on the screen, and I frown, unsure of what to do.

The background noise from the club's music flows into this room, and he'll probably wonder where I am. But if I don't answer, I'll feel bad because something could be wrong.

"Hello?" I say, putting the phone to my ear.

"Hey, good-looking. You still working?" He pauses. "What's that noise?"

I chew my bottom lip. "Uh, no. I'm, uh … I just got out and came to a little get-together with Ryann," I lie through my teeth. Something I'm apparently getting good at. "Did you win?"

"You know, if you didn't want to come to my game, you could have just said that," he says coolly. "Fake relationship or not, we can at least tell each other the motherfucking truth."

"No, I did. I wanted to come. I just—"

"I gotta go," he snaps.

He ends the call abruptly, leaving me alone in the dressing room of the strip club, feeling like absolute shit.

# HUNTER

Even though it's the last place I care to be, after my phone call with Sutton, I say fuck it and go out with the guys to Peaches. Contrary to what people might believe, all men don't get horned up over strip clubs. I know I don't. It's awkward to me to sit around and watch girls fuck a pole, knowing half the dudes around me are likely pitching a tent in their pants. Gross.

We take our seats on the leather bench that wraps around, making a U-shape, and within minutes, a chick takes our drink order. She's only in her bra and underwear, her asscheeks hanging out, and her face is covered with a mask.

I look around. All of them are wearing masks. Shit, these girls probably go to Brooks, and we'd never even know. It's a smart idea on the owner's side. Obviously, it protects the dancers, no one knowing who they actually are.

Once drinks are passed out, I sip on my beer. Taking out my phone, I pull Sutton's profile up on Instagram to see if anyone has tagged her in any pictures tonight that might indicate where she is. But I find nothing, which leaves me even more pissed. For all I know, she could be around a bunch of creeps, and they could even be trying to take advantage of her.

Stuffing my phone back in my pocket, I look around the entire club. It's nothing like what I imagined it would look like in here. The guys have been trying to get me to come to Peaches for years, but I was never interested. And I know the only reason why my ass is sitting here, looking like a pervert right now, is because I'm mad that Sutton is out somewhere, probably finding her Romeo.

"Glad you came out, brother," Cade says, throwing back another shot. "Scenery's pretty good, huh?"

"Yeah, I guess," I mutter.

"Don't sound so impressed. If you're more into meat, I'm sure one of us can take one for the team and go shake our asses for you," Walker teases, waving around. "Seriously, man, how can you not be happy? Titties and ass."

"Titties. And. Ass," Cade mimics, grinning like a fool. "Also known as heaven."

I shake my head at them, gazing around again until my eyes fixate on the girl dancing for the next booth over. She's wearing a sheer black bra, exposing most of her breasts, except for her nipples. Her thong matches her bra, along with her thigh-highs. But on her feet are some hot-pink high heels. Total fuck-me heels. There's something about her that draws me in.

Her chest glistens with some kind of shimmer she's applied. And her long black hair falls in waves around her face and down her back. But there's something familiar about her too. And when she lifts her arms up, gripping the pole ... I see a familiar tattoo—*5 ... 6 ... 7 ... 8...*

And when I watch her hold back a cough, clearly struggling to catch her breath ... I see fucking red.

Within a second, I'm on my feet, heading to her. And I don't even think about how it's going to look or that there's a bouncer when I make my next move. Frankly, I don't care. But before I can reach her, she walks off the stage, around the bouncer, and through a door.

Going to the same door she went through, I point in her direction. "That's my girlfriend, man. Help a guy out. She knew I was coming tonight to watch her."

He eyes me suspiciously before signaling to another bouncer and taking my arm. Walking me out back, he knocks a few times, and Sutton appears in the doorway, holding her inhaler in her hand.

"Yeah?" she says blankly before her eyes find mine and widen. "Hunter? Wh-what are you doing here?"

I open my mouth to answer, but before I can, the bouncer grips my arm tighter.

"You told me she knew you were here. That's strike one, puck boy." When I give him a surprised look, he shrugs. "Yeah, I know who you are. I like college hockey. What can I say?"

I'm so fucking mad at the girl standing in front of us right now. And knowing this fucker is probably looking at her body makes me want to take the bat from the rage room last week and attack him.

Nodding at my arm, I attempt a smirk. "Go easy on my arm, big boy. Be awful hard to carry a stick around when it's crushed."

"I haven't checked my phone," Sutton blurts out. "He probably texted me that he was coming, but I haven't seen the message yet." She looks to me. "Right?"

"Right. Yes." I nod but send her a glare because I'm fucking fuming right now, looking at her in this slutty outfit, letting every man in this motherfucker see her perfect body.

Eventually, he walks away. Leaving no one here besides me and Sutton. And when I back her up into the room, locking the door behind me, I press her against the wall with my body. It's just her and me.

And she has some fucking explaining to do.

And she'd better do it really fucking fast.

# SUTTON

His blue eyes are almost black as he glares down at me, his chest heaving. "So, this is what you do? When you tell me you're going to work at a restaurant, you actually come here and shake your fucking ass for strangers." He grits his teeth; his entire body is rigid. "Fucking creeps go home and jerk off to thoughts of you. Are you fucking kidding me, Sutton?" His voice rises with every word he says, and he's shaking.

Though it's hard, I stand tall. "Yep, I do. Because this," I say, waving my hand down myself, "is my body. And I'll do whatever I want with it."

Slamming his hands on the sides of me, he boxes me in. "I could set this fucking place on fire right now, Sutton. That's how fucking pissed I am." He radiates heat, anger seeping through his pores. "This was supposed to be a fucking fake arrangement. Hell, up until a month ago, we couldn't stand each other. Yet here I am, wanting to murder every motherfucker in this building who has the image of your perfect body stuck in their brain."

He drops his hand down, grazing my nipple with his fingertips, and I whimper.

"And knowing people can openly stare at these? Fuck. That." He puts his lips to mine, growling against my mouth.

Reaching between my legs, he cups me—hard. "Or the fact that this is almost on display when I've tasted it and it's as sweet as a fucking cupcake? Makes me fucking sick, Little Bird."

A vein in his neck sticks out, proving how angry he is as his livid eyes glare into mine.

"But you know what makes me even madder?" he grumbles, lips almost touching mine. "It's that I'm so distracted by how fucking hot you look that my cock is rock hard right now, begging to fuck you. Even though you lied and I'm fucking irate about it, all I can think about is bending you over and blowing my load all over your fucking ass."

"I'm sorry," I whisper, biting my lip. "I just didn't know how to tell you." I swallow. "And honestly, I didn't think you'd care."

His hands move to my waist, digging into my flesh. "Little Bird, I wanted to throw Elliot over the side of the boat for hitting on you. How the fuck did you think I'd feel about this?" One hand moves to my neck before gripping my chin. "You might have started off as a fake girlfriend. But you're still fucking mine. Act like it."

"You want me to act like it?" I hiss, tipping my chin higher.

"Yeah, I do."

The music pulsates through the changing room. I pull his hand, leading him to the corner of the room. My hands move to his chest, and I shove him down in the chair. Walking to the wall, I dim the lights before I walk toward him again. I've danced for hundreds of people in this club the past few weeks. Yet this is the only one where my legs shake and my heart pounds as the nerves overtake my body.

I climb onto his lap, straddling him. I throw my hips in rhythm with the pulsating music, tipping my head back.

His hands slide to my thighs, and he groans, "Fuck, Little Bird. It's hard to stay mad at you when you're grinding on my cock like that."

It crosses my mind that someone could be outside the door. But luckily, there are enough changing rooms in the building that if one's locked, someone could simply move on to the next one.

I feel his hardness growing, pressing into my thigh as I bend down, kissing his neck. I run my tongue to his chin, and suddenly, his hand grasps my nape, pressing our mouths together.

His kiss is possessive and angry. His hand moves up, taking a fistful of my hair tightly. I need him so badly right now. Desperation takes over, and I grind myself hard against him.

"You make me fucking crazy, Sutton. Do you realize that?" he growls, holding my hair harder as he pulls my head down and bites my neck. "Fucking. Insane."

"Fuck me, Hunter," I moan, biting my lip so bad that it hurts. "Please."

"You've been a bad girl though," he growls. "And bad girls don't get the cock, do they?" His hand comes down hard on the top of my asscheek, making me yelp. "Have you thought about sucking my dick since that night in your bedroom?" He presses his lips to my ear. "Or what about my face buried between your thighs? Has that thought run through that pretty head of yours? Imagining me feasting on you while you came on my tongue?"

"Yes," I cry. "Yes, so many times."

Dropping his hand from my hair, he reaches between my legs. "Fucking. Soaked, Little Bird." He works his fingers inside of me. "So tight and so ready."

"You're going to play by my rules. And my rules are, this body is for my fucking eyes only." Sliding his hand from between my legs, he drags a finger across his lips. "So sweet. And all mine."

In this moment, I'm not thinking about how irrational it would be to quit this job for someone who isn't even my real boyfriend. I'm just thinking about how, with one more touch … I'd come undone. I'm in the palm of his hand, and he knows it.

"You on the pill, Little Bird? Because I need to claim you with nothing between us. I need to fuck you raw and feel you clench my cock when I deliver you to heaven as you come on my dick." He leans forward, pulling my mesh bra to the side and taking my nipple into his mouth, biting it gently between his teeth. "And I need to come inside of you, filling you so full of my cum that you remember you're fucking mine."

"I am," I hiss, needing him so bad that I want to scream. "Please, Hunter."

"Well, since you said please, good girl," he says, pushing me upward as he stands us both up. Turning me around, he bends me over the plush chair. Pushing my cheek into the chair, he yanks his own pants down before shoving the fabric of my thong to the side and grazing his fingertips between my legs.

Using the same hand, he brushes his fingertips across my throat. "Feel yourself, baby. That's how ready you are for me to take you." His hand cups my neck, tightening slowly.

Pushing the head of his cock inside of me, he bites my shoulder lightly. Little by little, the sting becomes less and less until he moves in a rhythm. His grip on my neck tightens, and even though I never imagined enjoying being choked, the harder he does it … the more turned on I am. And he must feel how wet I am because he puts his lips closer to my ear.

"Dirty fucking girl, you love me choking you as I bend you over this way, don't you?"

"Yes," I whine.

"That's what I thought. Because you're practically dripping on my cock, baby."

I still hear the sound of the music from the club in the background, but my brain can only focus on the sound of his hips as they smack against my asscheeks.

Releasing his hold on my neck, he grabs a fistful of my hair and presses my face a little harder into the chair. "This ass, Sutton. Jesus fucking Christ, it looks good from this angle. Watching you suck my cock into your greedy pussy, squeezing me because you love it." He barks the words out as his other hand moves to my ass, digging his fingertips into it. "God, you take me so good. Like you were made for me to fuck."

That's all it takes. A combination of filthy words and him filling me to the max brings on a tsunami of an orgasm out of nowhere, making me grip the chair as a stabilizer even though it's useless.

"Coming inside of you," he mutters low, thrusting harder as he trembles above me.

I feel him release inside of me, drenching me more as I suck in as much air into my lungs as I can get. And after a moment or two, he leans down and kisses my back.

"You're making me lose my mind, Little Bird," his voice rasps.

"I could say the same about you," I whisper just as he releases me.

Standing up, I adjust myself before grabbing a robe that hangs on the rack. I open my mouth to say something—anything to fill the silence—when a knock at the door startles both of us.

"Sutton, I know you're in there," Ryann's voice hisses. "Open up. Now."

My eyes widen as I glance at Hunter, who shrugs. But I walk over to the door and open it a few inches.

"I'm going to tell the boss that you felt sick and had to leave right away." She narrows her eyes. "Go out the back and get the hell out of here." She sticks her head further in the door and looks at Hunter before her eyes move back to mine. "But figure it out, Sutton. Boss doesn't like messy drama, and I have a feeling that's what this shit show in here is going to be."

"I'm sorry," I whisper.

"Don't say sorry. Just get out of here before she comes back here and sees your puck boy in her changing room." She sends me a warning glare. "Go home, Sutton. Go home and figure your shit out."

"Okay," I utter.

And then she's gone.

# HUNTER

The start to the ride home is quiet, and I'm wondering what is going on inside that pretty little head of hers. This night is the complete opposite of what I thought would happen. I thought we'd win our game. I figured I'd find Sutton and give her the information about her mother. We'd kick it for a bit, and then I'd go home with blue balls. Instead, we lost our game, and Sutton wound up being a fucking stripper.

The thing is, if this were even a month ago, I would be impressed. I spent my life thinking she was a sheep, doing what she was told. Following her family's wishes blindly. Then, I got to actually know her. And now, I can't stand the thought of her doing that for a living.

"If it's about the money, I'll give you whatever you need," I blurt out, breaking the silence. "Just name it, and it's done."

Her head turns toward me right away, and she narrows her eyes. "You fucking asshole. *Of course* it's about the damn money! I'm a college kid with no family and a ton of medical bills! But do you really think I would trade being controlled by my parents to being bought by you? You actually think that? How dense are you?"

Pulling the truck over, I slam it into park. "I don't give a fuck, Sutton. Really, I don't." I glare at her. "You want me the same way I want you. I'm fucking done pretending."

"You don't know what you're even saying!" she screeches. "Up until a few weeks ago, you were set on making Paige so jealous that she would come crawling back to you! Now what? You think you and I should be together? That I'd actually agree to be your rebound?"

I slam my fist against the steering wheel. "I don't fucking know what I think, Sutton! You've clouded every fucking thought in my brain. And now, all I see is you." I shake my head, throwing it back against the headrest. "At practice, at the game—which we lost, by the way. When I'm with friends. Every. Fucking. Second. All I see is you. And now, I find out that there're hundreds of nasty fuckers looking at you? Seeing what should be mine? Jesus Christ, Sutton. How do you want me to feel?"

"I won't quit my job simply because you think I should," she snaps. "I'm not that pathetic."

Uncontrollable anger pulses through my veins, and I grind my back teeth, knowing I'm about to say something I shouldn't, but unable to stop myself. Because that's how fucking insane this girl makes me feel.

"Guess you're just like. Your. Fucking. Mother, Little Bird." I drag in a shaky breath, feeling my head spin. "Shocker. I was warned you're all alike."

"What the hell is that supposed to mean?" She scowls. "What does my mother have to do with the conversation we're having?"

Taking my phone out, I open my email, pulling up the file. "There you go, Sutton. Here's my end of the deal. A deal it seems you can't fucking wait to get out of."

Snatching it from my hand, she reads through everything. She's quiet as her eyes take it all in, and I watch her chest rise and fall.

"This doesn't make sense," she whispers more to herself than to me. "If this is true, then my dad ... isn't my dad."

"What?" I say, stunned because I didn't actually read it.

I only knew that her mother was a prostitute because when Jake called, he told me as soon as I answered my phone. And I certainly didn't think this was how I'd drop that bomb. But the girl makes me so fucking angry that I blurted it out. Now, I wish I could take it back and say it nicer even if she is pissing me off.

"My mom was pregnant when they met," she croaks. "He's not my dad. I'm not a Savage."

"Fuck," I utter, raking my hand through my hair. "Fuck."

"I have a brother from South Carolina." She keeps reading before her face pales. "He went to college here."

"What?" I grab my phone, trying to find where she left off. "Who?"

Her eyes lift, but they don't look directly at mine. "Brody O'Brien," she barely whispers. "Brody O'Brien is my brother."

I stare at her in complete disbelief. Unable to form a thought, much less a word. Because I was just a complete dick to someone who was about to learn that everything she thought she knew ... was a lie.

And she'll probably never forgive me now. I blew it before I even got a real chance.

# SUTTON

The rain pours on the windshield as we sit on the side of the road for close to an hour. Hunter's asked me if I'm okay numerous times, and I just keep nodding, telling him I'm fine. But the truth is, I'm not.

After I found out what our dancing fundraiser was for, I did my research on Brody since he had started One Wish. I learned that Brody O'Brien started this foundation because his childhood had been so bad that he wanted to make it his mission to help kids in similar situations. His father—who could be my father—was apparently a raging alcoholic who had beaten the shit out of him day in and day out. And his mother—my mother—had left him alone with that monster when he was a toddler. Brody shared all these painful things when he first started One Wish. Which is so incredibly brave.

If I ever thought my mother could be forgiven for what she did to me, I now know I'll never look at her the same after learning this.

"If you want to go see Brody and talk to him about this, I can take you. He's a good friend of mine, and I know he'd be open to seeing you. *If* that's what you want. If not, that's okay too." He reaches over, patting my knee. "Whatever you need, just tell me."

"I need you to take me home," I mutter. "And I need our deal to be off."

"Sutt—"

"No," I snap. "You are confused. You miss Paige, and now, sex between you and me has clouded your judgment. But at the end of the day, she's the one you love. Not me." I look out the window. "We have our dance down pat. You practice your steps on your end, and I'll do mine. In a few weeks, at the fundraiser, we'll meet up and get it done."

"And then?" he croaks. "What happens after that, Sutton?"

"We'll go our separate ways. And pretend none of this happened."

"You want to pretend like we never happened?" he growls. "That the past *month* hasn't happened? The yacht, your bedroom, the rage room?" He jerks his thumb behind him. "Back in that changing room?" His body turns noticeably rigid. "I can't fucking forget that. Don't you see that?"

"It's over, Hunter." I swallow back the lump in my throat. "It's not like it ever even began. Not really."

"That's not what I want," he murmurs. "And it isn't what you want either."

"Take me home, Hunter. I need to go home."

For what is likely minutes, he just sits there, looking at me. But when I continue ignoring him, he throws the truck in drive and peels away from the side of the road.

And when we finally get to my house, I bail out before he can say anything to make me change my mind. Because a few words from his mouth could easily do that.

I need to walk away from this. Because deep down, I know I wasn't his first choice. And I'll be damned if I settle for second.

## HUNTER

Practice is brutal, but I think we all knew it would be after we lost Saturday night's game. Yesterday, I spent the day texting and calling Sutton, asking if she needed anything after learning the truth about her family. She ignored all of my messages, so that was fucking awesome.

She's pissed that I offered to pay her to quit stripping. But I fucking would. I can't stand the thought of her continuing to do it. Turns out, Watson also learned this weekend that Ryann works at Peaches. And that's a problem for them because he's fucking obsessed with the girl. But on the bright side of that, he found out Sutton's work schedule through Ryann. So, I'll be able to at least go and make sure no one tries to fuck with her during her next shift.

"I might die." Cade grabs his side. "I think that's Coach's plan—kill us and get a new lineup."

"One that doesn't suck balls," I groan.

"Fuck you guys. I sure as hell don't suck." Walker shakes his head while we wait for Coach to decide that our fifteen seconds of rest have ended and barks another order. "Thompson, what the fuck happened to you at Peaches on Saturday? One second, you were there, and the next, you were nowhere to be seen."

Cade wiggles his eyebrows, dropping his voice to a whisper. "I saw you go to the door—the one the dancers use to go out back. So, about that, what did you say to that bouncer for him to let you out back? For future purposes, ya know. In case I find myself in a similar situation."

"Cade, shut up," I growl before pointing toward Walker. "And you, I had to go see a friend—that's all you need to know," I snap just before Coach starts yelling again after looking up from his clipboard and seeing too many of us standing idle.

For once, I'm thankful for Coach being the hard-ass that he is. Because he just got me out of a million questions from these guys.

For now anyway.

Now that practice is over and I've showered and no longer smell like someone's nasty, unwashed ass, we head out of the locker room. Link told us that we are having dinner as a team tonight, so that's exactly what we're going to do. Our bond is tight, but nothing like it was when Cam and Brody were here. Somehow, it seemed like Cam, Link, and Brody were the glue holding everyone together. Now, I guess we're sort of floundering.

"Look who it is," Cade mutters, jerking his chin toward the arena doors. "Who do y'all suppose she's here for?"

I look up, wishing to find Sutton, and I sigh when I see Paige smiling in my direction. But even with her lips turned up, I can tell she's nervous. I guess that's what happens when two people go from being together to pretty much strangers.

"For the love of fuck," I grumble under my breath. "I don't have the energy for this today."

Weeks ago, I would have been so excited to see her. It would have meant that maybe things were getting back to normal. Now ... I wish she'd just go away.

"Hunter," she says, looking up at me, smiling.

A sight that I used to count on to brighten my day suddenly does nothing for me besides irritate me. And eyes that I used to love to stare into make me cringe.

"I'll catch up with y'all in the parking lot," I tell the guys, and they all head outside, leaving me alone with the most up-and-down person I've ever met.

That is, until Poppy walks by, smirking so hard that it looks like it hurts her face.

"Paige, what are you doing here? I thought I made myself pretty clear the last time we talked that things were over. This shit's getting really fucking old."

"I know," she whispers. "And if that's really what you want … I'm gone. This will be my last attempt to right my wrongs. But I miss you. And I'm really, *really* sorry that I got scared and let your parents drive me away. But this time apart has made me realize that you're who I want to spend my life with. I want to be by your side when your dreams come true."

"No, it wasn't the time apart. We've had time apart for years now. It was seeing me with someone else—that's what it was." I look at her, shrugging. "It's okay, Paige. We were kids. I know my parents suck. But I also know that if we were as solid as I thought we were, you would have stuck by my side anyway. And if you had, I never would have realized just how wrong for each other we really are." I run my hand up the back of my neck. "You're a great girl … but you aren't my girl. Not anymore."

"And who is your girl, Hunter?" she asks, her lip quivering. "Sutton?"

"If I'm lucky, yes. Yes, she will be," I say honestly, done holding back. "Maybe not today and maybe not even tomorrow. But one day, Paige … she will be mine. And I'm sorry for that. But you and I, we're done. For good."

"Is there anything I can say to change your mind?" she whispers, tears spilling from her eyes. She wraps her hands around my waist and looks up at me. "I just want to go back to the way things were."

"We can't," I say quickly. "Weeks ago? Yeah … probably. Now? Not a chance." I peel her hands from my body and step around her, giving her one last look. "Good-bye, Paige. I wish you nothing but the best. But these interactions between us are over. I want off this ride."

I mean it when I say I want the best for her. She's not a bad person. She got scared. We were too deep, too fast, and she needed a way out. She used my parents as her scapegoat instead of being honest. But still, I want good things for her.

I also meant what I said about Sutton. Maybe not today, tomorrow, or even a week from now. But one day, when the smoke clears … she will be mine. And when she is, I'll never let her go again.

She just doesn't know it yet.

# SUTTON

"Ladies, as you know, we're less than two weeks out from the One Wish fundraiser and just three weeks away from your solo performances that will be held in front of the entire school." She puts her glasses on, glancing at her phone. "Looking at the dates, we have so many things to do in a short time. So, what I'm thinking is, the dress rehearsal for the fundraiser will be at the auditorium, where the actual event is. Let's utilize that space and arrive a few hours prior to the hockey players. This will give each of you time to practice your solo routine for the next event." She giggles. "The one where you don't have to worry about a massive hockey player landing on you and just worry about yourselves."

Pulling her glasses off, she puts them on the top of her head. "Another thing, we're going to be having some young ballerinas from a local studio joining us for the charity event. They'll be performing first, and their dance instructor will be leading them through their dance. But I'm sure they'd sure love some attention from you all as well. So, please, during rehearsal and on the night of the event, make them feel special. And help keep their nerves at bay."

She beams. "I am so excited!"

Finally, Jolene releases us from dance, and I gather up my things. I'm moping around like a toddler who didn't get the toy she wanted when her parents took her to the store. I'm grumpy, and you'd swear I was PMSing even though I'm not.

"Are you catching a ride home with me?" Ryann says, changing her shoes. "We can swing into the diner and get milkshakes."

I give her a weak smile and shake my head. "That's okay. I think I'll walk. I could use the fresh air. Besides, it's nice out today."

She gives me a look, telling me that she really wishes I'd just take the ride. But eventually, she shrugs. "If you say so. See you at home."

I walk outside, letting the sunshine beat on my face, warming my soul. I'm thankful that I don't have to work until the end of the week because, frankly, I'm just not feeling up to dancing at Peaches right now. I don't know if I'll ever love showing off my body to make a living, to be honest.

Hunter has reached out too many times to count. And I've come close to responding far too much. But at the end of the day, I feel myself falling for him—hell, part of me knows I've already fallen. I could let him in. I could jump in headfirst, not coming up for a single breath of air. But everyone knows that rebounds don't last. And when he woke up, realizing that was all I was, I'd be left with a broken heart, a shitty set of lungs, and an estranged family. This is better. This is the closest thing to a solution that I can come up with.

A huge part of me knows that I've never really liked working at Peaches. I have nothing against Ryann or the other girls who do it, but for me, it feels unnatural. But now that Hunter voiced that I should quit and have him pay my way—as if it were that easy—I'm being stubborn, and I don't want to quit. If I do, he'll assume it was for him.

And I really hate that he is a part of the reason why I'm second-guessing my damn job.

I look around the campus as I walk along the sidewalk. No matter how grouchy I am, I really have grown to love this place. And I love Ryann and Lana too. Even Poppy hasn't been all that terrible. And by not terrible, I mean, she ignores me, and I ignore her, and we pretend the other one doesn't exist.

It's great.

A loud truck zooming by makes me wonder what Hunter is doing and if he plans on practicing our routine. It will be tricky to practice alone, but it can be done.

It has to be done.

But eventually, we'll need to see each other. And when we do … yikes.

Once I'm home and I fix myself a snack, I plunk my ass down on the couch next to Ryann.

She glances at my sliced apples with peanut butter and a Slim Jim. "The diner cheese fries and chocolate milkshakes would have been *much* better than whatever you've concocted."

"Probably." I nod in agreement.

The door opens, and out of the corner of my eye, I see Poppy strolling in. Normally, if I were near, she'd take her ass to her room. Not today. Today, she takes a seat on the other couch.

"Hey, girl," Ryann calls to her. "Where'd you go after dance?"

"Just had to run to a few places," she says, not hiding the amusement in her voice.

I look at her nervously to find her actually, literally smiling. But instead of commenting on it like I want to, I turn my attention back to the television as Ryann flips through Netflix.

"You seem down, Sutton," Poppy says smoothly. "What's wrong? Sad that Hunter went back to Paige so soon?"

"What?" I mutter, narrowing my eyes at her. "What did you say?"

Holding her phone out, she shows me a picture of Hunter standing in front of Paige, her arms wrapped around him. "And if you don't believe me, check the date."

Glancing at the date and time, I see it was just taken a little while ago. My stomach turns, and I feel like I'm going to throw up. But I know what this comes down to. We have our solo performances in a few weeks, and it's crunch time for that. She's trying to get in my head.

Sadly, it's working.

Pushing the phone away from me, I attempt to level her with a harsh glare. Which does nothing. "You enjoy this, don't you, Poppy? You enjoy seeing people hurt?"

"Not people, just you." She shrugs. "You should have expected it when you rolled in here, acting like you owned the place."

"She never did that, Poppy," Ryann interjects, throwing her hand up. "You're being a complete bitch right now. And truthfully, it's not a good look."

I take a deep breath and let it out before I stand, walking till I'm nose to nose with her. "You can try all you want to get in my head. But at the end of the day, when we go to the solo event, everyone will know who the better dancer is." I glare at her. "Continue to fuel my fire, Poppy. I dare you."

And then I walk away because, frankly, the picture of Hunter and Paige is burning in my brain, making me feel sick.

I should have known he'd run right back to her. It was never me he wanted. It was always Paige.

# HUNTER

Do I look like a creep, sitting in this corner booth with my hat on and my hood up over it? Probably. But let's face it … I don't give a flying fuck.

It's been a week since I've seen Sutton, and despite coming off like a pathetic loser, here I am, at Peaches, because I know she has a shift tonight.

My eyes search the room, and it doesn't take long before I spot her, walking toward one of the small stages before she wraps her body seductively around the pole. It's hot.

*Fuck, it's hot.*

But what's stopping me from enjoying the show is knowing that there's about twenty to thirty other sets of eyes watching too.

If someone could catch heaven's saddest angel and bottle her up, they'd have Sutton Savage.

I don't know when it happened. Not the exact moment anyway. But somehow, everything that matters to me now begins and ends with this girl. The world spins not because she exists, but because I finally, truly know her. And if I never get my real shot with her, it'll be my biggest regret.

Song after song, I sit here. My eyes never leave her, and she never seems to spot me. I know, soon, she'll need a break. I wonder if her lungs get tired when she's constantly moving like that. Or if she ever gets scared or uncomfortable. She's brave to get in front of this club and show herself the way that she is. I have to give her credit for that. But I still fucking hate it.

When she steps away from the pole, slowly moving her body as she dances closer to the edge, I watch some drunk motherfucker grab her leg. And when she kicks him away, he goes in for another grab, this time trying to reach higher.

I see the bouncer headed his way, but I don't give a fuck. He won't be here fast enough. Taking some large strides, I pull the dumbass who grabbed her leg backward by his hood, smashing the back of his head off the chair.

Standing over him, I lean forward, gripping his shirt. "If you *ever* touch my girl again, you stupid cocksucker, I'll make sure your arms don't work for the rest of your life."

"Chill out! It's not my fault your girlfriend is a slut who wants to be looked at!" he grunts. "She's basically begging for me to fuck—"

My fist connects with his face over and over as I clench the fabric of his shirt. I'm just about to go in for another punch when I'm hauled backward by what I'm sure is security.

"I will fucking kill you, you dumb motherfucker!" I growl, sucking in a breath as adrenaline courses through my veins. "I will fucking bury you alive if you ever touch her! Do you fucking hear me!"

Shoving me through the door, one of the guards points his finger in my face. "You listen to me, you little punk. The only reason why we haven't called the cops is because we know who you are. You're Hunter Thompson, starting winger for the Brooks Wolves. We're not about to fuck the team's season up more than it is." He points a finger in my face. "But the boss isn't going to be happy. We have a way of taking care of customers like that." His eyes widen as he jerks his thumb toward the door. "And that shit you just pulled? That ain't it!"

"Can I just see her?" I pull my arm from his hold, dragging my hand through my hair. "Can I just fucking see her to make sure she's all right?"

"They deal with that shit every night, kid." He shrugs. "She signed up for this job. It often involves drunk, entitled dickwads like that one. We handle it. The night goes on."

"Hunter, what the fuck?" Sutton wails, pushing through the door, wearing a long black robe. "What the hell was that in there? Huh? Now, you're stalking me?"

"Miss Sutton, do you need us to remove this boy from your presence?" one of the guards says.

"He'll leave soon, trust me. You can go back inside. I'm fine," she hisses, never breaking eye contact with me. When they walk off, she jabs her finger into my chest. "You have no right, showing up here and causing a scene. No. Right."

"What the fuck do you want me to do, huh? Let assholes like that grab you?" I grind my back teeth together. "I can't do that. Who the fuck else is going to keep you safe?"

"The fucking bouncers!" she screams. "The. Fucking. Bouncers!"

"Oh, yeah, it looked like they were doing a stellar fucking job at it. That asshole could have had his hand between your legs if I hadn't been sitting where I was."

I shake, dragging in ragged breaths. "This is what you really want?" I wave my hand. "To be fucking grabbed every night of your life? To be scared?"

"I'm not scared," she utters.

"You should be," I say before my eyes float to her lips and I move closer.

"Don't," she whispers.

"Don't what, Little Bird?" I reach up, tilting her chin up with my thumb. "Don't kiss you?"

"Don't kiss me," she breathes out. "Don't you fucking dare!"

I lean closer, my lips hovering over hers. "Why? Because you might like it? Because you might figure out how much you miss me?" I kiss the corner of her mouth, and she doesn't move. "Because you might agree to leave with me right now when you remember how much you miss me?"

"No, I won't." She shakes her head.

"You'll remember how you fucked my tongue while you sucked my cock like it was a fucking Popsicle, won't you? Or maybe you'll remember how I fucked you from behind, hitting you so deep, yet you squeezed my dick, greedy for more."

She shivers, staring up at me. "No."

"You'll remember swallowing every ounce of me down when I came down your throat. And you fucking loved it. You were soaking wet, Sutton."

"No," she whimpers, her knees growing noticeably weak.

Taking her lips with mine, I kiss her, sucking her tongue into my mouth gently. She moans against me, and I'm about to lift her up by her asscheeks, throw her over my shoulder, and take her home, making her come a minimum of four times before the sun comes up.

"Sutton," a female voice growls, and she pulls away from me.

"Ginger, um … this isn't what it looks like," she says to the lady who must be her boss. "I was just … we were—"

"Save it. Come with me. Before you guys make another damn scene at *my* business," she hisses at Sutton before leveling me with a harsh glare. "You, get the hell off my property. And don't come back. I know you're a puck boy at Brooks, but that doesn't mean jack shit to me. I'm more of a basketball fan."

When Sutton turns, I catch her hand. "I'm not leaving without you."

She sighs, giving me a sad look. "Then, you'll be waiting a long time." She looks down. "Just go home, Hunter. You've caused enough problems for one day." She shrugs her shoulders. "Besides, isn't Paige waiting?"

Before I can ask her what the fuck she means, she bolts. I watch her disappear into the club, trudging behind her boss. I have no intentions of actually leaving. I'll sit in my truck and make sure she gets home safe.

# SUTTON

"Shut the door behind you," Ginger mutters, sitting down at her desk.

Closing the door, I sigh. "Look, I really am sorry. I don't know what got into—"

"Do you think I didn't know about that same boy following you into the changing room last week?" She narrows her eyes. "Or that you weren't actually sick, but that Ryann—one of my best employees—lied for you because she didn't want you to get in trouble?"

I open my mouth to speak, but before I can, she holds up a finger at me.

"This place might be just a strip joint to you, somewhere you feel degraded and embarrassed, but to me … it's everything. It's a place for girls to earn a helluva lot more money than they would serving tables. A place where my workers shouldn't be embarrassed for just doing their damn job." She exhales slowly, her nostrils flaring. "And a place where I don't need drama to follow my dancers around like the plague."

She reaches in her drawer. Pulling out a check, she scribbles on it before sliding it across her desk. "This is more than what you would have made for your next few shifts. Take it and leave. I've worked too hard to build this place to what it is for nights like tonight to happen."

I could argue. I could promise her that it wouldn't happen again and that Hunter was no one to me. But the truth is, she just did me a favor. I'm not cut out for this industry. The first few shifts made me feel mysterious and daring. But now, I just want a job where people don't stare at my body for pleasure.

Offering my hand to her, I wait for her to take it. "I am really sorry for how things went down. I look up to you for building something from the ground up and for giving your dancers a safe place to make money while also keeping their integrity."

Slowly, she takes my hand, and I give hers a shake.

"Thank you for giving me a chance, Ginger. I'm really sorry it didn't work out."

Releasing my hand, she shrugs, giving me a lopsided smile. "Hey, it's happened before, and it'll happen again." Standing, she gives me a small nod. "Have a good night, Sutton. Best of luck to you figuring out your crap with that boy."

"Thanks," I mutter before I turn and walk out.

There's nothing more I'd like right now than to run outside to the parking lot and jump into his arms. I know he's still here. Waiting to make sure I'm safe. But then I remember that if his ex hadn't dumped him to begin with … none of this would be happening.

So, instead, I text Ryann and ask her to come pick my pathetic ass up.

# Hunter

The guys and I climb out of my truck, heading into the auditorium for dress rehearsal. And thanks to Watson telling us the wrong time because he was the one who actually read the email, we're here forty minutes early. By the time he figured it out, we were pulling into the damn parking lot. So, we said fuck it, and here we are.

The past week has dragged some major ass. Ever since I watched Ryann pull up in her old, beat-up car, pick Sutton up outside of Peaches, and drive away, I haven't seen Sutton. Watson and Ryann must be getting closer because she told him that the owner of Peaches, Ginger, fired Sutton that night. I should be happy. After all, I didn't want her working there anyway. But instead, I feel guilty for fucking up her income and what was paying for her medication.

Here I am, ready to face a girl who might or might not hate me. One I can't get off my fucking mind.

"Huff, are you drunk?" Watson scoffs, looking at Cade. "Please say no. It's one fucking night out of your life where we need to show up and get it done right. It's for charity."

"Technically, it's two nights," Cade says. "Tonight and tomorrow. But, no, I'm not drunk. A little buzzed—that's all." Reaching up, he squeezes Watson's nipple. "Don't be a Negative Nelly, Watson."

"Fuck off," Watson grumbles, rubbing where Cade assaulted him. "Just keep it together. This entire thing is for Brody's foundation. Let's not embarrass one of our own, got it?"

"You heard Miss Jolene," Cade drawls. "She said I had the best moves out of all y'all. So, piss off, sit back, and let me carry this shit while you all suck balls."

Pulling the door open, Link looks back at both of them. "Just shut up, would you?"

"Sorry, Cap," Watson utters, and Cade, of course, says nothing.

Walking into the auditorium, I look onstage, and when I do, my breath hitches.

"Holy shit," I mutter.

I stare as Sutton dances by herself. Jolene is standing off to the side, observing her, bobbing her head up and down randomly, and jotting notes on a pad of paper. She moves, and I swear the world stands still. Every set of eyes in this entire place is drawn to her, nothing but the sound of the music playing as she gracefully moves around.

Her presence is big. So big that she'd easily fill any room she was in. And I love that about her.

When the music finally stops and I watch her chest rise and fall as she inhales sharply, she looks my way. Her shoulders slump, and suddenly, she doesn't look as graceful. Instead, she looks like my Little Bird. My *broken* Little Bird.

How did I ever hate something so beautiful? I wasted years not allowing myself to fully see her, afraid I'd fall for the girl my brother loved. And look where it got me. Here, tortured and wanting to kiss her.

# SUTTON

My whole world stands still when I stop dancing and my eyes spot Hunter in the crowd. My pulse races, and every cell in my body feels his stare. It's like my entire being wants to give in to him, and my mind is the only part of me sane enough to know that I can't. It's been close to a week since we saw each other last, and yet none of it—walking away, staying away, or even getting through the days—has gotten easier. I miss him. I miss him so much that my entire body is feeling the loss.

Looking away, I make my way off the stage. But not before Jolene stops me.

"Great job, Sutton. I have to say, watching you dance is quite magical. I have a few notes. We can go over them later."

I give her a small smile. "Thank you."

I practically feel Poppy's eyes in my skin. Lasering me to death like I'm a damn target or something.

Now that he's had time away from me, I'm sure he's seeing things more clearly. And he has Paige back, so I guess I helped him achieve his goal after all. He got the girl. And I ... well, I got a bunch of insane information about my mother. Information I don't know what to do with.

Technically, my father could be anybody. I mean, for fuck's sake, the woman was working as a hooker for six weeks before my father—well, my fake father—swept her off her feet. But after I read the files and thought about the timeline of things, something tells me ... I likely share the same father as Brody. Which would make us full siblings.

By now, I could have gotten his number from so many people. Heck, I could have borrowed Ryann's car and gone to find him. But from what I've heard about Brody, it took him a long time to find his happily ever after. The last thing I want to do is drop a bomb on him. I mean, it hurt me that my parents cut me off for being a loser. But she left him when he was a toddler. With a monster nonetheless. Even imagining the type of pain he must have felt kills me.

Heading to my seat, I wait for what will be either the most painful or most awkward dance of my entire existence.

We aren't moving like we usually do. I'm cold and closed off. And he's acting nervous, shying away from digging deep and going to the place we need to make this performance our own.

His hand grazes my hip, and I swear my skin must smoke from catching on fire. Chills run up my spine, making my head spin.

The music stops mid-song, and Jolene steps in front of us.

"Take five minutes. Go talk. Or fight. Or whatever the heck you need to do to pretend like you like each other." She shakes her head. "You two are *not* the pair I watched a few weeks ago. So, go away and rehearse again, and when you come back, you'd better be that couple from before."

I groan silently, just wanting to get this whole debacle over with. I know we suck right now. But I don't think either of us can help it.

Walking behind the curtain, I feel him behind me. I'm almost to my water bottle when his strong hand turns me around so that my body is facing him.

"Kiss me, Little Bird," he mutters, tilting my chin up with his fingers.

Shoving his chest, I snarl, "No! I'm not kissing you!"

Anchoring me, he brings my lips to his, and that's when I slap him—hard.

"Get away from me," I growl.

"No," he mutters. "That's not what you want."

This time, when he brings my lips closer to his, I don't slap him. I just continue sucking in air, trying to keep my emotions in check.

"Kiss me, Sutton. It doesn't have to mean anything to you, but when we're dancing on that stage, I want you to remember this kiss."

"Is this a game to you, Hunter?" I glare at him. "Bouncing between Paige and me? Making it seem like you're over her, and then the second you and I end whatever the hell we had going on, you run to her? Are you that incapable of being alone?" I feel my face heat with anger, and I will myself not to slap him again. "Well, I'm not playing your game anymore. I'm a grown-ass woman." I laugh bitterly. "I mean, lately, as childish as this bullshit between us has been, it hasn't seemed like it. But I am. And the last damn thing I'm going to do is kiss you, asshole."

"What the hell are you talking about? And why did you say that to me outside of Peaches?" He scowls. "Run back to Paige? I don't want Paige."

"From the picture I saw of you guys at the arena ... y'all looked mighty cozy," I snarl. "It's okay, Hunter. But please, fuck off now."

When I start to pull away, he stops me. "I haven't run back to her. I never will either." Something flashes in his eyes, and he sighs. "She showed up at the arena the other day, and I told her I didn't want her. I told her the truth."

"Which is what, Hunter? Do you even know anymore?"

"That I want you," he snaps back, glaring down at me, his body touching mine because he's so close. "That anything she and I *ever* had is done. And that I will get you back, Sutton."

"Get me back? You never had me," I say through gritted teeth. Smoke is all but coming out of my ears, but I swear I could also cry.

"Maybe that's fucking true, Little Bird," he growls against my lips. "But you had me. You *still* have me."

And then, gripping my nape softly, he kisses me harshly. And even though a huge part of me wants to, I don't push him away. Because honestly ... I can't. I'm frozen. A victim of Hunter Thompson's charm.

Once his lips leave mine, slowly, I step back. "Let's go get this rehearsal done. We should talk about this another time. A time when everything has

172

settled down." I shake my head. "Showing up at my work, this, right now"—I wave my hand between us—"everything you do is too much."

"I just want to keep you safe."

"That isn't your job."

"I wish it were," he says instantly. "So fucking badly."

As I look at him, my brain tries to think of what to say back. And just when I open my mouth to try, Jolene tells us it's our turn to rehearse again.

*And, yeah … I'll probably be thinking about that kiss the entire dance.*

# HUNTER

I hold her in my arms like my life depends on it. Like, if I let her go, I'll never hold her this way again. And the thought of that really fucking bothers me.

Every ounce of her being drives me to the point of madness. But to be honest, being totally sane sounds pretty fucking boring without her next to me.

Our song ends, and our faces are so close by the time I bring her down from the air that her nose almost touches mine.

I miss her. I *really* fucking miss her.

As we head offstage, I follow her out back, and she walks into one of the small changing rooms, pulling the curtain across.

"Are we going to talk? Like, really talk?" I ask, trying to keep my voice as soft as I possibly can even though a part of me wants to throw her over my shoulder and force her to go home with me.

"What do we need to talk about, Hunter?" she tosses back.

"I miss you," I tell her, meaning it so much that it fucking hurts. "And I have every fucking second since the last time I kissed you before today. All I do is fucking miss you." Pulling back the curtain, I step inside with her. "And I've been worried about you. Before Ginger fired you, I was worried about you getting assaulted at work. I've been worried about the information I gave you. I'm worried about your shitty fucking lungs." I shake my head, looking down. "I'm worried all. The. Fucking. Time. And I don't want to be this way, Sutton. I never have been before, not really anyway." I sigh. "With you, I'm so fucking scared. Nonstop."

Her expression softens as she pulls her sweatshirt onto herself. "I'm fine, Hunter. I promise." She steps toward me, looking up. "I want you to go be happy. You deserve that."

"You know what would make me happy? If you are up for it, let me take you to see Brody tonight. He's in town, and I told him I'd have a drink with him after I leave here." I move my hand to her cheek. "This is your chance, Sutton. Your chance to know your brother." I laugh lightly. "He's a crazy motherfucker, but he's got a heart made of gold. I promise you that."

She looks nervous, her eyes dancing between mine. "What if he doesn't want to know me?" she whispers. "What if he gets mad?"

"He won't," I assure her. "He might be shocked, and it might take him a few minutes to understand, but he won't be mad. I know that much."

She looks up at me, eyebrows pulled together. "I never thought I'd say this, Thompson, but ... I missed you." She wraps her arms around me. "Like, really, really missed you."

"I missed you too. So fucking much." I tuck a loose piece of hair behind her ear. "I'm sorry I acted like a dick. I just ... I don't know. I guess that even though I have no right, I was worried about you working in a place like that." I shrug. "But I'm also really fucking jealous. I hate that your job meant men got to rake their nasty eyes over your perfect body, Sutton. It made me sick because I know what kinds of thoughts they were thinking. But I am truly sorry that I'm the reason you got fired." I shake my head. "That wasn't my intention."

"I understand," she whispers. "I didn't love the job either, Hunter. Not because I felt embarrassed—because, honestly, that wasn't really it. There are women working there to provide better lives for themselves and some for their children. There is nothing shameful about that. But I didn't like being looked at like that either. Not by random people. But it was good money. *Really* good money. So good that, luckily, I banked enough to pay for my meds for a few months."

"I wish you'd let me help you," I murmur against her hair. "I know you won't. But I would—in a heartbeat."

"I know you would," she says softly. "I'll go see Brody. What do I have to lose, right?"

"I guess that's one way to look at it," I say, pulling her against me. "He's going to love you. You'll see. Just be warned ... he's a crude dude."

She laughs. "Great. My birth brother is a perv."

"Yeah, but lucky for you, since he fell in love and is going to be a dad soon, he's a completely different man than the one I knew before Bria. Bless that girl for sticking around."

"They are having a baby?" she whispers, her eyes widening.

I nod. "Yep. Looks like you get a two-for-one deal. Brother and niece or nephew, all in one." I pull her into my side, throwing my arm around her. "Now, let's go, Little Bird. Time to meet your brother."

She has enough going on right now, and I don't need to add on to that and tell her that I've fallen in love with her. So, I hold it in.

For now anyway.

She'll find out soon enough.

# SUTTON

My stomach churns at the same rate as a soft-serve ice cream machine. I know my armpits are probably sweating. Heck, even my forehead feels like it's gathering drops of sweat on it.

*I feel like I'm going to throw up.*

Here we sit at this bar, next to Brody and his pregnant fiancée, Bria, and I literally feel like I'm going to puke. How am I supposed to drop the bomb that we are siblings? It's clear his life is going great. He's in the NHL now, and he has a baby on the way. And now, I'm about to stir all of that up. But maybe he wants to know. Maybe he would like to know that he has actual blood out there that isn't his messed up, abusive father.

For the past twenty minutes, Hunter and Brody have been talking hockey while Bria and I have made small talk about everything—from her pregnancy to life as the significant other of a professional hockey player to my dancing career. But when Hunter gives me a side-eye, I know he's wondering when I'm going to bring it up.

Patting Hunter's shoulder, I give him a look, telling him I'm ready. I feel more nauseous, knowing I need to just get the words out. I'd ask him to walk outside, but the bar is completely dead. So, I feel like it's a safe place to bring it up in here.

"So, look, man, as much as I wanted to see you to catch up and shoot the shit, I actually did this more because Sutton needs to talk to you." Hunter puts his hand on my leg, letting me know he's here. "She's got some important shit to tell you. And she means a lot to me, so please just listen."

Brody's eyes move to mine, and he looks confused. "Yeah? What's, uh … what's up?" He laughs nervously. "Nobody is trying to sue me or some shit, right?"

I chew my lip nervously, my throat seeming to close up, not wanting to let the words out. Inhaling, I tilt my chin up and look right at him.

"No. No. Nothing like that." I fumble, sounding like a moron. "I think … well, I think you're my brother," I say quickly. "We have the same mom and dad." I cover my mouth after blurting out the information I confirmed earlier this week. "I'm sorry. I had no idea how to do this. In a card. Or in person. Or at your doorstep. Maybe an email." I suck in a breath. "I'm blabbering. Fuck, I'm nervous."

Because she is his comfort, his first instinct is to look at Bria, who looks just as shocked as he is but tries to remain calm—for support.

She takes his hand in hers and runs her hand through his hair. "It's okay. Just ... just listen to her, okay?"

Taking out the papers I printed off from the information Hunter had gotten, I slide them to him. "My mom—*our* mom—was a prostitute when Sam, or Samuel Savage, the man who I thought was my biological father, met her. She was pregnant with me. And you ... you were—"

"Back in South Carolina with my old man," he mutters, staring at nothing.

"Yeah." I nod somberly. "I'm so sorry. I had no idea you existed until recently."

"Jesus," he mutters, swallowing thickly as his eyes skim through the papers. "Fuck. This is ... this is a lot." He clears his throat, running his hand over his shaved head. "No ... this is a fucking dumpster fire, started with dog shit. Wow. Wow ..." His hand moves from his head to his chin. "Yep ... wow."

"Brody ... just breathe," Bria whispers. "It's okay."

Looking at her again, he shakes his head lightly before standing from his stool and walking outside.

"Just give him a minute," Bria says softly, patting my hand. "His mother—well, your mother too—as you know, she left him as a toddler with that monster of a man. And I think ... I think this is just a lot of information for him to process. I think, deep down, he sort of assumed she was dead. Or maybe hoped that she was. That she hadn't stayed away from him his entire life for no good reason."

Climbing from her own stool, she nods toward the door. "We will both be right back. I promise." Before walking off, she puts her hand on my shoulder. "You did the right thing, coming to him." Tears gather in her eyes, making it clear how much she loves this man who shares the same blood but is a stranger to me. "He's never really had family. Well, besides me. I'm really happy for him, Sutton. I'm happy for you too."

As she walks outside, I look at Hunter. "I hope I did the right thing," I whisper. "What if I just ruined years and years of healing for him?"

Leaning forward, he cups my cheeks. "You didn't, Sutton. And I can't imagine how hard it was for you to come here tonight and tell him." When he kisses my forehead, I wonder if he'll ever kiss my lips again or if I'm being friend-zoned forever. "You are pretty incredible, Little Bird. I'm proud of you."

"Thanks," I utter. Looking at him, my eyes fill with an unfamiliar wetness. Emotions flood my body, but I'm not sure if it's from my newly found brother or knowing that Hunter is by my side, carrying my ass through this. "Thank you. For making this happen. I think … I think it'll be okay."

"It might seem like a shitstorm now, but it's going to be good." He winks. "I promise."

# HUNTER

Once Brody comes back, looking as pale as Casper the damn Ghost, he sits down and looks at Sutton.

"All right. So, I'm going to need you to go over that again because it sounded to me like you just said you're my sister. And I guess I've kinda always just assumed I was the only offspring that came from my father's fucked up nutsack." He looks from Sutton to Bria and back to Sutton. "How sure are you?"

Sutton's chest rises as she pulls in a breath. I see her hands shake the smallest bit, and she tucks her fingers into the palm of her hand.

"Obviously, we can do a DNA test to know for sure. But Hunter had someone look into my mother for me. This is what they found." She glances at me. "And I know Hunter's family enough to know that when it comes to who they hire, it's nothing but the most reputable. So, yeah … I'm pretty damn sure that what he found is accurate."

Brody rocks forward and back on his stool for a moment, processing it all before his eyes move to hers again. "And so … what do you plan on doing? I mean, are you going to call your mother out on it? Are you going to travel to South Carolina to meet our dad? Because I have to tell you … he's not what you've probably painted in your head. He's a bad, *bad* dude. You might think you realize how ugly he really is, but trust me, I lived with him, alone, for eighteen years. It's much worse." He swallows. "So, whatever it is you plan on doing with this information, think it through. I'm warning you, Sutton, just be careful."

She rakes her teeth over her bottom lip as she stares off into the distance. Finally, she looks at him again. "I don't plan on meeting our dad—ever. I've heard the backstory on why you started One Wish to begin with. It's obvious our father isn't a good man, and meeting him isn't what I want to do. And as far as our mother goes, she hasn't spoken to me in months. I was cut off when I transferred to Brooks, so she was already on my shit list. But now? Well, now, she's dead to me for leaving you the way she did. But I do need some sort of closure. I need to speak my mind and tell her how I feel and how vile of a human being I really think she is." Her voice grows thicker, and I can tell she's doing her best to push through. "I have no family anymore. None at all. But I'd like to have you as my family. And Bria and your unborn baby." A tear rolls down her cheek. "I'd like to know you, Brody. I'd like to actually be your sister. And I'd love to have a brother. But I'm not naive enough to think it's going to happen overnight. We're strangers. But we don't have to be forever."

His eyes move from her to Bria's, and I know he's trying to keep his emotions in check. Brody O'Brien has never been a dude who likes to show when something affects him. Everything has always been masked with humor or violence.

But finally, he stands. "Well, fuck it. I mean, you've got the same fucked up blood running through your veins as me. Do we hug now? Or what the hell do we do? I'm new to this touchy-feely family shit."

She shrugs, standing. "I'm not usually a hugger of people I've only just met. But in our case, I think that would be a good place to start."

As they hug, she looks at me, giving me a small smile. I'm really happy for her. Because maybe she won't have to feel so alone now. Maybe she'll feel like she has someone on this earth who's family.

I just hope that, one day, maybe I can be her someone too. Because as crazy as it sounds, she's already mine.

# SUTTON

Heading home after meeting Brody and Bria, Hunter puts the music on low and doesn't say much. I've come to realize how respectful he is. And sometimes, he doesn't want to overstep. I appreciate that, but right now, with the thousand thoughts running through my head ... I just want him to be close.

"I can take you home, if you need space," he says softly, glancing over at me. "But honestly, I'd rather you stay the night with me."

I'm quiet for a minute, and he shrugs.

"I'm trying to be softer. Not so psychotic and shit. But ... fuck, I hate the thought of dropping you off right now."

"I don't want to go home. And I don't want to be alone," I utter. "At least not without you."

I hate that he doesn't have a bench seat in this fancy truck. Because right now, all I want to do is get as close to him as I can. I might have just found my sibling and the only family I have, but I've never felt more alone in my life. And the small space between Hunter and me feels like a million miles. And I can't stand it.

As if sensing my feelings, Hunter reaches over, capturing my hand in his. Bringing it to his lips, he kisses my skin. "I'm right here, Little Bird. And I'm not going anywhere."

I want to melt into his words and allow myself to just jump into whatever the hell we started headfirst. But at the end of the day, this whole thing began from fake dating.

*Is he still faking it now?*

The thing is, I love him. I think I have since we danced together for the second time. But I'm afraid of rejection. Because my whole life, that's all I've known.

I've never been talented enough. My posture isn't perfect. My skin is far from flawless. I'm stubborn and oftentimes self-conscious. A million little things have been picked apart since the day I was born. And I'm scared. Scared that when he sees the real me … he'll decide he doesn't like what he sees.

We pull into his driveway. Releasing my hand, he gets out and jogs to my side, opening my door. As I follow him into the house, I know something is about to change between us. The energy is shifting. It's no longer about lust or sexual tension. Sure, those are there too. But now, it's about the fact that we found love in the most unlikely circumstances. And I think—I *hope* we both feel it.

Cade sits on the couch, half-asleep, and doesn't hear us come in. Watson is nowhere to be seen—same with Haley. And when Hunter leads me to his room and closes the door behind him, my heart skips a beat.

Going to his drawer, he pulls out a T-shirt and hands it to me. "You can sleep in this, if you want."

I nod silently, too emotionally exhausted to form a word. And when I sit back on the bed, he kneels down before me, gently taking the fabric of my shirt in his fingertips.

"Let me help you, baby," he whispers before slowly peeling the shirt over my head. Leaving me in my bra and leggings.

He swallows thickly, his Adam's apple bobbing as he touches the strap of my bra. "Do you want to leave this on or …"

I look up at him and shake my head. "No."

He nods slowly before reaching behind my back and unclasping my bra. By now, even though we've had sex—among other things—he hasn't seen me completely naked. Right now, I'm being stripped to nothing. Physically and emotionally. He's going to see it all.

When my bra falls, exposing my bare breasts, there's no mistaking the sound when he sucks in a breath. But I know he's trying to keep it together because he probably doesn't think this is an appropriate time to push things further after what we've dealt with all night.

Slowly, he takes the Brooks hockey shirt and pulls it over my head, dressing me like I'm a damn baby. And I don't fight it because I know Hunter enjoys doing nice things for people. It's who he is.

When his fingers find the waistband of my leggings, I lift my ass up slightly to help him wiggle them from my legs. Tossing them to the floor, leaving me in only my thong, I reach under his shirt and rest my hand against his abdomen.

"Hunter," I rasp, years of bottled-up emotions laced in my voice. "Please, even if this is fake … love me tonight. Love me like it isn't."

Kneeling before me again, he cups my cheek, his eyes burning into mine. "Little Bird, there is *nothing* fake about this. I promise you that."

Tears flow down my cheeks as he brings his lips to mine.

"Are you sure you want to do this tonight?" His forehead presses to mine. "We don't have to. I could hold you in my arms and be happy."

Reaching out, I slowly unbutton his jeans and brush my lips to his again. "I'm sure. All I want right now is you. I want to be as close as we can get."

Once his jeans and briefs pool to the ground, he kisses my neck. With one hand, he pushes my thong down, letting it fall to the floor before he gently hooks his arm around my back and lifts me to the head of the bed.

Keeping his body over mine, he nudges his dick between my legs, continuing to rest his forehead to mine. Slowly working in and out, he pushes in deeper, and my legs wrap around his waist.

"Hunter," I whisper, biting my lip.

"You're so beautiful, Sutton," he rasps against my lips. "And strong. And smart. Bold. Funny. Everything anyone could ever want."

"Even you?" I croak.

"*Especially* me," he says, kissing me again.

This doesn't feel like fucking. Not the way that it did when we were in the changing room. This feels like … love. But even though the three words linger on my lips, I don't say them. Because maybe it's too soon. It would probably scare him away. And truthfully, I don't want to scare him away. I want him to stay. Maybe forever …

My fingertips find the flesh on his back, and he drives his face into my neck.

"Hunter," I breathe. "Please. Don't. Stop," I cry out softly, dragging him deeper with my thighs over and over again as his hips thrust to match mine.

I hug him tighter as our bodies thrash together. I squeeze hard, wanting to just climb inside of him and never leave because I've never felt more at home than I do in this moment.

"I'm … I'm …" I moan, moving one hand from his back and gripping the bedsheets.

"Me too, baby." He chokes the words out. "Coming with you."

His body movements start to slow, becoming more dragged out as he kisses my neck. Trembling, he lifts his head and looks down at me before pressing a kiss to my forehead.

I know sex can't fix everything. But I just learned that sex with the perfect person can sure make you feel a lot less alone.

Hunter Thompson has become my person. And in a way, a muse in the story that is my life. I just hope I can keep him.

## SUTTON

I dress in the outfit Jolene chose for me. A pale blue princess-cut leotard with a bodice made of sequins and a sheer skirt that glimmers when I move, paired with matching ballet slippers. After, the stylist applies a little makeup and fixes my hair into a French braid, pulled to the side of my head.

This dance is strictly for charity. There's no golden ticket to becoming a professional dancer. It likely won't go on a résumé or win me brownie points with Broadway if I do good. Yet here I am, nervous as hell.

Nervous because I'm dancing with someone who makes me feel so dang giddy that I'll probably forget our routine. Afraid that I'll look like a moron in front of my newfound brother, who happens to be famous and über-talented. And petrified that this dance will make me fall deeper in love even though I'm too chicken to tell him how I feel.

The show is about to begin, and I haven't seen Hunter since both of us dressed in our outfits, and the pit in my stomach keeps hatching more butterflies.

"Wow, you're so purrrty," a little girl says, coming next to me. "I wish my hair were in a braid instead of this stupid bun."

I giggle, looking down at her in her pale pink leotard and her perfectly made ballerina bun.

"I love it." I smile. "Plus, with that bun, you're like a real ballerina." I point to my hair. "Unlike me."

She ponders my words, pulling her lips to the side. "Yeah ... but your hair looks like Elsa. Only with black hair. And Elsa is the most powerful Disney character ever."

"This is true. But Elsa isn't a ballerina, is she?" I pat her bun lightly. "I think you have the best hair here tonight."

"You do?" she whispers, looking around. "Even better than that girl with the red dress?"

"Definitely," I mutter, knowing she's referring to Poppy. "What's your name?"

"Carter," she says proudly. "Carter Anne."

"Well, Carter ... Carter Anne, are you excited to go onstage?"

She looks down, wringing her hands together. "I'm scared. There're a lot of people out there." Her eyes look up at me, pulling at my heartstrings. "What if I trip?"

"You won't." I smile, kneeling down to her level. "And if you do, no one will remember it because they'll just be thinking how cute you are." I stand up, whirling my finger around. "Want to practice your steps? I'm nervous too. You'll be helping me out."

She nods quickly, and before long, there we are, practicing her performance as she giggles. I watch her in awe because there's no pressure. No expectations. It's just for fun. That and her love of dance. And I'm envious.

After I help ease Carter's nerves—or maybe she helps me with mine—her instructor comes to get her and the other adorable ballerinas, and shortly after, the other performances begin. I poke my head out the side curtain every so often, ensuring no one sees me. But remain out back until it's our turn.

I'm getting slightly concerned where my dance partner is. Heading toward my bag, I begin to search for my phone.

"Wow, you look beautiful," Hunter's voice says behind me, and when I turn, I find him in a pale blue dress shirt and slacks. His hair is its usual tousled mess, and he looks delicious. And when he pulls me in for a hug, he smells equally as good.

I set my bag back down with a smile so big that it hurts my cheeks. "Thanks. You look nice too."

Giving me a boyish grin when he pulls back, he holds out his hand. In his palm is a beautiful corsage made up of the most stunning flowers. "I know this isn't the prom, but since you never got to go to one, I figured this would be the next closest thing." Taking my wrist in his fingers, he slides the corsage on. "One dance tonight isn't going to be enough, Little Bird." Sliding his hand up my neck, he smiles. "Dance with me now? Because to be honest, I'm really fucking nervous to go out there on that stage. And the only thing that could possibly calm me down right now is you."

"Perfect" by Ed Sheeran plays in the background from one of the performances, making its way to the back of the stage. I wrap my arms around his neck, and his hands fall to my waist. We rock slowly, and my face actually hurts from smiling so hard.

A thousand times, I've danced. But this dance … it's my favorite.

The craziest part is, no one is even watching, and that somehow makes it even better.

I rest my cheek on his chest and breathe him in. Never wanting the song to end. I've had relationships in my life, but nothing has ever been so sacred. And I've never loved another human being this much.

When the song ends and we hear applause, we know we're next up to take the stage.

Looking up at him, I kiss his cheek and give him a small grin. "We've got this. And remember, it's for charity, right?"

"Right." He nods. "But if I trip, you have to too."

"Deal." I giggle. "Same to you."

"You know it. If you go down, I do too."

Seconds later, our names are announced, and we walk onto the stage, hand in hand. And when the music begins, I know I'm about to put on the performance of my life.

Because with the love I have for Hunter now, there's no way the crowd can't see it.

# HUNTER

As our song comes closer to the end, I'm thankful as fuck that Sutton literally built this routine to make me not look like an idiot. Because in doing so, she stole the whole damn show.

I'm basically here to lift her when she needs lifting and for her to dance around while I throw in a few moves to not look like a dead animal in the center of the stage.

The moment comes for her to leap into my arms, and I catch her with ease, spinning slowly until I gradually bring her down, running my hand from her neck upward until I'm cupping her face. But unlike her usual smile that greets me, she's stifling a cough. And when a small wheeze escapes her lips just as the curtain closes, I pick her up again, running toward where I know her bag is with her inhalers in it.

Her wheezing becomes worse and more audible as she struggles to catch her breath. I grab her two inhalers, and she points to the rescue one. I hold it up to her lips, pushing my thumb down on it to release some medicine into her lungs. I have no fucking idea how much is too much or too little. I wish I had taken the time to learn more about what to do in these situations.

Her wheezing continues, even after more medicine. I can see the sheer panic in her eyes, and I notice her lips quickly turning blue.

I pull her phone from her bag and dial 911. And seconds later, when someone answers the phone, I fail when I'm trying my best not to fucking panic.

"I need an ambulance. My girlfriend has asthma, and she's having an asthma attack." I look down at her, tears forming in my eyes as people start to gather around, trying to help.

And after what seems like the fifth question from the lady on the other end, I break down.

"Just fucking send someone here! We're at Nickerson Auditorium, and she doesn't have time for you to ask me more fucking questions!" I growl, seeing the life leaving her slowly. "She is starting to lose consciousness!"

"Sir, please try to remain calm. We have someone en route. They are about three minutes out," she tells me. "Stay on the phone, please."

When Brody walks into the room, I hand him the phone. "Talk to the dispatcher. The ambulance is almost here. I'm going to carry her outside."

Just as I reach the door and push it open, I hear the screaming of the ambulance sirens. Looking down at her, I hold her closer. "It's okay. You're going to be okay."

Ryann runs next to me. "Oh my God, Hunter. I had no idea," she sobs. "Is she okay?"

"I—I don't know."

She makes a few small wheezing sounds, her eyes shut as I hold her against me.

"I tried the rescue inhaler. I don't know what else to do! I don't fucking know what to do for her."

The ambulance comes to a halt, and I run toward it. They open the back doors, and I set her down on the stretcher.

"I love you, baby. Please, please just be okay." I wipe my eyes, stepping back so they can give her what she needs.

"Sir, if you aren't immediate family, I need you to step out," the paramedic says, never looking at me.

"I'm her—"

"He ... stays," Sutton's voice barely whispers before wheezing. "He ... stays."

The paramedic glances at me, and the other one points to the small bench. "Sit there and let us help her."

"She's losing consciousness!" the girl yells to her coworker. "We're losing her!"

My throat closes up, and I collapse on the bench, crying harder than I've ever cried.

"Please," I sob like a baby. "Please just be okay."

# Hunter

One week. Seven days. Ten thousand eighty minutes. Six hundred four thousand eight hundred long-ass seconds.

That's how long it's been since Sutton has opened her beautiful blue eyes. Every day seems like Groundhog Day. Bringing the same fucking thing as the day before. And I'm ready for it to be over and for my Little Bird to wake the hell up.

The thing with asthma I never considered is that when it's severe and your brain doesn't get the oxygen it needs … you can go into a coma. Or worse, die. But the doctors can't figure out why her body didn't respond to her rescue inhaler. Or why she hasn't recovered yet.

Right now, Sutton isn't breathing on her own. And I'm fucking terrified she isn't going to wake up. I never even got the chance to tell her that I love her when she could actually fucking hear me. And if it hadn't been for her forcing those words out in the ambulance, I wouldn't be allowed to even be here right now.

Besides for practice, I haven't left her side. I've done all my classes remotely, and I will until she walks out of these hospital doors. But this weekend, we have away games. And as much as I want to camp out here and not play, that's not really an option. I know Sutton would kick my ass if I did that too.

She has to wake up. Because if she doesn't, I don't think I'll believe in the good of anything anymore. Because if she doesn't come back to me, what the fuck would the point of that be?

I loved Paige. I'll never say that I didn't because she was my first love, and I really did think I wanted to spend my life with her. And I guess that's because she was everything I thought I wanted. But the love I have for Sutton isn't anything I've ever felt before. She makes me feel shit inside of me I never even knew I could feel. Some good, some bad. The girl drives me batshit crazy, but she's the only person I can imagine being with from here on out.

I considered contacting her mother, but I don't know if that's what Sutton would even want. Her mother hasn't called her in months. She knows her daughter takes medication daily for her condition, yet she can't be bothered to check on how she's doing, which is fucking insane. And when she learned that Helena—who is actually Helen—left Brody behind as a toddler, it really hurt her. So, I don't think she wants her mom around her. Maybe even ever. For her to have done all the things she's done, I consider her to be one coldhearted bitch. And I don't really want to look at her face right now.

Looking at Sutton, I lie my head next to her hand. "Just open those pretty blue eyes, baby," I whisper, kissing her hand. "Open them up and call me an idiot or tell me I'm dumb. Anything. I just want to see your eyes and hear your voice."

Standing, I walk to the window and look at the sky.

"Please, Holden, if you're listening … which you probably aren't … I don't fucking know." I scratch my head, feeling awkward as hell. "If you meant what you said … if you really do give me your blessing, like you told me you did, give me the chance to love her the way she deserves. Please. If you have any pull up there or … if you can do anything to bring her back to me, do it." I wipe my hand across my eyes. "I wish you had gotten your shot. I have no doubt that she'd choose you over my ass any day of the week. But I'm begging you, man. I need her. I really, really need her."

## SUTTON

There's nothing worse than waking up with a tube down your throat. I wouldn't wish it on anybody. I try to avoid it at all costs. Yet here I am, for the second time in my life, waking up in a full panic because it feels like I'm actually choking on a dildo made of plastic.

I vaguely see Hunter as he watches me struggling, and he runs out of the room. Seconds later, a nurse rushes in—thank God.

"Shh, don't fight the intubation. It only makes it worse," she whispers, trying to calm me. "Relax, Sutton. Please."

I want to listen—really, I do. But every cell in my body is telling me to fight it. Fight it like it's a giant sword being shoved down my throat, cutting me wide open. Feeling someone take my hand, I hear Hunter's voice.

"Just be strong, baby. You're the strongest person I know. I'm right here."

The feeling of circles on my hand calms me the smallest bit, but it's not enough. Tears stream down my face, and I feel like I'm literally suffocating. A feeling I've become used to, yet I still haven't mastered my reaction.

Squeezing my eyes shut, I feel him stroking my hand and imagine him smiling at me. I pretend we're not in a hospital room but instead swaying to a slow song.

He looks down at me before whispering the words that I dreamed he said to me in the ambulance. And all seems right in the world. I relax my body, letting myself live in my imagination.

The pressure of the intubation tube lessens, and when the tube slips out of my throat, I feel a sensation that is both as nasty as it is relieving. Coughing a few times, I grimace at the sting of the sheer rawness from my throat.

Opening my eyes, I find Hunter at my side, still holding my hand.

"Hi," I croak.

"Hey there, Little Bird." He grins, tears pooling in his eyes. "You scared the shit out of me, you know. Pretty pissed about it actually."

I attempt to shrug, but my body is as frail as a one-hundred-year-old's on their deathbed. "My bad." My voice barely croaks the words out. "Did we win? The charity? Did we get the most points?"

He barks out a laugh, tears streaming down his face, and he kisses my forehead. "We did. I mean, it probably had everything to do with my talent and not yours, but ya know." He laughs before his face grows serious. "We all know you stole that show, Sutton."

"You weren't so bad yourself, Thompson."

"When you were lying in this bed the past nine days, I told myself a thousand times that if you woke up—if you opened your eyes and looked up at me—I'd make sure you knew exactly where I stood when it came to us." He inhales. "Little Bird, what started off as training for one stupid dance with someone who was supposed to be my enemy turned into something bigger than I'd ever imagined. And I have to tell you, a few measly dances will never be enough with you. Because I want a lifetime's worth." He kisses my lips, and I taste his salty tears. "So, please, don't ever scare me again. I don't know if I can take it."

"I'll try my best." I smile.

"You'd better." He kisses me again. "I'm sure, by now, you've figured it out, but I'll tell you anyway. I love you. I'm so fucking in love with you." He grins down at me. "You make me absolutely insane, but you're on my brain every second of every day. I told you before that there was nothing fake about this, and I meant it."

I lick my dry, cracked lips. I'm sure I look like dog shit, but the way he's looking at me … I don't feel insecure.

"I love you too." I inhale. "Even if you drive me crazy too."

"Keeps it interesting, right?" He shrugs.

I giggle, but when it makes my entire body hurt, I flinch, although I still smile through the pain. "I suppose it does."

I guess when the universe wants two people together, it finds a way to make it happen. Never did I think I'd fall in love with someone with the last name Thompson. Never mind Hunter Thompson.

Two people who couldn't stand each other are suddenly relying on each other for happiness. An unlikely bond made, even in unfortunate circumstances. And an impossible arrangement that blurred every single line. And a hundred roadblocks later … here we are.

We can fight how we feel. Hell, we can even try to ignore it. But one thing is for certain: love will always find a way to knock you on your ass and land you right where you belong.

And I belong with Hunter.

# HUNTER

I bolt around my room, trying my best to get my shit together quickly for practice after spending last night with Sutton at her place.

It's been a few weeks since she got out of the hospital, and I've been spending a lot of time with her because, honestly, I haven't wanted to let her out of my sight.

The doctors found out she had a rare form of asthma that didn't respond well to certain medications. Even ones that had worked for her sometimes wouldn't always be the answer. Especially in times when she needed her rescue inhaler. That's why she ended up in the hospital those other times. It's extremely rare and also hard to diagnose. Hence why my uncle, as well as a few other pulmonologists, missed it. But now that she has an actual answer to what she has, she has been put on proper medication. And her new doctor is extremely hopeful that she'll live the life she wants to live.

She told me that before this diagnosis, she was considering throwing in the towel when it came to dance. But now, she doesn't have to slow down. She can dance the way she wants without the constant fear that she'll end up in a coma again. Sure, it's possible. But now that she has the right medicine to help her, it's a lot less likely.

I walk downstairs to find Haley curled up on the couch. At first, I think she's just watching TV, but when I move closer, it's clear she's crying.

"What's wrong?" I say, standing in front of her. "What the fuck happened?"

When she sees me, she quickly wipes her face and shakes her head. "I'm fine, really." She tries to smile, but I know it's fake. "I didn't know you were home. I thought you were with Sutton."

"I was earlier, but I had to leave to come here for my practice stuff." I narrow my eyes at her. "Are you going to tell me what's going on or what?"

"Please, Hunter," she says, her bottom lip trembling. "Leave it alone for now. I'll talk to you soon enough."

I grind my back teeth together, feeling uneasy. But I don't want to push her too hard because then she'll never come to me when she actually wants to talk.

"Fine. But promise me that if you need me, you'll tell me. All right?"

She nods quickly, wiping her eyes again. "I will. Promise."

Watson walks out of his room. "You ready?" He looks around. "Where's Cade?"

"Fuck if I know." I shrug, looking at my sister. "Have you seen him today?"

Her facial expression only saddens, and she puts her hands over her face. "I don't want to say anything. He'll never forgive me."

"Forgive you?" Watson rears his head back. "What the fuck are you talking about, Haley?"

She sniffles, peeking over her hands. "I think he's passed out in his room." Her lip trembles. "I think he needs help, Hunter. I think … he's been taking drugs."

"Fuck," I mutter.

I've been so wrapped up in everything with Sutton and me that I really haven't been paying attention to Cade lately. I know he has a history of drug abuse. Hell, he was in a rehab facility for six weeks before he even turned eighteen.

Cade carries a lot of shit from his past with him. I don't think he's ever gotten over his best friend dying. In fact, I think he blames himself.

Dropping my bag, I head to his room, Watson hot on my heels and Haley right behind him.

"Please, don't tell him I said anything," she cries. "He'll hate me so much."

When I push the door open, there he is, passed out. I shove him, and he stirs the smallest bit, only to fall back asleep.

This time, Watson rips his covers off, slapping him on the back. "Wake the fuck up, Huff! We have practice. And after practice, we're going to figure out a plan for you to get your fucking life together."

196

"Fuck off," Cade groans, pulling a pillow over his head.

"No, fuck you," Watson growls, grabbing his arm and flipping him onto his back. "Get the fuck up, Cade! We're on a team. Together. You don't fucking get high or drunk and sleep all fucking day."

Cade's up on his feet within seconds. But instead of getting dressed, he grabs Watson's shirt. "Fuck you, Gentry! You're such a Goody Two-shoes." He shoves him, veins popping out of his neck. "Get off my dick, pussy boy."

Watson has him in a headlock, and they crash into the dresser. Haley wails, covering her mouth. And I know it's up to me to split them up.

Grabbing Cade, I pull him backward. "Cut the shit, Huff," I yell into his ear. "We're just fucking worried!"

"Let me go!" he screams, and after a bit of fighting, I release him.

Looking at the three of us, he laughs bitterly. "You're worried? You don't know the first fucking thing to be worried about when it comes to me." He shakes his head. "I'm fucking done with hockey. And I'm done with all of you."

Grabbing his keys from his desk, he starts toward the door.

"Cade!" Haley screams. "Please, stop!"

Continuing to stalk out of the room, he blows by her and runs down the stairs. Seconds later, we hear the door slam, and we know that he's gone.

But I don't think any of us knows what the fuck to do next.

# SUTTON

I stare down at the message from Hunter, telling me he's coming over after practice and that something's wrong with Cade. I frown, not really knowing what to expect because as far as I can tell, Cade's sort of a mess. But I never thought he'd get to the point where his friends were this worried.

The past few weeks have been a whirlwind. One that included me trying to catch up after missing so much class, dealing with the emotions of missing my first solo performance at Brooks, and also thinking about the future when it comes to dancing. And I've come to the conclusion that maybe I don't want to do it anymore. Not competitively anyway. When something loses its sparkle, it might be time to hang it up.

Dancing with Carter Anne at the One Wish event, seeing the excitement in her eyes to be on that stage … I realized that I want to be there when young girls and boys feel that joy inside of them as they move their bodies to music. I want to remind kids what we're all there for.

Fun and wonder.

Maybe it was the near-death experience or finding out I had a brother—one who's actually really cool. Whatever it was, it made me grasp what I want in life. And what I want is to be a ballet instructor for young children. Before they become overly competitive brats.

I was going to tell Hunter all of this when he came over later, but now, I feel like it would be the worst time to talk about myself when he's worried about his friend. But I will tell him. Maybe just not tonight.

The hockey team is like a band of brothers. One that sticks together through thick and thin despite the disagreements they might have. Whatever Cade is going through, he's lucky to have Hunter and the other guys on his side.

I meet Hunter in the driveway the second I hear his truck pull in.

As he gets out of the truck, he pulls me against him with one arm, kissing my forehead. "Is anyone else home?"

I look at the house, nodding. "Yep. Poppy and Lana are both inside."

"Can we maybe go for a walk?" he mutters. Looking down, he slides his hand up my neck and into my hair before bringing his mouth to mine.

I'll never get tired of kissing Hunter. That much I know.

"Sure." I nod, taking his hand and stepping back.

Heading toward the sidewalk, I glance nervously up at him.

"Is Cade okay?" I whisper, giving his hand a squeeze. "And you? Are *you* okay?"

He inhales a deep breath, his chest rising. "Watson, Link, and I just had to talk to Coach. We didn't want to tell him, but when Cade didn't go to practice today, Coach somehow knew what was going on with him." He shrugs. "Guess he'd noticed it a few weeks ago." His body stiffens, and I know he's upset. "Cade's going to have to go to rehab. He'll be off the team until he can pass however many clean drug tests that Coach says." He grimaces. "Maybe even forever, if he doesn't take Coach's help and just go to rehab."

Stopping, I turn to face him, wrapping my arms around his waist. "I'm so sorry, Hunter. But … maybe he'll agree to rehab. I'm sure he'll do whatever it takes to keep his spot on the team."

He gives his head a small shake, squinting his eyes. "You didn't see how he acted today, Sutton. He … he wasn't even the same Cade I've known since freshmen year."

Guilt fills my stomach. "If you hadn't been so wrapped up in my health crap, you probably would have noticed sooner. I'm sorry, Hunter."

"No, it wouldn't have changed anything," he assures me, rubbing his fingertips against the tops of my arms. "At the end of the day, Cade's a big boy. I just really hope he'll let us all help him instead of fight it." He kisses the top of my head. "Since this shit happened earlier, all I've wanted to do is come see you."

I nod slowly, moving my hands to his chest. "It'll be okay. You're a good friend, Hunter."

"I'm not so sure about that." He cringes. "I've gotta go see him. But first, just walk with me for a little longer. We don't even have to talk. I just want to be near you."

"Okay." I give him a small smile.

He looks down at me. "Okay," he mimics me.

And we walk. Ignoring life's issues for a few minutes.

# HUNTER

As Cade leaves the house with his parents, ignoring Watson, Haley, and me, there's a darkness in the room. A void that I know isn't going anywhere until he comes back. And even then, I have to wonder if he'll forgive me. If he'll forgive any of us.

My sister cries, but I don't really get why. She's lived with us for a few months, sure. But I didn't think this would hit her this hard.

Once their car pulls out of the driveway, Watson shuts the door. The look on his face is the same as mine. Lost. Like we have no fucking idea what to do or how to do it.

Finally, Watson glances at my sister before frowning. "Haley ... you don't look so good. Are you all right?"

When I look at her, she breaks down, gripping her chest.

"Hunter, I'm pregnant," she croaks.

My eyes widen, and my heart stops.

"I'm pregnant ... and it's Cade's baby."

Once the words are out, she bolts into her room, and Watson and I stare at each other.

*Well ... fuck.*

# SUTTON

I daydream about the conversation I plan to have with my mother when I see her next week. She won't know it's coming, and it'll be in the middle of a stupid, fancy luncheon that I've gotten word she's attending an hour from Brooks, but I'm going in … guns blazing.

I wish I didn't need this closure, but deep down, I know I do. For some strange reason, it's something I need to do before I can leave the past in the past. Once and for all.

Hunter's parents came to see me multiple times while I was recovering. And the more time I spend with them, the more I realize that I don't think they are even aware of how negative they've been when it comes to Hunter's dream to play in the NHL. In their defense, I think they just truly believe him following in their footsteps would be best.

When class ends, I gather my things, letting a yawn out before I walk outside.

Hearing my phone ring in my bag, I take it out and swipe my thumb across the screen.

"Hey, how'd it go?" I ask nervously because I know how scared Hunter was for Cade's parents to come physically take him away to rehab.

"Where are you right now?" he says instantly.

"I'm by the Sawyer building."

"I'll be there in two minutes. Stay there."

He ends the call before I have a chance to say anything back, and I know that whatever happened, it wasn't good. Sitting on the bench, I wait anxiously for him to arrive.

# HUNTER

After the fucked up news I just received, I needed to find Sutton and vent. I don't really care that my sister might not want her to know. Because, one, I know Sutton would never repeat it. And, two, I just need a distraction from all of the shit happening around me. And my distraction is Sutton. My beautiful Little Bird, who I can't get enough of.

I pull up against the sidewalk, and for once, I don't even get out because before I can reach for the handle, she's inside the cab of my truck.

"Are you okay?" she whispers, touching my hand.

"I am now." I nod. "Cade's gone to rehab. He hates my guts. Probably won't talk to me ever again." I suck in a breath. "What if he never forgives me, Sutton?"

"He will. I promise." She moves her hand to my cheek.

"Oh, and my sister is pregnant." I cringe. "*With* Cade's baby. So, while the dude's just trying to get sober, he's going to also have to learn that he's about to be a fucking father. To a human fucking being when he can't even take care of himself." I point to her seat belt. "I don't want to talk about any of that shit though. For days, all my world has revolved around is Cade Huff and his issues. I love him. I really do. But right now, I just want to be with my girlfriend." I look at her. "Deal?"

"Deal," she whispers, winking. "Hey, thanks for the title. I was beginning to have a complex. Glad to hear that you actually like me."

"What?" I frown.

"You said *girlfriend*. First time you've used the term, big guy." Leaning forward, she kisses my cheek. "I'll think about it. Ya know, the whole … girlfriend thing."

Sitting back in her seat, she taps her chin. "All right, I've thought about it. And … yeah, sure. I mean, I guess I'll go out with you."

She's trying to make me smile, and she's succeeding. Shaking my head, I pull her toward me, kissing her as she giggles against me.

When she pulls away, the same guilt from today's event creeps in. She must sense it, too, because she pats my shoulder.

"It's my turn to take you somewhere. To take care of you."

"You always take care of me. You're what keeps me going."

"That's sweet and all, but get your ass out of the driver's seat and just trust me."

She pushes her door open and jumps down before coming to my side. When she pulls my door open, she tugs my hand, bringing me out of the truck.

Shoving me up against the truck, she kisses me so hard that my dick twitches, and I wish I could bury myself inside of her right now despite everything going on.

"Hunter, I love you. I love you more than I've ever loved anything in the whole wide freaking world. But it's my turn to do something for you, okay?"

I swallow, offering her a weak nod. "Yeah. Okay."

Giving my ass a swat, she climbs behind the wheel. "Good. Let's roll."

"Yeah. Uh, babe … this isn't really what I had in mind." I run my hand up the back of my neck. "I thought maybe we'd get naked. Perhaps you'd feel bad and give me a blowie. Maybe even sit on my face." I point to the brick building. "But this? Nope. I didn't really have this in the list of possibilities."

I stare at the soup kitchen, looking at the line of people outside the doors. A lot of them are clearly high, and some are just really dirty. A few have kids. My stomach sinks.

"If you wanted to make me feel worse though, you've succeeded." I cringe. "Fuck, even I might need an antidepressant after this day."

Shoving me, she glares. "I promise you'll understand why we're here shortly, Hunter. But for now, just stop whining like a little bitch before I withhold sex for a month."

Taking her hands, I pull her toward me, putting my lips to her ear. "We both know you couldn't wait a month. Hell, Little Bird, you couldn't last a week without me." I nibble her ear. "In fact … if you want to go find a place to park, I'd love to drive my dick so far—"

Pushing me back, she puts her hand over my mouth. "Shush. Shush your face." Lacing her fingers in mine, she starts walking. "You're gonna look so cute with a hairnet on, babe."

Coming to a stop, I scowl. "A fucking hairnet? Are you serious?"

"Yes. No one wants a hair in their soup. Ew." She scrunches her nose up. "Let's go. And if you're a good boy and you don't complain again … I'll give you a reward."

"Better be a good reward," I grumble.

"It will be."

"Like … anal?"

"No!" she hush-yells, shooting me a glare.

"Maybe I can fuck dem titties?" I shrug. "I'd settle for that."

"You'll see. Now, shut up," she says as we reach the door and she pulls it open.

"Sutton! Hi!" An older lady smiles when she spots her. "I didn't know you were coming by to help." Her eyes move to mine, and she wiggles her white eyebrows. "Oh, and you brought some eye candy with you. The gals will love this."

As she pulls me behind her toward the kitchen, I tug her hand. "What gals?" I whisper. "What fucking gals?"

Putting her finger over her mouth, she silently shushes me … again. And when we walk into the kitchen, I know exactly who the "gals" are. In fact, I'm pretty sure they might be the actual fucking Golden Girls. Maybe even

204

older. And the way they are looking at me, I'd say they haven't seen a young man in ages.

And I can tell by the look on Sutton's face that she fucking loves it.

# SUTTON

For the first half hour, I know Hunter had no idea why we were here. He didn't understand why I chose a soup kitchen out of the countless other things I could have taken him to when he was upset. But slowly, I think he's starting to understand.

Most of the customers in this area are drug addicts who live on the streets. I don't volunteer here nearly as much as I wish I did, but the few times I was here … I left feeling like I'd done something important that day. Something that mattered.

Some of the customers recognize him from the team, and they applaud him. A few shake his hand, and some tell him how incredible of a player he is. They look at him with stars in their eyes, likely envious that his whole future is at his fingertips, waiting for him.

Once everyone is fed and Gloria and the other ladies are done flirting with him, he comes next to me.

"You were the highlight of a lot of people's weeks just by being here," I tell him, washing off some bowls. "Thank you for being so kind to everyone."

He peers into the dining room before kissing the side of my head. "Thanks for bringing me here. I actually really liked hearing people's stories. Made me realize I'm a judgmental prick too much of the time."

Pulling him out of view from everyone, I stand against a counter. He puts his hands on each side of the counter next to me and pecks my cheek.

"So many people we just saw tonight probably don't have a loving family waiting for them at home. Good friends to care enough to call them out on their shit and help them get better. They went down a bad road, and there was nobody there to stop them." I cup his cheek. "You know what Cade Huff has that none of them did when their life became what it is now?"

He swallows thickly, his eyes growing misty. "What?" he croaks.

"You," I whisper. "A friend like you to have their back. To have uncomfortable conversations that could be life-changing. Even life-saving." I press my lips to his before dipping my forehead down. "Cade might not see it right now, but one day, he will. He'll know that you, Watson, Haley, and Link saved him." I point toward the chattering voices in the dining area. "I bet if you asked all those people if they wish they had a friend like you in their life, they'd say yes. So, stop beating yourself up, Hunter. I promise, it's all going to be okay. Cade is going to be okay."

His nostrils flare with emotion as he gives me a small nod. "Thank you," he whispers, "for always making me see the silver lining."

"Thank you for being my silver lining." I smile. "I love you so damn much, Hunter Thompson."

Stepping back, he winks. "Let's go clean up. Because if my memory serves me right … you owe me something."

Rolling my eyes, I giggle. "Yeah, yeah."

Hunter is the type of friend you want in your corner. A fierce protector. The best listener. And a guy who carries the weight of other people's pain on his shoulders without thinking twice.

And the magnitude of love I have for him scares me. Because I've never loved or adored a person this much. And one of these days, his phone's going to ring, and the pros will be calling him up, handing him the keys to the kingdom.

And I don't know where that'll leave us.

# HUNTER

"I know this game doesn't feel right to you guys," Coach LaConte says, looking around at us in the locker room.

It's quiet. Too quiet. Ever since Cade left, that's how it's felt. We don't have him constantly joking around and saying dumb shit. And truthfully, it really sucks.

"It doesn't feel right to me either. And if you're feeling pissed off at Huff or maybe even mad at me for the decision I made for him to step away from the ice for a while, well, that's something I can live with." He sighs. "What I can't live with is something happening to one of my guys. Something that could have been prevented if someone had just spoken the hell up." He pauses. "I'm not going into detail about Cade Huff because he's not here to defend himself, and it ain't right to talk about his shit while he's away. Just know that when you step on that ice, every one of you is going to feel the shift. The burden of not having him out there."

He nods slowly, his lips forming a tight line. "And that's okay. But what's not okay is if we use that as an excuse to play like shit tonight. Huff wouldn't want you to throw it all away. He'd want you to go out there, balls to the wall, and get it done." His eyes move to each and every one of us. "You all think you can do that? Can you go out there and play hard? For Cade Huff?"

"Yes, sir," we all chant, but it's weak, and he shoots us a glare.

"Well, fuck. If that's how this is going to be, I'll go tell them we aren't even going out tonight. We'll fucking forfeit." He stands up on the bench, clapping his hands together. "Are you going to go out there and play hard?!"

"Yes, sir!" we yell, louder this time.

"Good!" He points to Link. "Go on, Sterns. Remind these boys who they are!"

Link smacks his palm on the locker. "Who are we, fellas?!"

"The Wolves!"

"And what the hell are we going out there to do tonight?"

"Take them down!" we scream out.

"Because whose fucking house is this?!"

"Our house!" We all stand, clapping our hands together, a few tipping their heads up and howling.

It doesn't feel right, playing this game without Cade. But I guess I'd better get used to it. Because from the sounds of it, he might not even make it back at all this season.

# SUTTON

There's just something about being in the stands, wearing a jersey with *Thompson* written on the back, that just feels … good. A sense of pride runs through me when he scores and the crowd goes wild. So many people in this arena adore him because of his ability to play a sport. At one time, not long ago, this sport was the only reason I respected him. Because athlete to fellow athlete, I knew he loved the game. Now, I'm seeing him for so much more than his talent on the ice.

His body turns to face me, and even through his helmet and shield, I can see the grin on his face when he looks up at me. My sweet, sensitive, protective, and—at times—jealous man. I know he's hurting, given this is the first game back since Cade left. But his energy—along with Link's and Watson's—has been carrying them through, keeping them in the lead as the clock winds down in period three.

Hunter is one of those people who absorbs other people's pain and problems. When the ones he loves hurt, he hurts. It's one of his qualities that I love. He feels things deeply, and he isn't afraid to show it, unlike so many other men in this world.

I know he's worried about his sister. He has every right to be, too, because I feel the same way. I tried to get her to come with me tonight, but she wasn't feeling up to it, so I didn't push. But whatever I can do to help, I'm going to do it. She's Hunter's sister, so I know she'll be just fine. And if she isn't, she'll have Hunter and me to help her through. Heck, I truly believe the entire hockey team will be there for her. After all, she's carrying Cade Huff's baby. And each and every one of them loves him like a brother.

I watch eagerly as the puck goes into play. At one time in my life, I didn't really think of this game as an art, but now, I see it as something beautiful. The rage and aggression, the coordination, speed, agility, and fierceness that come to the arena every game is pretty magnificent. And I'm loving being a puck boy's girlfriend.

They win the game, and I'm the first person he looks at, giving me a grin. I hope, one day, his parents will come and watch him. And they'll remember just how talented their son is on the ice. And that just because he isn't going to be a doctor, it doesn't mean he isn't extraordinary.

Because he is. He *so* is.

But no matter what, whether they support him or not, I'll be here. Cheering him on as loud as I can.

# HUNTER

"You good?" I say to Sutton.

She's looking out the window of my truck, her hands clasped in her lap, the way she does when she's nervous and trying not to fidget. Something those etiquette classes probably taught her.

Glancing at me, she gives me a small smile. "Yeah, I'm fine." Frowning, she sighs. "Okay, that's a lie. I'm freaking out. Like *armpit sweat, boob sweat, probably breaking out in hives* freaking out."

Reaching over, I take one of her hands and pad my thumb across the top of it. "It's going to be fine. And if we get out here and you change your mind, we'll say fuck it and find something else to do. Deal?"

Nodding once, she sucks in a breath. "Deal. I just … is this too hard-core? Showing up at their freaking elaborate luncheon, dropping a big bomb, and then being like, *Deuces. We out.*"

"It's hard-core, but it's not like you're going to do it in front of a table of fancy fucks, are you?" I look at her. "Wait, are you going to say it in front of her stick-in-the-ass country-club friends?"

"I mean … I thought about it," she squeaks. "But you're right. Too far. No, I'll simply tell them I need to talk to them, pull them to the side, and, *bam … I know the truth, bitch.*"

I nod slowly. "I like it. My baby is ruthless."

She thought about going to their house, but it's a long-ass drive, and if we got there and they didn't let her through the gate, that would probably be more traumatizing than anything. My parents are frequent visitors of the club the luncheon is at today. So, I know we'll have no problem getting in.

Not once in the length of time I've been around Sutton this year have her parents reached out. It's literally like they've forgotten about her. Cutting her off altogether. I'll admit, I expected it from her mother, but Sam Savage has always seemed better than that. Sure, he's always put his position as the senator before anything else, but he's never been degrading to Sutton the way Helena—or Helen—is.

Slowly, with no warning, I pull off to the side of the road.

"Give me your phone." I take my hand from hers and hold it out.

"What?" She frowns, looking confused. "Why?"

"Just trust me." I shake my hand waiting.

Slowly, she takes her phone and slaps it into my hand.

Plugging it in, I open her Music app. Scrolling through, I smirk when I find the perfect song.

She and I couldn't have more opposite taste in music if we wanted to. I listen to everything from country to a little rap and some old-school shit. She's a Taylor Swift fanatic.

Hitting play, I grin over at her, trying not to laugh as a song that I've been forced to memorize starts to play. But even though I'm not a big Swiftie, this song isn't *that* bad.

I turn the volume up, and "Bad Blood" screams through my speakers just before I pull back onto the road.

"Come on, girl. Get it." I wink at her, bobbing my head back and forth. "Get down with your T. Swift–loving self."

When she's hesitant to sing, I take one for the team and start belting out the lyrics. I take my bottle of water, holding it up like a microphone. Sutton laughs at first, covering her face in pure embarrassment for her man. But by the time the chorus starts, she's singing along with me. Well, more like screaming out the words as we both act like complete morons.

She rolls her window down, letting the wind blow her hair around into a completely tangled disaster. Her cutoff jean shorts and blue tank top aren't exactly fancy luncheon attire. Which is exactly why I told her to wear them. She could climb out of a dumpster, wearing a garbage bag, and she'd still be ten times the person her mother is. She'd also still be the most beautiful woman in any room.

The song ends, and she glances over at me. No longer looking like a scared puppy dog, shut in a cardboard box. But a damn warrior, ready to fight.

"Thank you." She leans across the console, kissing my cheek. "I needed that."

"I know." I give her the side-eye. "I know when you're in need of one of your T. Swift jam sessions. I've come to accept it now."

"And I love you for it." She giggles.

If I had to listen to Taylor Swift on repeat for the rest of my life to keep her smiling—my ears might bleed inside, and I might mentally lose my mind—I'd do it. For her anyway.

# SUTTON

Call me a gutless, codependent coward for needing Hunter by my side when I confront my parents. I don't really care. There was no way my ass was walking into the devil's realm alone. Hell no.

After Hunter gets us through the door, we walk to the outdoor area out back. But not before the hostess flicks her gaze up and down my body and gives my boyfriend a seductive sex-kitten look.

"She wants you," I mutter, rolling my eyes. "I feel dirty, just watching her eye-bang you."

"Eh, well, I'm taken." He shrugs. "Besides, I'm not really into redheads."

"You're not into anyone besides your girlfriend, asshole," I hiss, nudging his side.

"Obviously, babe." He throws his arm around me just as we walk around the corner and see the tables spread out on the lawn.

Big, fancy hats, suits, and designer clothes fill the yard as I glance around.

"Time for another jam session?" I gulp.

"Nope. Just a bitch session," he utters, dropping his arm from my body. "To your left, third table over. Hideous blue dress."

My eyes move until I find my mother and Sam sitting with two other couples. I pull a deep breath into my lungs, wondering if I need my inhaler.

*No. I've got this.*

Tipping my chin up bravely, I begin to walk toward them. My legs shake, and my heart thumps in my chest. I pray Hunter won't grab my hand because my palm is probably slimy with sweat.

My mother looks past me first before she takes me in, and her eyes widen. There's no mistaking the sheer panic on her face.

Does she deserve for me to pull her away from her ritzy friends and talk to her? No.

So, am I going to make a scene in front of them? Hell yes, I am.

"Sutton." She plasters on a fake smile, glancing around at her company to see who's looking. "How ... nice of you to show." Her eyes move down to my outfit, and there's no hiding her disdain. "But, sweetie, what in the world are you wearing?"

"Sutton." My dad—Sam—stands, instantly walking to me and putting his hands on the tops of my arms. "What a surprise." I can see the emotion in his eyes as he takes me in. Hugging me, he whispers, "Thank you. Thank you for finally coming back to us."

I rear my head back. "*What?*"

He looks confused. "You haven't taken my calls or emails for months. Your mother said you just needed time, that you had asked that we stay away from you. But I have to tell you, it's been hard." He swallows, his eyes moving to Hunter. "I'm sorry for what I said to you on the phone, Hunter. I was just pissed. Mad that you were spending time with Sutton when she had cut me out."

Hunter scowls. "Yeah, uh, I think your story is twisted, Sammy. Better ask your wife what the truth is." He glares at my mother. "Right, *Helen?*"

By now, we're causing a scene. And even though a few of their table partners have gotten up and left, two remain, watching every move.

Standing, my mother walks to me, grabbing my elbow. "Let's talk somewhere more private."

"No," I snap. "I'm not going anywhere with you."

I point to Sam. "Does he even know the truth, *Mother?* Have you lied to him throughout your entire marriage? Does he know who you really are? The monster you are?"

"Helena, what is she talking about?" He frowns. "I'm so confused."

She opens her mouth to talk, but I hold my finger up, pointing it in her face.

"He's not dumb enough to not know that I'm not actually his kid. Because he can do math," I growl. "But does he know that I'm not the only child you abandoned?"

I glance at Sam, and his face pales.

"Sutton," he whispers. "I'm sorry we didn't tell you. Your mother ... she told me how awful your father was. I never wanted you to try to find him." His face fills with regret. "I didn't know what else to do." He looks at my mother, and his eyebrows pull together. "What is she talking about? Do you have another child?"

"She sure as fuck does," Brody says, appearing out of nowhere with Bria at his side.

I swear I hear a few people gasp when they see him—in his faded blue jeans, white T-shirt, and tattoo-covered arms. Though I know the old biddies are raking their eyes over him like a dang snack while clutching their pearls.

When I called him a few days ago, telling him what I was going to do, he told me he didn't think he was going to show up. He said he didn't care about finding closure with our mother. Looks like he changed his mind.

"Brody O'Brien?" Sam's eyes widen. "Defensemen for the Tampa Bay Lightning?"

"In the fucking flesh, Senator." Brody nods, pointing to me. "I'm only here for Sutton."

My mother pales, appearing like she could pass out as she looks at Brody. Emotion is all over her face, but I can't dissect what the emotion is.

"Brody was abandoned as a young toddler by his mother," I say, my voice small. "Left with an abusive, alcoholic maniac of a man." My gaze shifts to my brother before moving back to Helen. "*You*, Helen, left him." I give my head a slight shake. "It was bad enough that you abandoned me, cutting me off like I was nothing just because I no longer fit into your perfect little world." I wave my hand around, raising my voice. "This fake, shallow, conceited world." My hand motions to Brody. "But the fact that you didn't take him with you when you fled?" Tears pool in my eyes because I know I am the product of an absolute monster. A true villain. "You are a bad person, Helen. And I hate you for what you did."

"Helena, is this true?" Sam growls, putting his hands on her arms and giving her a soft shake. "You left a child—*this* child—behind?" He stumbles back, dragging his hand over his head. "And for months, you told me that Sutton cut us off. That she blocked our numbers and needed space." He looks at her, disgusted. "That's not true, is it? It was you all along."

"Samuel, please," my mother cries. "She was never going to listen to what I said. She was determined to do things her way." She shifts her eyes to me, snarling, "You were going to wind up *just. Like. Me*, Sutton. I could tell you were throwing your life away and you were going to be stuck, never knowing what could have been."

"Brooks University is a far cry from throwing my life away," I say bitterly. "And no matter how many colleges I transfer from—or hell, even if I drop out altogether—I'll still be twice the person you will *ever* be." I inhale, standing tall. "I didn't come here to tear your life down even though … honestly, this right here is exactly what you deserve. I came here for me. To look you in the eyes and say that I don't care what you think of me. And I don't care that you couldn't love me enough to stand by my side." I grab Brody's hand. "*We* don't care. We're moving on."

"I didn't have a choice," she hisses, looking at Brody. "That man was going to kill me."

Brody's eyes dance with mischief, and he moves in a little closer to her. "Yeah? Well, the only reason I'm glad he didn't is because if he did, I wouldn't have Sutton. If it wasn't for her, I'd just have assumed your plastic, Botoxed ass was rotting in hell." His lip turns up. "Remember, when Sammy here shitcans you after we leave … you can go back to riding cock for a living."

Turning toward me, he gives my hand a squeeze before releasing it. "You ready to get out of here, away from these losers?"

"Hell yes." I smile through the pain that radiates throughout my body. Slowly making its way out of my being.

"Sutton, wait," Sam says, catching my hand. "Had I known that your mother was lying, I would have come to you much sooner. I had no idea that this whole time, you thought we … or I cut you off." He dips his head. "I would never do that. Blood or not, you're my daughter. You will *always* be my daughter."

Even though I know he wants me to say it's all fine, I can't. Because even though it was for my own protection, he lied to me. And he believed in the good of his wife when he should have known me enough to know better. That I'd never cut him from my life the way she led him to believe.

"I can't," I whisper. "Not right now anyway."

He nods slowly. "Take all the time you need. But when you're ready … I'll be here." He glances at Brody. "I'm sorry that I played a role in keeping your mother away."

Brody shakes his head. "You didn't. She wasn't coming back either way."

And then he turns and leaves. And I follow. Because, damn it, that's my family.

Hunter brings my hand to his lips. "I love you so much. You know that, right?"

"I do. And I love you too." I smile. "Now, take me home. I've had enough crazy for one day."

"Same, babe. Same."

# SUTTON
## SEVEN MONTHS LATER

I drag a long, exaggerated breath of beach air into my lungs, closing my eyes and soaking in the sunshine as it hits my face. Even the air seems easier to breathe. Or maybe it's just that today is the first day of our new beginning. Because today, we moved into our new home in Florida.

Right. On. The. Freaking. Beach.

And I'm not talking about a yucky, smelly, seaweed-covered beach. This is fine white sand that massages your feet while you walk in it.

When the Tampa Bay Lightning called Hunter last winter, offering him a spot, I was so happy for him. And he was excited too. But he was also concerned because I still had two more years left before I was graduating, and the last thing he wanted to do was ruin any future plans I had. But after taking some time—a week, to be exact—where I thought long and hard about what I wanted and what would make me happy, I realized I didn't have a real reason to be at Brooks. I no longer wanted to dance competitively. And I had no idea what degree I was trying to go after. And then I said, *Screw it*. Because I knew what I wanted, and that was Hunter. The rest we'd figure out when we moved.

And we did. Because when we came to Florida to see our house, we got to swing by the arena, where I met Hunter's coaches. And after they learned my past with dancing, it turned out, they knew a dance studio nearby in desperate need of an instructor. After a few phone calls ... I was in.

I had never considered working with children until the night of the charity event. And now, I couldn't be more excited.

Not only is Tampa Bay an amazing opportunity for Hunter, but it's also going to provide a better environment to keep my asthma at bay. And the cherry on top is that my brother, Brody, plays for the Tampa Bay Lightning. Truthfully, I wonder if he put in a good word for Hunter to get him the offer he received. Even so, Hunter is a damn good player, and they are lucky to have him.

Now, Hunter and I will get to be close to my brother and his adorable family. And there's no greater blessing than that.

I miss the hell out of Ryann. And I feel terrible for leaving her. But somehow, I think Watson is keeping her plenty busy. Who would have thought that my friend who claimed to hate athletes would fall for the Wolves goalie? I talk to Lana from time to time, but we never really had a chance to get close anyway. And Poppy ... well, surprisingly, she apologized for being such a bitch to me. Her words, not mine. But we both knew we'd never consider ourselves friends. Sometimes, you just don't like someone, plain and simple. And the truth is, I don't like her. And she certainly doesn't like me.

I've kept in touch with Sam, who I actually call Dad again even though he didn't father me. Right after everything went down between my mother and me, he filed for divorce. And though I have no idea where she is now, he's put in the work to remain my family. Besides, he beats the hell out of my real father from what Brody has told me.

Not only did my dad find out that my mother had lied about Brody and me, but he also learned that his relationship with the Thompsons had been sabotaged by Helen because she was the one who planted the seed to start the drama. Apparently, she didn't want Sam to give them the land because she felt like her and my father weren't getting enough money for it. That all might suck in some ways, but now that everyone knows the truth and the one rotten apple in the batch—known as Helen—is gone, my dad and Hunter's parents have become friends again.

Hunter's parents are far from perfect, but after he got the call from the Tampa Bay Lightning last winter, they took the news strangely well. And not only that, but they also even came to a few of his games. Including the Frozen Four, where his team won. I think it finally clicked that their son was never going to be a doctor and that it was time to accept him for who he was. Which is an incredible athlete who is going to be a lot of people's hero.

Arms wrap around my waist, and Hunter buries his face in my neck. "Thought I might find you out here, Little Bird."

I giggle, putting my hands on his. "I'm procrastinating. Because honestly, I don't want to unpack."

"So, don't," he mutters, kissing my neck. "I can think of a few other things we could do to pass the time."

"Oh, yeah?" I blush, thinking he means sex. "What's that?"

"Well, for starters, we're probably sweaty after moving in today. Could use a wash."

I shiver. "Mmhmm …"

Just when I'm about to turn toward him, going in for a kiss, he lifts me onto his shoulder, running down the beach and toward the waves.

"Don't you dare, Hunter Thompson!" I squeal. "I will kick your ass clear to Tuesday!"

"Well, seeing as it's already Monday, I can deal with that," he says, slapping his hand on my asscheek. "My baby loves the ocean. Let's go test it out!"

When he runs us into the waves, laughter, mixed with screaming, comes through my throat as my dress becomes soaked.

He releases me, and our bodies rise up with the swells.

I splash him. "You're going to pay for that, you asshole."

"Don't worry; I'll make it up to you after this—in that walk-in shower you like so much." He winks. "You dirty girl. We were on the beach, and you were ready for me to take you right then."

I scowl. "Was not!"

He wiggles his eyebrows. "Oh, you were. Your thighs were clenching, and your body was begging for my cock." Grabbing my legs, he pulls them around his waist and kisses me. "Good thing for you, I'm not going to make you wait much longer. You know I want to fuck you against that tiled wall."

"No way." I shake my head. "You blew it, buddy. I was ready. I was going to do *allll* the things. Now? Nope. Forget it."

His lips twitch in amusement, and I hate that he knows me too damn well to know that I'll give in. He's too freaking irresistible.

"Is that so? So, you don't want me to lick those perfect tits while I fuck you against the wall so hard that your back is bruised tomorrow?" He shrugs. "I mean, all right. That's fine."

Splashing him again, I walk back onto the sand before I start running toward our house. Laughing, I look back at him, coming up on me fast.

When he scoops me up, I scream as he carries me up onto our porch and pulls the door open.

"We're going to get sand and water everywhere!" I shriek, still giggling.

"I don't give a fuck. I'll clean it by hand if I have to." He pushes the bathroom door open, setting me down on the seat.

After pulling my dress over my head, he kneels down, unclasping my bra and pulling down my panties, slipping his fingers between my legs. "Fuck, baby. You're squeezing my fingers so hard. Just imagine what you'll do to my dick. You're so ready, aren't you?"

I nod slowly, dragging in air. "Yes. Yes, please, Hunter."

"Fuck … me. You're so beautiful," he groans, peeling his own clothes off before turning on the shower.

Lifting me up, he walks us in and pushes my back to the cold tiles before his mouth lands on mine. He tastes minty as his tongue moves against mine before he drops his head to my neck, kissing my skin.

His erection presses into my belly. I reach between our bodies, stroking him a few times, and he groans.

I will never get enough of this man. Ever.

He pulls back slightly, pushing the head of his cock inside of me little by little. I throw my head back against the wall, straightening my back on the tiles as he presses his forehead to my chest, moving harder and faster.

I moan, biting down on my bottom lip from pure desire as my fingernails move to his back, pushing into his skin as he thrusts in and out of me. And just like he said, I know my back will likely be bruised. But I don't care. Not even a little.

The water sprays over our bodies, and he takes one hand and grips the back of my head, bringing our mouths together. My nipples harden to the point of pain, and his movements become more erratic.

"Squeeze my dick, baby," he growls into my mouth. "Come all over my cock. I want to feel you drip down my legs."

On demand, I come undone at the exact moment that he does. His moans are muted by my screams. And it doesn't matter because we live alone. In our own house.

He sucks in some ragged breaths before he slowly releases me from his hold and smirks.

"Yeah, I knew that what you said down on the beach was bullshit. My baby never turns down a chance to fuck my cock."

I slap the back of my hand against him before pinching his nipple. "Shut up. You're annoying."

"Yeah, well, annoying as I might be … what's that glow on your cheeks? Huh?" He winks, grabbing some soap and spinning me around before washing my hair. "That's right. That's the *Hunter's glorious dick* afterglow. And you're welcome."

I laugh, shaking my head and rolling my eyes as he continues to lather my hair. "Whatever you say, Thompson. *Whatever. You. Say.*"

Hunter's love has filled a void inside of me that I never even knew existed. I thought love this big only happened in fairy tales. Turns out, I was wrong.

I've found my fairy tale. Hunter *is* my fairy tale.

# HUNTER
## THREE YEARS LATER

I sit on the patio, holding my newborn, wondering if he's too hot. Or maybe he's cold. I don't know. These things need to come with an instruction manual.

"Say good-bye to that baby face of yours." Brody grins, looking down at our baby boy, Easton. "Now that you have yourself one of these little bastards, you won't be getting much sleep. All that sleep deprivation is gonna lead to some wrinkles on that super-soft skin of yours."

"Babe, shut up," Bria hisses from the pool before smiling at me. "Hunter, don't listen to your knuckleheaded brother-in-law. You know he's just jealous that you still have a baby face at your age."

Brody moves closer, poking his finger into the side of my face. "Yep, I see a wrinkle starting right there."

I scowl. "Fuck off."

The sound of a loud snore has all three of us turning our heads to the hammock, where Sutton's mouth is hanging open while she sleeps. I'm pretty sure I see a line of drool. A few minutes before, she was part of the conversation. But given that, ten days ago, our lives completely changed and no one in this household is getting much sleep, she's exhausted.

Brody smirks, pulling his phone out and snapping a picture. "I'll get her back for that prank she played on me at Christmas. Took me days to get all that fucking Sharpie off my face."

Iris, Bria and Brody's oldest, jumps into the pool to her mother, and Brody shakes his head.

"That kid has no fear, I swear."

"Wonder who she gets it from," Bria deadpans. "Hopefully, our little man won't be like that. But something tells me with that O'Brien blood in his veins … I'm doomed."

Before anyone can answer, Isla runs around the corner, barreling toward me and the baby with Cam hot on her heels. Addison's last to make an appearance with their son on her hip.

"Slow your roll, Isla girl," she calls out. "We need to talk about rules before you hold the baby."

Cam stops in front of me. "Yeah, like rule number one. Your dad gets to hold the baby first," he says. Holding his arms out, he grins. "Come to Uncle Cam-Cam, little buddy!"

Handing him off, I shrug. "Yeah, I think he just shit his pants anyway, so that's all you, big guy."

"Seriously?" Cam groans. "Not cool."

The baby stealer, also known as Cam, takes off inside with my smelly kid. Out of all of us guys, he's the one who took to fatherhood so easily. It's like he was made to do it, and I look up to him so much. I also ask him for advice more than I'll ever admit.

In the midst of all the commotion, Sutton wakes up, wiping her face with her sleeve. "Oh shit. I dozed off."

"You say it like it's a surprise." I laugh. "Babe, I found you asleep in the laundry room last week."

Sutton rubs her eyes as Addison walks to her, giving her a hug.

"Congratulations, Mama. How are you doing?"

"Honestly, how the hell did you do this as a teenager?" She frowns. "I'm tired. My boobs are achy and leaking. He only sleeps during the daytime, like some sort of vampire. Oh, and my body looks like stretched-out pizza dough."

"Truthfully, it wasn't easy. But I had a lot of help from my parents. And as hard as the newborn stage is—and I don't care what anyone says; it's hard—it also goes by really fast." She sighs. "Don't sweat the small things. The laundry, the housework. Any of it. Just get through the days and try your best to snuggle that little nugget and soak it in."

"It's so much harder than I thought it was going to be," Sutton says, and I can hear the emotion in her voice. "I'm so scared all the time. And I'm tired. And then I get grumpy." Patting her chest, she pouts. "And seriously, are my boobs ever going to look normal again?"

"You're sexy as hell, Little Bird. And I love dem boobies," I call out, winking. "Not me counting down the days till you get that six-week check."

"What check?" Isla says, looking around, and Addison widens her eyes at me, giving me a dirty look.

"Isla, baby, grab your swimsuit in my bag and go change into it. You can swim with Auntie Bria and Iris." Addison smiles. "Go on."

"Yes!" Isla squeals before looking at Cam as he walks back outside, narrowing her eyes. "It's my turn after I swim. You can't hog him the entire time."

"But I'm the baby whisperer." He grins, and once she walks away, he looks at his wife. "I'm putting a baby in you tonight. It's been decided."

Addison shakes her head, completely ignoring him as she looks back at Sutton. "It'll be okay, I promise. Also, want to know a secret? I bet that most all new mothers have felt the same way that you are feeling."

"Preach!" Bria calls from the pool. "I cried for, like, three weeks straight. It was great."

Addison nods. "See, told you. Your hormones are just wacky right now, and it's all normal. Be patient with yourself." She pats her back. "And your body is still bangin', babe. Your husband is right; you look really good."

"Damn right you do," I chime in. "You're hotter than ever."

When she walks away from Sutton and goes to steal Easton from Cam, I walk over to Sutton and pull her onto my lap in a lawn chair.

"You're doing great, Mama. I know you're tired, and I know you feel like your body isn't the same, but I promise, you look more beautiful than ever." I kiss her cheek. "And I love this life we've built together. You and me."

Craning her neck, she looks up at me, crying. "Why'd you have to go make me cry?" She sniffles. "I love you too. Even if I look like shit these days and you have your baby-ass smooth skin."

She snuggles into my chest, and I wrap my arms around her, looking around at our friends and family who showed up just to check in on us. Cam came all the way from fucking Boston just to meet Easton. And Link and his family are arriving tomorrow.

I'm a lucky man. And it all started with one dance.

More puck boys are coming!

Ready for an emotional read?
Preorder Cade's story, *Lost Boy*, at https://mybook.to/lostboyHG

Is a marriage of convenience your thing?
Preorder Watson's story, *Perfect Boy*, at https://mybook.to/perfectboy

# acknowledgments

You all didn't really think I was going to leave Brooks University after just three books, did you? Of course not! I had to bring you more puck boys. And after the emotional havoc I wreaked with Brody, I thought I owed you Hunter, who, in my eyes, is an angel! I really enjoyed writing Hunter and Sutton's story. To me, it's the perfect amount of sweet and spicy!

I always have a heap of people to thank because, let's face it, without them, this whole thing wouldn't be possible. Everyone I thank has played a pivotal part in my career even if they don't realize it.

To my beautiful, adorable, crazy, tiring children—We have the best adventures, and I'm so thankful this career allows me to take trips with you guys. And to snuggle you when you're sick and be there for all of your biggest moments. I love the three of you so very much.

To my husband, who oftentimes gets left with the tired, overwhelmed, mentally drained parts of me—Thank you for loving me through it. And for the hugs in the kitchen when I'm frazzled and about to fall apart. You're always there to hold me together. Sometimes, true love isn't flowers, cards, and candy. I've learned, sometimes, it's just about getting each other through the "thick of it," as we say. And I can't imagine getting through it without you. I love you.

Thank you to my mom. She is the world's slowest reader. She started reading when my first book came out, and she is just now reading *Playing Dane*.

Which … yeah, I'm bad at math, and even I know that's awful. But either way, she always reads the Acknowledgments. So, eventually, years down the road, she'll be reading this. So, Mom, I hope you know how important you are to me. I call you when something good happens. When something terrible happens. And sometimes just because I need to hear your voice. I love you more than words could ever say.

Autumn Gantz—I might not always like what you have to say, but no matter what, I always listen. Because at the end of the day, I value your opinion so much, and I learned long ago that you truly want the very best for me. I put my trust in you three years ago, and you've helped me grow into the author I am today. We still have a long way to go, and I'm ready to work. Thanks for keeping me on my toes. I love you, my lifer.

Jovana Shirley at Unforeseen Editing, who gets the pleasure of cleaning up my messy-ass manuscripts—Damn, lady. You are good at your job. I love that we have created such a comfortable flow when we work together. It works much like a dance, and to me, it always runs smoothly. Together, we've brought thirteen books into the world. Love you and can't wait for many, many more.

Candice Butchino—You started off as a reader who made the sweetest posts about my books. And then you became a bookstagrammer who shared so much of my promo. And then you became an incredibly good friend who I know I can text or call anytime. Now, you're making my swag and beta-reading my books, and you are a huge emotional support for me. I love you, lady. I'm so glad that the book world connected us.

Jaimie Davidson—Thank you for being my trusty proofreader! No matter how busy you are, you make the time to be an extra set of eyes for me, and I can't thank you enough. Your love and support for the authors you adore is unmatched. And I appreciate you so much. Love you, babe.

Thank you, Jenn Phelps and Megan Smith, for being an extra set of eyes! And for all you do in the book community. You rock!

Thank you, Renie Saliba, for providing me with the gorgeous cover photo. I love it so, so much. It was a pleasure working with you. I know I didn't make it easy, and I certainly made you work for my business. But I am so happy with how it came out.

Sarah Grim Sentz with Enchanting Romance Designs—Girl, you hit it out of the park again. I always love working with you. I adore your creative mind and am always blown away with your work.

Special thanks to Amy Queau, Q Design—As always, you are ahhhmazing to work with. I love how communicative you are with your clients, and I can't wait to work together again. You make it so easy.

Thank you to my readers for taking a chance on my work. Now, let's all prepare ourselves for Cade. Because, well, he's going to wreck you. Consider yourselves warned.

That's all for now! XO

# about the author

Hannah Gray spends her days in vacationland, living in a small, quaint town on the coast of Maine. She is an avid reader of contemporary romance and is always in competition with herself to read more books every year.

During the day, she loves on her three perfect-to-her daughters and tries to be the best mom she can be. But once she tucks them in at night—okay, scratch that. Once they fall asleep next to her in her bed—because their bedrooms apparently have monsters in them—she dives into her own fantasy world, staying awake well into the late-night hours, typing away stories about her characters. As much as she loves being a wife and mom—and she certainly does love it—reading and writing are her outlet, giving her a place to travel far away while still physically being with her family.

She married her better half in 2013, and he's been putting up with her craziness every day since. As her anchor, he's her one constant in this insane, forever-changing world.

Made in the USA
Columbia, SC
25 June 2024

37498499R00128